COME ONE, COME ALL

A dark fable of raw ambition, quiet complicity, and the fall that everyone sees coming but no one tries to stop.

M.K. MILLIGAN

Published by Best Hands Publishing LLC

For Mom,

who fought her way back,

R. Maxine Milligan, 1942-2022.

TABLE OF CONTENTS

PROLOGUE

Autumn.

The Big Top smells of sawdust and animal musk and the kind of exhaustion that comes at the end of a long season of work and travel.

Helena releases from the bar and completes two, two-and-a-half, three full rotations before Marco's hands find her wrists. They suspend artfully for a split second, then swing back toward Marco's platform.

"Sloppy," Ace bellows from below. He is standing in the center ring, hands on hips, shaking his head. "Do it again," he yells. As if there's a chance they can't hear him.

A loud bray cuts off Ace's command; he bristles at the sound and turns to glare at the clowns in the third ring. Bongo and Freckles are juggling fake chainsaws back and forth. Patches is brushing one of the two donkeys. Their names are Ravioli and Ziti. Born into this circus, they're beloved by everyone except Ace; he has never bothered to learn which is which, though they look nothing alike.

There are several more clowns, but the only other one rehearsing right now is a child. Pip is a lean eight-year-old girl with two golden braids. She is not wearing her wig or makeup yet, but she is wearing her costume. She climbs on Ravioli's back and wraps her small hands into his mane, then he takes off in a gallop around the ring. Her bright, musical giggles echo through the tent and Ace scowls at the noise.

"Stick to the script, kid," he yells at top volume. "We're rehearsing, not goofing around!"

Pip pulls on Ravioli's mane and he stops abruptly. Forlorn, she climbs off and makes a halfhearted kick at the sawdust. Her shoulders drop in defeat. She does not look in Ace's direction.

Another loud bray erupts from the third ring. Ziti is tired of being groomed, but Ace always thinks their hee-haws are meant to mock him. He grits his teeth in aggravation but refrains from yelling at the donkeys themselves. Even though of every living thing in this, his circus, they are the ones who get on his nerves the most.

The remaining clowns return from their smoke break. Their easy banter quiets when they see Ace, and they walk to the third ring to resume rehearsing.

Bruno's unexpected roar pierces the air. The apex predator is frustrated as he prepares for his sixth performance in five days, and a seventh will happen tonight. He's expected to jump through hoops a dozen times a day, in addition to other tricks, and he's finally had enough. His handler—Charlie, who's worked with big cats for twenty years and knows better than to turn his back even on the most reliable lion—reacts fast, but not fast enough. A single claw from Bruno catches his forearm in a quick slash before Charlie can jerk away. Blood wells immediately, bright red against his fair skin. It drips onto the sawdust that will absorb it, the way it has absorbed so much else.

Ace storms toward the cage, his face tight with fury, but not at the exhausted lion who's just injured someone. "Get your act together!" he screams at Charlie, pressing his other hand against the wound. Ace is pleased with his own wordplay, the double meaning of 'act,' and he's already walking away before Charlie can respond. Bruno retreats to the back of his cage and paces restlessly. Charlie leaves to search for a bandage.

A crash behind Ace echoes through the Big Top and grabs everyone's attention. All eyes turn to see a nineteen-year-old crew hand named Tommy. His face is red from both embarrassment and exertion, and a heavy piece of rigging equipment lies at his feet.

"Dammit you imbecile," Ace barks, "that's a four-thousand-dollar piece of equipment... if it's broke, that's coming out of your paycheck!"

Tommy makes an apology but Ace has already turned his back on the boy, having delivered his judgment. The rigging is undamaged, but Tommy will check it three times before the afternoon show, just to be sure.

The remaining crew members continue setup with practiced efficiency despite the tension. No one wants to be the next target of Ace's attention.

Two of the crew hands grab supplies and move to the area Charlie just vacated. One sweeps up the blood-soaked sawdust and scoops it into a garbage bag. The other sprinkles fresh sawdust on the patch of bare cement, blending it in with the rest.

The audience will never know. The show must go on.

ACT I

Spring, six months later.

Theodore James Crane—Theo to those who know him—approaches the dark green trailer. Each step brings the mural into better focus. The words "Donahue's Traveling Circus" are carefully spaced across the top of the modest building to run the entire length. Beneath that, a variety of animals are coming into view… a lion, a donkey, a llama. Strangely, they are not at all proportional; the artist painted them all of similar size. Only the bright colors of their sashes reveal any realism to their respective appearances. The royal blue of the cartoon lion's sash is the same color as the pedestals from which the real lions leap when commanded to pass through flaming hoops. The red sash on the laughing donkey matches the red sombreros the real ones wear during their act. And the green sash on the llama matches green saddles that all three of the real llamas wear while they're performing.

By the time Theo arrives at the trailer's door, he is close enough that he can no longer see the colorful painting on the trailer's side… just the buzzer, a doorknob, and a small window. Mounted in the window, indeed taking up almost the entire glass, is a white sign that reads:

100 CIRCUS ROAD
OFFICE AND DWELLING SPACE
OF OWNER AND
RINGMASTER ACE DONAHUE

It's as if Donahue places more importance on his ringmaster role, keeping that word tied to his name, than his ownership of the circus. Theo finds this curious and tucks it alongside everything else he's gathered in the last few minutes: the colorful artistry displayed on the trailer, the crisp lettering above the animals, and the sights and sounds all around this trailer whose wheels have been cleverly integrated into the design.

He knocks and waits several seconds, then briefly presses the buzzer. Theo winces at the shrill sound it makes, then takes a step back. He can hear footsteps approaching. Unable to see anything in the window except the sign, he wonders if Ace Donahue himself will answer the bell.

Just before the door swings open, Theo hears the familiar beckoning of Razzle and Dazzle. They've been fixtures outside the entrance of this circus for decades—greeting guests as they enter the Big Top, announcing changes with varying degrees of volume and vigor. Sometimes they speak in unison and other times they argue over one another, each thinking her announcement is more vital than the other's. He can't quite make out what they're yelling at the moment. It is early afternoon; the next show does not start for several hours. But that doesn't matter. They've always got something to say for anyone who cares to hear it.

An attractive older woman answers the door, to Theo's surprise. She is wearing an expensive suit with even more expensive high heels. If Theo had been raised around wealth, he might know the designer brands she is wearing.

"Please, come in, Mr. Crane," the woman beckons in a kindly tone. "Ace is expecting you." She steps aside and gestures for him to enter.

Ace? She calls him Ace? He wonders if this is meaningful.

His eyes absorb the sights he has already seen in magazines, but seeing the office in person is very different. Every inch of wall space is covered with framed photos of Mr. Donahue in varying stages of his career. His years as a late-night infomercial announcer, then his years as a gameshow host. Compared to the quantity of photos from his circus years, however, there are perhaps ten frames for each one of the ones showing his past.

"My name is Patty Angstrom. I am Ace's office assistant."

When she holds out her hand, Theo takes it with a grip he's spent years perfecting—firm, then yielding, his left hand briefly covering hers before letting go. The day Theo realized two seconds were vital to first impressions, he'd practiced his technique. Practiced until he knew with certainty he could adjust in the moment.

"Pleasure to meet you, Ms. Angstrom." He warmly cups his left hand over her right as they do this ritual dance. Her smile tells him he made the right choice to give that extra second of contact.

"Just Patty is fine," she smiles. "I will let Ace know you're here. Have a seat."

She gestures and he looks in the direction she is motioning. A solitary wooden chair rests near the front wall of the trailer. He turns back to thank her, and suddenly realizes she is at least ten years older than he first thought. Impeccable makeup sets her apart from most of the women in Donahue's orbit. It is not caked on thickly or intended for an audience to view from afar. Her appearance is cultivated like a pearl.

Theo takes a seat, and Patty walks around her desk to sit in a fancy swivel chair. Her posture is so vertical it looks as though she's a compass needle. The way her space is arranged suggests to Theo that she is efficient, from the tall filing cabinet by her desk to the printer sitting adjacent to her monitor. She's wearing a modest necklace, and an even more modest wedding ring. He twists his own wedding band reflexively and is instantly aware he's done this—and he notices that Patty glanced at his hands in that moment as well. She is paying attention, as is Theo, and he wonders if this is a skill Mr. Donahue values.

For a moment, Theo allows himself to feel a quiet satisfaction. Less than two years ago he'd excoriated Ace Donahue in print—called him a fraud, a snake oil salesman, a cautionary tale in satin lapels. And yet here he sits, in the antechamber of Donahue's empire, invited by the man himself. *The right words, delivered with the right humility, can open any door. Even doors belonging to those who should know better.*

He waits. Patty busies herself with paperwork, her pen moving in precise strokes across a ledger. The silence stretches comfortably; she seems as accustomed to it as he is.

"Is Mr. Donahue in the Big Top?" Theo finally asks, keeping his tone light. "I wouldn't mind watching him work, if there's time."

Patty looks up and gives him a polite smile—warm enough to be gracious, cool enough to establish boundaries. "Ace is here in the trailer. Another room. I'll bring you back to meet him shortly."

Another room?

Theo glances around, seeing only walls covered in photographs and press clippings. No visible door.

Interesting, he notes.

As if on cue, a faint buzz emanates from somewhere on Patty's desk. She rises and gestures for Theo to do the same. He follows as she crosses toward the far wall, toward what appears to be nothing more than another cluster of framed magazine covers. But Patty's hand finds a handle cleverly disguised as part of a gilded frame, and she pushes inward. A hidden door swings open.

From somewhere in the dim interior, a voice calls out. Unmistakable. The voice Theo has heard in countless clips and interviews, always a few decibels louder than necessary.

"Come in, Teddy."

Theo steps through the doorway into a room where the light seems reluctant to gather. He grits his teeth at the absurd nickname. In his lifetime, there have been perhaps three people who called him Ted or Teddy. Yet some people make assumptions, and he decides to tolerate the error for now. This is not the moment for correction.

The first thing that hits him is the smell. Cigar smoke, thick and stale, hanging in the air like an unwelcome guest who's overstayed by hours. Theo loathes cigars… the performative masculinity of them… the way the smell clings to fabric and hair. He breathes through his mouth and moves forward.

Through the haze, a shape assembles itself: broad shoulders, that red coat, a figure seated behind a desk that seems designed to make visitors feel small. Theo strides toward him with a confidence he does not entirely feel.

"Mr. Donahue." Theo extends his hand. "An honor."

Donahue's grip is immediate and crushing—tighter than necessary, held longer than comfortable. A dominance ritual, as subtle as a sledgehammer. Theo recognizes it for what it is and yields to it, letting his own hand go passive, waiting. He will take his hand back when this man decides to release it, and not a moment before.

Finally, Donahue lets go. They settle into their respective chairs: Donahue behind the fortress of his desk, Theo in a seat positioned just low enough to require looking up.

Donahue stubs out his cigar in a crystal ashtray, and Theo feels a small wave of relief wash through his lungs.

For a long moment, Donahue simply looks at him. Sizing him up. Taking inventory. Theo holds the gaze, keeping his expression open, pleasant, mildly admiring.

Then he begins.

"I have to say, Mr. Donahue, seeing this operation in person…" Theo shakes his head slowly, as if words are failing him. "It's something else. The energy out there. The way you've transformed this place. I thought I understood it from my research, but being here..." He pauses, lets the silence do its work. "You've built something extraordinary."

Donahue's watery blue eyes brighten. His posture shifts, barely perceptible. Shoulders back, chin lifting.

Theo continues. "The vision it must take. The stamina. Most men would've sold off the pieces and retired. But you saw something nobody else saw."

He watches Donahue lap up every word. The man is parched—a dog who's found a puddle on a scorching summer day, drinking and drinking without pause. Theo wonders if he should dial it back, if the excess might trigger suspicion.

But Donahue gives no indication his thirst is quenched. Instead he leans forward, wanting more.

So Theo gives him more.

* * * * *

Has it already been a full hour? Theo wonders, sneaking a glance at his watch. He is in no hurry. After all, this is quite possibly the most important meeting he's ever had in his life.

In this short span of time, he and the owner of Donahue's Traveling Circus are now on a first-name basis. Well. Except Ace is still calling him 'Teddy'. He lets it slide for now, and instead continues smiling and nodding.

For seventy-two years old, Ace has an impressive amount of energy when it comes to congratulating himself.

Careful, Ringmaster, Theo thinks. *If you pat yourself on the back much harder you'll tip over.*

Ace clearly thrives on praise; he is animated as he gestures to emphasize his heroics. "Old man Leo's numbers were in a free-fall when I saw the potential. All his sentimental crap about 'tradition' was killing his business. If I hadn't plucked it out of the sky, it would have crashed and burned. But I knew I could steer it back to glory. And beyond, even. It's more profitable now than anyone ever thought possible. Thanks to me." Ace draws in a breath to continue. "And now? Now the other circuses are trying to copy me. But I'm way ahead. They'll never catch up."

Theo's eyes are wide with amazement, and he hopes his expression reads as impressed and not incredulity at Ace's bombastic ego. "Amazing, sir. Remarkable vision." He lays his palm flat over his heart and shakes his head slowly, as if overwhelmed by the brilliance before him.

With this, Ace grins widely. Even in this dim lighting Theo catches the gleam off his over-bleached teeth. "Exactly. You get it, Teddy. That's why I wanted to meet with you."

"The honor is all mine, sir." But Theo's mind snags on one phrase: more profitable than anyone thought possible. He makes a mental note. *Worth looking into.*

Ace rolls his neck left, then right. Both crack audibly. "Ahh, I needed that," he sighs with relief. "I'll have to see if Greta can do my shoulders tonight. The tension builds, y'know?"

Theo notes the stiffness, the effort. Seventy-two years is catching up.

Ace pushes himself up from the massive desk and draws a deep breath. The air has cleared somewhat; Theo hopes he's not about to light another cigar.

"Now, I promised you a tour of the lot earlier. You sure you don't want a bottled water?"

Ace is already moving toward the door. Theo rises quickly to follow and says, "I'm good, but thank you for offering."

When they exit through Patty's office Theo squints in the late morning sun, grateful to be out of the haze in Ace's lair. He has to walk quickly to remain by Ace's side, and is surprised by Ace's energy. He realizes this is not from vigor but from necessity; Ace is at the stage in his life where remaining still allows everything to seize up. Theo files this detail away with the others.

They wind through the back lot. Rows of RVs are parked, all in varying states of repair. The Big Top looms beyond them and the smell of animals and diesel and sawdust remind him of the time he spent researching the history of the circus. This work led to *Sawdust and Lies: An Industry in Decline*. His book remained on the bestseller list for over a year, in part because of his harsh criticism of the once-great Ace Donahue.

Ace is a few paces ahead and still talking, so Theo picks up the pace and catches the last words of his sentence.

"... didn't think I could pull it off, but I did. Owner *and* Ringmaster. Dual roles. No one had ever tried it before, until me."

Theo bites back the temptation to correct him. Ringling Brothers. Barnum. Countless family operations. The dual role is not Ace's invention; it is a common tradition in the industry. But Ace doesn't want facts. He wants validation, so Theo gives it to him.

"Of course, sir," Theo says, nodding vigorously. You've definitely proved it's not only possible, but that you are the only person who could ever pull it off."

Performers glance up as they pass, curious, cautious. Ace waves like royalty. Theo catalogs everything.

Then, standing outside the lion enclosure, watching the trainer work, Ace stops. Turns to Theo, suspicion etched in the lines of his face.

"So, Teddy. Let's talk about why you're really here." There is a pause. Ace is watching him carefully, then continues, "You wrote a book about me. Made a lot of money criticizing circuses, criticizing me specifically. Sixty weeks on the bestseller list, wasn't it? That's... what, six figures? More?"

Theo starts to respond but Ace continues.

"And now you show up. All smiles. All compliments. Wanting a 'tour.' I've been in this business long enough to know how this works. First book is the takedown. Second book is the 'I got access' insider tell-all. Am I right?"

Theo meets Ace's eyes. "You're absolutely right to ask, sir. And if I were in your position, I'd be asking the same question." He pauses to take in a breath, then continues. "Here's the truth. I *could* write another book. You're right about that. But I don't want to write about success from the outside anymore. I want to be part of success."

Theo leans forward slightly.

"That first book? I was an outsider looking in, making judgments based on research and interviews. But spending time here… seeing what you've actually built, watching you operate..." He shakes his head admiringly. "There's only so much you can understand from a distance. You have to be inside to really see it. And I realized—I don't want to be the critic in the cheap seats. I want to be in the ring."

He holds Ace's gaze.

"I'm not here to write about you, Mr. Donahue. I'm here to work for you."

Ace's expression hardens slightly. "Work for me. Doing what exactly?" And then Ace studies him for a moment before adding, "You did your homework about me, so I did my homework about you. Undergrad from Yale, MBA from Wharton. All on scholarship."

Something about the way he says 'scholarship' makes it sound like an insult. Judgment. To Theo it sounds like Ace is saying: *You're not really one of us.* Again, Theo knows silence is his ally and he fixes a bland expression on his face, waiting for Ace's next words.

"So... you think you're a smart cookie. And so far, you're doing all right. Making money off other people's hard work."

Theo has to bite his tongue… resist the urge to defend himself. Instead he smiles easily and chooses his words carefully.

"'Smart' is a subjective term, Ace, and I don't consider myself smart. I consider myself a fast learner. Call that whatever you want."

He waits a beat to create a dramatic effect, then drops his voice down lower when he adds, "But I know I can help you. For instance: you're following a standard circus schedule. Eight months on, four months off. Why? Why not maximize your revenue? I've got solid ideas on extending the season without degrading your assets. You protect your investment while increasing returns. More shows, more markets, same cost structure. Pure margin expansion."

Ace studies him for a long moment.

"So. You're angling for a job, hmm? And you think I hadn't already considered these options yet. Interesting."

Theo doesn't hesitate. "Maybe you have considered them. But you have not implemented them. And that's why I'm here. I can help you build this great enterprise into something unstoppable. You've already done what most couldn't. But I see so much more potential."

"Unstoppable, eh?"

Silence stretches into long seconds. Ace strokes his chin thoughtfully. Then grins. The angle of the sun makes his teeth practically glow.

"You've got my attention. Why don't we head back to my office and discuss terms. Patty can draw up a contract."

Ace's phone rings. He takes the call and walks away, leaving Theo standing in the dusty road outside the lions' enclosures.

Theo watches him go, then notices movement to his left. A little girl walks past. Honey-blonde braids. Coverall shorts. Skinned knees. She's holding a rope that's dangling behind her, but whatever is attached to that rope is not within his view yet.

She stops when she sees Theo, looks up at him and squints in the sunlight. Adjusts her position so her greenish-gray eyes are shaded. She has infinite freckles across her nose and cheeks.

"Hi," she says.

A donkey appears from behind a temporary wall… it's a dark gray beast, with impressively large ears twisting this way and that. Theo is startled by the beast's sudden appearance but recovers quickly. The donkey moves to stand at her side and rubs its head affectionately on her shoulder. The rope is now mostly slack on the ground, where it had been stretched between them.

"Hi, my name is Mr. Crane. What is your name?"

"My name is Pip." She scratches the donkey between his long ears. "This is Ravioli."

Theo remembers from his research. "Ah. Ravioli... and Ravioli has a brother named Ziti, right?"

Pip's face lights up. She's clearly thrilled he knows this detail, and suddenly her words are tumbling out quickly.

"Yes! They've been in the circus way longer than me. I was two when me and my daddy joined the Trentini family. Except now it's the Donahue..." She pauses for just a moment before finishing her sentence. "Family."

Something about her tugs at him. A feeling he can't quite identify. She reminds him of someone… someone he might have known a long time ago. *Before. Before what?* The thought surfaces and vanishes before he can grasp it.

A shadow passes overhead and Theo looks up. A huge crow lands on a nearby pole, tilts its head, and watches them from one black eye.

Theo looks back down at Pip. She has skinned knees, scabbed over and dusty. He smiles despite himself.

"You must work hard and play hard, to have knees like those. What do you do here?"

"I'm the youngest clown!" Pip announces with pride. "Glitter and Sprinkles? They're little people. But they're grown-ups, and I'm taller than them. And they play Cupcake's twins. They're really funny. And I get to do a number with Ravioli and Ziti in the grand parade. And sometimes Bongo lets me juggle, and—"

"Teddy!" Ace's voice cuts through her enthusiasm. He's off the phone, already moving. "Let's go. Patty's waiting."

Theo nods and starts to follow. But something makes him stop, turn back.

Pip and Ravioli are already walking in the opposite direction down the dusty road, her small hand resting on the donkey's neck. His long ears twitch as she sings to him. The crow watches from high atop the pole.

Then Theo turns toward Ace, toward the office, toward the contract.

*****

Blue folders. Six of them. Theo picks them up, returns them to alphabetical order, then slips them into the hanging files drawer inside his desk. There are two more reviews scheduled this afternoon, and therefore two blue folders still on his desk. He takes the one labeled Hodges, Brandon and sets it on top of the other files in the drawer. This leaves one—Richards, Virginia.

He has already scanned through her file twice. Nothing inside hints at what Ace told him earlier today about this woman. "Watch out, she's a whale," he'd harped. "And highly bitter. Prone to yelling."

Theo has seen and spoken with Virginia numerous times over the six months he's been with Donahue's circus. He has yet to see her yell at anyone. He wonders if Ace's perception of her has anything do with… Ace's perception of her.

There is a soft knock on his office door.

"Come in."

She is a bit out of breath as she navigates her way through the doorway. "Made it. Right on time." After closing the door behind her, she turns and offers a wary smile.

Theo realizes in this moment she is, indeed, a large woman. *Probably over four hundred pounds*, is his best guess. Her size is more noticeable up close. He returns her smile, a few degrees warmer than hers, and gestures to the reinforced chair he brought into his office today, just for this meeting. It holds up fine; there are minimal creaks and groans under her girth.

Her clown name is Cupcake, but he makes sure to call her Virginia during their meeting. In spite of Ace's warnings, he finds her agreeable and friendly. She is pleasant while he reviews the terms of her contract for next season. She is especially grateful for the modest raise she receives. Theo had requested this for all the performers; Ace had approved.

"Thank you so much, Mr. Crane," Virginia says, sliding the signed paperwork back toward him along with the pen.

He smiles warmly at her, making sure to maintain eye contact and not let his gaze fall below her numerous chins. She returns his smile as she pushes herself to a stand.

"And you said I should just… talk to Gloria about my new costume?"

"That's correct. There's no need to keep stitching up that seam over and over. I'll make sure you get a replacement."

Briefly, her large brown eyes well up with tears. "Mr. Donahue… he just…" But she does not finish the sentence and only shakes her head.

"I know. He could definitely use some lessons in tact. But don't tell him I said that," Theo teases, holding out his hand.

Virginia smooths down her bright blue dress and Theo thinks he hears her sniffle. She grasps his hand and shakes it once before letting go. "Thanks again."

"My pleasure, Virginia. We do appreciate your talent and dedication. Would you mind sending Brandon and his daughter in next? If they're out in the waiting area, that is."

Brandon Hodges' clown name is Zippy. The records Theo has been reviewing indicate Brandon's daughter is named Piper, though he's already met her and is aware she goes by Pip. He's been working on how to frame the news about Pip's employment status; he thinks he has settled on a solution.

"Sure thing, Mr. Crane. You have a nice evening."

Virginia squeezes out the door, careful to pull her caftan tight against her side so the cloth won't catch on the doorknob. It crosses his mind she must go through life navigating doorways and other narrow spaces with the same caution.

Just before the door latches closed, Virginia swings it back open again. "Mr. Crane? Looks like they're not here yet."

"Thanks for letting me know. You can just leave the office door open, then."

"And your trailer door, too? It was open when I got here."

"Yes. That's fine."

Virginia lets go of the doorknob and is on her way out when Theo hears the unmistakable sound of a lion's roar.

Bruno, Theo thinks. *His roar is deeper and louder than Hazel's.*

The sound carries through the entire lot and reminds Theo of the strangest disagreement he's had with Ace since coming on board as Operations Manager at Donahue's six months ago. He's used to hearing "no" from Ace, but this particular day there'd been a loud contempt that came with it.

At approximately half of their shows, especially the ones in bigger cities, animal rights activists show up to protest just outside their lot perimeter. They are not loud. They are not confrontational. They just walk around carrying signs that say things like "wild animals belong in the wild" and "no cages, no stages, no animals in the circus."

Theo saw a middle ground and offered a suggestion to Ace. "What if Donahue's came to some sort of an agreement with these groups? Allow them access to send a couple of their advocates through. Maybe once or twice a year. Let them see the training process, meet the handlers. See their living conditions and traveling conditions. And in return, they stop protesting right outside the fairgrounds."

"Hell no," Ace had bellowed at a surprisingly high volume. "I am *not* going to kowtow to any crunchy granola hippies. Those are *my* animals, I follow all the state laws, and they are not going to tell me how to run my business."

Theo got the gist of Ace's objections, but Ace continued the rant anyway.

"It's bad enough Trentini's had to get rid of their elephants. Magnificent creatures. People come to the circus for magnificent. And these animals, and what they do… is pure magnificence."

"Noted." Theo had said, then changed the subject.

That incident had happened maybe two months ago, when they were in Wisconsin. He'd simply catalogued it and moved on.

Now it's been more than six months he's been with Donahue's. As Theo had promised during their initial meeting, he'd quickly gotten up to speed on knowing both the administrative and the performing sides of Donahue's. For now, Ace had explained, he wants Theo to focus on the performers, and he will continue handling all admin and board matters.

The extensive research he'd done to write *Sawdust and Lies* was proving useful, and he's made sure to continue dropping breadcrumbs for Ace to indicate how thoroughly wrong he'd been about him when he wrote the book.

Theo glances at his watch; almost six o'clock. He hopes this last meeting of the day, the one with Brandon and Piper Hodges, goes quickly. He's been up since five-fifteen this morning. Except for a brief meeting with Ace around noon, he's been doing contract reviews all day.

Voices become audible and he hears footsteps. One more glance at his watch tells him it is six on the dot. He appreciates their punctuality and calls out.

"C'mon in, Brandon. Door's open."

Pip enters ahead of her father and stands to the side. She seems reserved compared to the other times he's seen her; he attributes this to the formality of his office.

"Hello, Mr. Crane," Brandon says, holding his hand outstretched.

Theo clasps Brandon's hand and cannot contain a wince.

"Oh, sorry 'bout that. I'm a little nervous," Brandon says, quickly pulling his hand back to wipe it on his jeans.

"It's okay," Theo says through a terse smile. He leans down to open the bottom drawer of his desk, pulls out a Kleenex, and wipes Brandon's sweat off his palm.

After crinkling the tissue up and tossing it in the trash, he looks back to see that the little girl is now holding out her own hand.

"It's okay, Mr. Crane. My hands are dry."

He notices flecks of gold in her green-gray eyes as he accepts her small hand in his, and is careful not to squeeze too hard.

"Have a seat, you two," Theo motions. In a practiced gesture, he runs his hand down his tie as he takes his seat.

Brandon sits in the reinforced seat; his little girl climbs on his knee despite the two chairs on the other side of his desk.

"I know I've met with you before, Brandon," Theo says. For some reason it makes him uncomfortable that she preferred to be in her father's lap. It complicates the room's dynamics, makes it harder to read Brandon's responses. "What was that… maybe five, six weeks ago?"

"Uh, yes, sir. That's correct."

"Were you able to get things worked out with your parents?"

"Yes, sir. Thanks again for allowing me and Pip to take a couple days off to go visit them."

"We got it all worked out on our end. I hope they've gotten settled into their new environment."

Both of Brandon's parents fell ill within days of each other and ultimately needed to go into a nursing home. With no other siblings, the logistics fell to their only child. Ace grumbled when Theo mentioned it, but Theo knew giving him the time off was necessary. Even though it was peak summer season. Even though he was gone over the weekend and missed four shows. Sometimes the best thing for the business is to accommodate an inconvenient request. This is something Ace does not accept, so Theo is glad he had the authority to grant it directly.

"Yeah, they're doing okay. Big adjustment and all."

Theo can tell he wants to say more but is glad Brandon stopped there.

"I can only imagine," Theo offers, his voice a little too chipper given the sentiment. He checks himself and drops to a softer tone when he adds, "It's good of you to look after them."

A sound escapes Brandon's mouth that might be a whisper or a sigh. Theo reaches into his bottom drawer and pulls Brandon's file out. He sets it on his desk, opens it, then pulls out the four top pages which are stapled together.

"I trust you've had a chance to look through next season's contract?"

"Yes, sir. I did. I have a couple of questions for you, though."

"I'm happy to hear your questions, but let me give you some information first, which may well answer those questions."

"Okay."

Pip wiggles on her father's knee and Theo tries to ignore her.

"Hold still, Pip. We'll go get supper as soon as we're done with Mr. Crane."

Theo forces himself to meet her eyes and smile. "This won't take long, young lady."

"I'm not fidgety because I'm hungry, Daddy. I want to ask a question."

"You heard Mr. Crane, darlin'. He said he's going to tell us some stuff, and it will probably answer any questions we've got. So, let's sit tight and listen to what he has to say."

Theo clears his throat and smiles at Brandon. "Yes, thank you. So, I need to inform you that Mr. Trentini was a bit… lax… about handling your daughter's status here, and when Mr. Donahue took over, he was likely unaware that he should address her role within the company."

Brandon's dark eyes show concern and Theo sees him clench his jaw. "What do you mean?"

"I don't mean to cause you any alarm, Brandon. There's no problem with Piper—"

"Pip," the child interrupts. "Everyone calls me Pip."

Theo looks toward her, trying to keep his expression neutral in spite of his annoyance. Her face radiates pure innocence; she has no idea that interrupting the adults is rude. He bites back the urge to correct her. Even gives her a halfhearted smile.

"Pip. Of course." He returns his attention to her father. "As I was saying, there is no problem with your daughter being here with you, Brandon. The issue is that most states have strict child labor laws. She should not be a paid performer within Donahue's."

"What… but…" Brandon stumbles over his words.

"But I'm a clown," Pip insists. Her conviction is large compared to her petite frame.

Brandon gives an indignant nod and finally has found his own voice. "Yes. Pip is one of us. A performer. Started when she was just four years old."

"Whoa, whoa," Theo says, holding his hands up in defense. "Of course she is. I'm not saying she can't still participate in the acts."

"Oh. Then what are you saying?"

"We will just need to switch her from contractor to volunteer. She can continue doing everything she's been doing. And to be honest, this change will actually give her more freedom to help in other areas, if she wants. She can be more involved in animal care. Help the other performers with props, if that interests her."

Theo watches Pip mull this over. He can tell the idea is growing on her, but Brandon is not on board. An idea occurs to him and he decides this is the perfect time to mention it.

"The llamas, for instance," Theo starts. "As you know, their handlers often have them doing photo shoots before the show."

This practice generates revenue beyond the tickets and concessions. Some people want a photo standing next to a llama. Others want a photo of their child sitting in a llama's green saddle. But sometimes, the child is not nearly as interested in sitting on a llama as the parent hopes. It is in this spirit that Theo suggests, "Maybe Pip could reassure the little ones that the llamas are gentle.

Or… if they're still not convinced… maybe Pip would like to pose with the child instead. I bet the parents and the kids would love that."

Brandon does not look excited about this opportunity, but Pip clearly has her own opinion.

"That would be so *fun*, Daddy." Her eyes are wide as the two of them regard each other. Brandon smiles at her enthusiasm, then turns his head to look at Theo again.

"Mr. Crane, she's been receiving wages since she was just four years old. She has a savings account and everything."

"And we fully appreciate that, Brandon… which is why Donahue's is going to roll her wages into your paychecks. Along with the raise that was mentioned earlier this year, when Ace announced that the season was going to be adjusted."

Brandon is quiet for a moment. His hand rests on Pip's knee, and she stops fidgeting. She is looking at him hopefully.

"Hang on." Brandon's voice is measured, but there's a tightness beneath it. "So… she can still perform with the clowns. And now she can help with the other animals, and be part of the photo ops, and…" He trails off, his brow furrowing as the words catch up with his thoughts. "You're saying she can do more than she was doing before."

He stops. Looks down at Pip, then back at Theo.

"You're telling me my daughter is going to be doing more work around here, and none of it counts as work?"

Theo opens his mouth to respond, but Brandon isn't finished.

"How come it was never a problem in the past? All these years, nobody once said a word about it. And now suddenly it's a legal issue?"

"I can't speak to how things were handled before I got here, Brandon. What I can tell you is how we need to handle them going forward."

Brandon turns this over. Theo watches him do it—watches the gears work behind those dark eyes—and shifts his weight in his chair. He's ready to wrap this up.

"I think I understand," Brandon says slowly. "We are all going to be working an extra eight weeks this season. And only have eight weeks off—basically the holidays—and then we start the new season early. And my daughter isn't going to get paid anymore, because the real work she is doing can't be counted as work, or Donahue might get fined." He pauses. "And Pip's earnings getting rolled into my paycheck now… that's my raise? Because Donahue did say with the extended season we would be getting a raise."

Theo's patience thins visibly. He straightens in his chair and his voice drops into something more formal, more final.

"Mr. Hodges. You *are* getting that four percent raise. Plus your daughter's earnings. Plus the income from the extended season." He holds Brandon's gaze. "All I'm doing is making sure we are in compliance with the law. The onus of your daughter's earnings needs to be yours, because of her age. Period."

Brandon opens his mouth. Closes it. Theo can tell he's trying to understand, and he wonders if he should have used a different word than onus.

The clown's jaw works like he's chewing on something that won't go down. He looks at Theo for a long moment—long enough that Theo shifts slightly in his chair—then drops his gaze to the top of Pip's head.

She's been sitting on his knee through all of this, swinging her legs, half-listening. The way kids do when adults talk about money and rules.

She looks up at him. Patient, trusting. Waiting to be told what this means.

Whatever was building behind Brandon's teeth, he lets it go. Not because Theo won. But because his daughter is on his knee and she doesn't need to watch her father lose a fight he was never going to win.

He breathes in slow. Out slower.

Then he forces a smile and wraps his arms around Pip from behind, giving her a squeeze. "Well, little Pip, you heard the man. We're getting a raise. I think we should get some ice cream after supper tonight. To celebrate."

Pip twists around on his knee. "Really? Can I get two scoops?"

"Of course, Pip. Heck, I might have three scoops myself."

She giggles and settles back against him, satisfied. The world is good. Daddy got a raise and there will be ice cream.

Over her head, Brandon's eyes find Theo. The smile is gone. What replaces it isn't anger—it's something quieter. More permanent. The look of a man filing something away that he will never forget.

Theo holds the gaze just long enough to acknowledge it. Then he slides the contract across the desk toward the man. He even uncaps the pen before holding it out to Brandon. He watches this thirty-something father with short, dark brown hair—perhaps a decade younger than himself—sign his name with a flourish. He grins at Theo with what looks like recognition, rather than gratitude for a raise and another year of work secured. And Theo offers him an equally large smile, though there is an emotion behind it he cannot name.

As they leave Theo's office, Brandon picks up his daughter and turns to him to ask, "Would you like me to close your door?"

"No, thank you," he replies. "I'm heading out shortly."

A few moments later he hears the outer door of his small but efficiently designed trailer click shut. Ace provided this trailer for Theo a month ago. The old one was adequate. Perhaps even a little bit bigger. But this one is brand new and top of the line. Certainly not as nice as Ace's. But still nice.

A buzz from his cellphone is barely audible from the top drawer of his desk, and he pulls it out to see his wife's name and image on the screen.

"Hi, hon," he answers. "Between meetings?"

"Of course," she answers. Her tone is breezy and light. "I've only got a few minutes."

"Me too. One more meeting tonight."

"Wish I could say I only have one more meeting tonight."

"Still in Boston?" His wife is Senior VP of Strategic Partnerships at Advantra Pharmaceuticals, and she travels even more than he does.

"Yes," Sophia answers. "Until Wednesday. Then in Tampa from Thursday through Saturday."

Theo twists open the blinds in his office and sees Brandon and Pip in the distance, walking hand in hand. Probably heading to the Dairy Queen he'd noticed yesterday; it's just a couple of blocks off the back lot.

He scans left and right before closing the blinds again. "I should get going, babe."

"Of course. Still going to be home on the fifth? And leaving on the morning of the eighth?"

"That's the plan. Talk soon. Love you."

"You too. Bye-bye."

Ten minutes later, Theo locks his trailer on the way out and slips his sunglasses on. He descends the three steps of his trailer and heads toward the company vehicle Ace leased for him recently. The dark gray Chevy Tahoe is parked facing away from him, and it is not until he climbs into the driver's seat that he notices a white splotch on the windshield. It is an eyesore on the otherwise pristine SUV, and before closing his door he gets out again, wondering if it might be something other than a bird dropping. From outside, however, it is undoubtedly an ugly, fried-egg-shaped mess.

He removes his sunglasses and scans the area to see if the guilty party might still be around. Glancing up at a utility pole, he sees a solitary crow staring back at him. They regard each other silently for a few seconds before Theo finally points at his windshield and asks the large bird, "Did you do that?"

The bird fluffs its feathers and lifts its wings once, but then settles again and looks in a different direction. And that's when he sees the crow's beak has a stark white line that crosses from one end to the other. A scar, perhaps. Or a pigment variation, like a birthmark.

Theo sighs and shakes his head, mildly exasperated. After putting the sunglasses back on, he climbs in again and closes the door. The new car smell hits him. He starts the Tahoe and squirts the windshield with wiper fluid, then turns the wipers on high. Most of the mess disappears, but a streak of white remains. He repeats the process but it's still there. After turning off the wipers, he glares at the streak.

I'll go through a car wash tonight, he tells himself.

And with that, he leaves the lot and heads to Roger Weber's office, which is in a small suburb of Omaha. Ace arranged for Theo to meet his accountant while they are making their way through Nebraska; he hopes this means Ace is ready for him to have an in-depth understanding of the admin side.

Traffic is light this Tuesday evening. The last of their caravan arrived early this morning, and show setup is well underway. Their next performance will be Thursday. He should have all the contract and performance reviews done by tomorrow night, he estimates.

The Tahoe's windshield is gleaming; he found a carwash on the way out of town and is watching the sun slowly move below the horizon.

Theo always uses drive time to sort through his thoughts... to review procedures, to work out some problems, to preempt others. Today is no different.

In just half a year, he has streamlined the advance work by cutting underperforming stands and replacing them with better markets. He's renegotiated three vendor contracts. He even got Ace to bring on a staff veterinarian by feeding him the numbers over the course of a few weeks—telling him the cost of sourcing local vets at every stand, plus transport and emergency fees—and letting Ace connect the dots. Ace finally said "You know what? We should just hire our own vet." And Theo had three résumés on Ace's desk within the hour. Whittled down from dozens. He'd asked Ace if he wanted to conduct the interviews himself, or if he would prefer that Theo handle it. Ace had waved him off. "You've got a good eye, Teddy. Just pick the best one." And so Dr. Block joined Donahue's a few months back, and Ace told the board it was his initiative.

Theo had even managed to expand the season. More stands, tighter routing, better margins. A couple of months back he noticed Ace had started introducing him to people as "the best hire I ever made." Which Theo understood was Ace's way of taking credit for the improvements. That was fine. The man who gets the credit and the man who holds the power don't need to be the same person.

When he arrives at the office complex, he notices the parking lot is deserted save for a few vehicles scattered about. But one row back from the entrance, in the spots in front of the building number Ace gave him, is a white Toyota Camry. As nondescript as nondescript can be. Theo makes a mental note, then parks close to the front entrance of Roger's building. He shuts off the engine, then closes his eyes and brings up the mental image of the one and only photo he'd found of Roger Weber, Omaha, CPA, online. It will be interesting to see how much Roger has changed in the ten years since that photo was taken, back when he was with a big firm. Theo's research revealed Roger had opened his own office around the same time Ace bought Trentini's. And he's sure that's not a coincidence.

Roger's office is in a squat brick building wedged between a print shop and a vacant storefront. Theo pulls the glass door open, and a small bell jingles overhead. The reception area is tidy but uninspired: two upholstered chairs, a low table with fanned-out magazines, and framed inspirational posters mounted on the wall.

There's a desk with a dark computer monitor and a nameplate that reads LORETTA KIRBY. The chair behind it is pushed in. No purse on the hook. No coffee mug. The lights are on, but the room feels like it's been exhaling for a while.

This is going to be an interesting evening, Theo tells himself.

Several seconds later, he calls out. "Hello? Anybody here?"

A door opens down a short hallway, and a neatly groomed, middle-aged man emerges. He's already smiling too wide for the occasion.

Roger Weber looks exactly like the person central casting would send if you asked for an accountant. Pale, tidy, buttoned up. Glasses with black plastic frames. His salt-and-pepper hair looks like he just combed it. He's even got a pocket protector in his white dress shirt; Theo has not seen one in years.

One detail seems at odds with this otherwise stereotypical look for a numbers guy. He's of average build, but he has a gut. Theo is not sure if this detail supports his theory, but he plans to find out.

"Mr. Crane! Welcome, welcome." Roger's handshake is enthusiastic and slightly damp. "I let Loretta go home already. She's great, but it gets pretty quiet around here after four. Can I get you a coffee? I've got a Keurig in the back. Probably should've gotten the good stuff for this, but I didn't know what you drink. I've got some of those little creamer cups too. Loretta got a variety pack of the flavored ones. French vanilla, hazelnut, Irish crème—"

"Black is fine," Theo answers with an agreeable smile.

"Black! A man after my own heart. Come on back." He waves his hand and turns down the hall.

Roger talks as they make their way to his office down the hall. He points out a framed photo of himself shaking hands with a local news anchor. "That's Cherise Waters. Channel Six. She did a segment on small business tax prep and I was one of the featured accountants. Good exposure. Got three new clients off that piece."

"Impressive," Theo offers, and Roger beams.

His office itself is orderly in a way that borders on compulsive. Every file labeled. Every pen in its cup. The diplomas and certifications are arranged in perfect symmetry on the wall behind Roger's desk: CPA, CMA, CFE, EA. Four frames, evenly spaced, perfectly level. Theo's eyes move across them all, then he takes a second look at the CFE.

Certified Fraud Examiner... interesting, Theo observes, and he wonders if there is any irony to the credential.

Roger settles into his chair and launches into a joke about an accountant, a lawyer, and a bartender. Theo can tell from the setup that the punchline will be mediocre, but he laughs anyway—a generous laugh, slightly louder than necessary. Roger lights up like a man who rarely gets that reaction.

They spend the next hour going through the books. It is during this time that something shifts. His nervous chatter falls away. His slender hands stop fidgeting. His eyes sharpen behind his glasses. He knows every number, every line item. He effortlessly recalls every contract, every vendor, every seasonal fluctuation in revenue. He does not need to reference any files. It is all in his head, and Theo realizes Roger is a living, breathing map of Donahue's financial architecture.

During this hour, Theo watches the transformation with genuine interest. This is not the same man who offered him hazelnut creamer minutes ago. This is someone else entirely.

"You've got a hell of a handle on this operation, Roger."

He looks up at Theo and blinks, as if the compliment caught him off guard. "Well. That *is* what Ace pays me for."

"No," Theo says, leaning back in the chair. It squeaks as he does so. "I've worked with a lot of people who do what they're paid for. This is different. Ace is lucky to have someone who understands his business this thoroughly."

And there it is. A flush creeps up Roger's neck. His chin lifts almost imperceptibly. His fingers stop tapping the desk. For just a moment, the man with a pocket protector looks like someone who's been waiting a very long time to hear those words.

Theo files it away. *Achilles.*

"Listen," Theo says, glancing at his watch as if the idea just occurred to him. "I've been going since five-fifteen this morning and I haven't eaten since lunch. Any chance you'd want to grab a bite? My treat. I saw a Chili's a few miles back."

Roger hesitates for exactly one second. "You know what? Sure. Why not. There's nobody waiting for me at home." He laughs—the self-deprecating kind—and Theo smiles.

Theo nods once, pleased. "I'll drive."

The Chili's is nearly empty this Tuesday night. A few families are finishing up. A couple at the bar is watching baseball. Theo requests a booth in the back corner, and the hostess obliges without question.

They order buffalo wings and fries, and Theo asks the server to bring a bottle of Maker's Mark to the table. Roger raises his eyebrows but does not object. By the time the wings arrive, Roger is two bourbons in and his posture has changed for the third time this evening. The rigid accountant from the office is gone. The eager-to-please jokester from the lobby is gone. What remains is looser, warmer, and—Theo notices—hungrier.

It started with Ace. Small complaints at first. The way Ace never reads the reports Roger prepares. The way Ace calls him at odd hours demanding numbers he should already know. The way he introduces Roger to people as "my numbers guy," as if years of his carefully constructed fortress could be reduced to a title that sounds like a bookie.

Theo matches him gripe for gripe. Nothing too sharp. Just enough to signal: *I see what you see. I deal with it too.* The bourbon did its work. The complaints got more specific. More honest.

"The man doesn't understand half of what I do for him," Roger laments, shaking his head. "Not half."

Theo shakes his head in sympathy and pours him another finger, but he is still nursing his first drink. "I believe that," he offers, his tone earnest.

"I mean it. The structure I've put in place? The way everything flows? It's not just bookkeeping. It's architecture." Roger's eyes are bright again, the way they'd been in the office when the numbers took over. "And he just... he just waves his hand." Roger waves his own hand and does a decent imitation of Ace's rumbly baritone. "He says, 'Just handle it, Roger. Make it work, Roger.' Like I'm fixing a leaky faucet."

Theo holds back a smile and instead reaches for a fry. Chews it thoughtfully. Then he casually offers, "When Ace told me you handle the full sponsor lifecycle—the intake, processing, and reconciliation? I thought wow, that's a ton of responsibility, and it takes a very specific skillset to manage it all properly."

Roger freezes. He's holding a half-eaten wing in one hand from which he just took a bite.

There it is, Theo thinks. *Funny how a carefully worded sentence can expose a cleverly hidden room. And here I am, already inside before Roger thought to lock the door.*

His eyes flicker to Theo's face, searching for something.

Theo keeps his expression mild. Interested. Nothing more.

Roger resumes chewing and sets the wing down carefully on his appetizer plate. Looks back up at Theo, his expression a mix of calculation and curiosity. Finally, he licks wing sauce off his thumb and smiles at Theo before he says, "Well, well. I already knew Ace trusts you. But I didn't know he trusts you *this* thoroughly."

Theo reaches for another fry and pops it in his mouth, then leans against the back of the booth. Chews, swallows.

"For all his faults," Theo says lightly, "Ace does know how to find good people and keep them loyal to him."

That's when the dam breaks. Not all at once. But Roger spends the next forty minutes quietly laying it all out. The four shell companies. How he routes the money. The method of cash from ticket sales getting split into legitimate revenue and a shadow operation to move money through entities registered in a handful of states. Theo learns that Roger keeps the second set of books himself—no software, no cloud storage, nothing digital. Just handwritten ledgers kept in a safe in his office. And he's the only one with the combination.

And the pride. God, the pride. Roger talks about the structure the way an architect talks about a cathedral. Every decision is deliberate. Every layer has a purpose. He has built this thing over the years, refining it, stress-testing it, adapting it as tax law evolves. It is, by any objective measure, brilliant.

Michelangelo, Theo thinks. *Ace handed him a ceiling and told him to make it look nice. Roger built the Sistine Chapel.*

"You want to know something?" Roger asks, leaning in. The bourbon has loosened his jaw and his tie. "When my wife divorced me, she hired a forensic accountant. A good one, too. Cost her a fortune." He pauses for effect. "They never even got close." And then Roger's voice drops to a confident whisper when he adds, "This thing? It's bulletproof." He shakes his head, amazed by his own prowess.

Theo raises his glass to Roger. A toast without words.

"Your office," Theo says several moments later. "It's pretty spartan. And the space you're leasing is low-rent because of the location. It's good you're keeping a low profile. But I'm curious where you're putting your piece of the pie." He meets Roger's eyes and adds with a grin, "No offense, but it doesn't appear to be your wardrobe or your car."

Roger smiles. It's a real smile, not the eager-to-please kind from the lobby. "I've made a few investments over the years. Quiet ones. Nothing flashy."

Theo nods slowly. Of course. He's got an exit plan. Disciplined enough to build it incrementally, patient enough to wait. He respects that. And he also understands what this means. Roger has something he wants to protect.

"Hey," Theo says, leaning closer to Roger and lowering his voice a bit. Roger takes the hint and leans in also. "I noticed that Patty has a small filing cabinet in her office that she keeps locked.

It's right next to the tall one, which she doesn't keep locked. Does that mean what I think it might mean?"

And then Theo sits upright, having baked conspiracy into the question.

Roger sits back slowly and tips his chin upward slightly to gaze at the light above their table. One eye squints, and his mouth twists to the side; he is putting serious thought into what Theo has just implied. "Hmm," he finally says, and then he shakes his head slowly. "No. There is no way she knows anything. I'm the only one… well, besides you too, now… who's aware. I'm sure of it."

"That's good," Theo offers, his words light. Congratulatory, even.

They finish the wings with light banter. The fries are cold, and the bottle is two-thirds empty—most of it in Roger.

After Theo settles the tab, he leans back in the booth and says, "Roger. Just for the sake of clarity." His voice is low and reassuring. Gentle, even. "I suspected what was going on. But I wasn't sure until you confirmed it tonight."

The color drains from Roger's face, and his eyes are blank.

"This is a little bit concerning," Theo continues, "but don't worry. I won't tell Ace that you let it slip. For now, my knowledge is just between us." He pauses to let that settle. "When the time is right, I'll tell Ace what I know, and I'll make sure he doesn't blame you for anything."

Roger opens his mouth. Closes it. Gives a small, bouncing nod.

There is small talk for the next couple of minutes, and then Theo offers to get him an Uber. Roger agrees, though he still wears a bit of a shellshocked expression. When the ride pulls up to the front doors, Theo walks him to the curb. He watches the car pull away. Roger's pale face is visible through the back window, still processing what just happened to him.

Theo turns around, goes back inside to their booth, and leaves a generous tip. He heads to the exit again and pushes open the door.

The September night air has a bit of a chill, but it feels cool and clean.

He is tired from his long day but smiles to himself and thinks just one word.

Bonus.

ACT II

Autumn, eight months later.

"Dammit, Teddy, shut those jackasses up!"

Theo is holding his left hand over his ear and his phone is pressed against his right ear when Ace's bellow nearly makes him drop his phone into the sawdust.

"Hang on," Theo says. He presses mute and directs one of the clowns to take Ziti and Ravioli out of the Big Top. Ziti is the one complaining at the moment.

Usually their hee-haws and snorts draw laughter from the crowds, but Ace has never had any tolerance for their noise. "Those jackasses are laughing at me," is a common refrain Theo hears from Ace. He knows it's simply not true. They're just being donkeys. But he always obliges his boss and agrees they can be quite loud and annoying.

There is still plenty happening in the Big Top while crew hands shuffle supplies around and performers ready their props for this afternoon's performance. But the donkeys are no longer around and Theo can resume his call with Ace now.

"Sorry, sir. What were you telling me?"

He hears shuffling noises for a few seconds. Finally Ace barks, "Why hasn't Liz received her tickets for tonight's show yet?"

Theo's mind sifts through a dozen situations he's dealing with in the moment. Ensuring that Patty followed through on his request—which he'd delegated—to handle comped tickets is not on the list. But, he adds it and pushes it to the top three.

"I'll check into that, sir. I thought it was already taken care of, but I will make sure your friend gets VIP treatment tonight."

The call ends abruptly. Ace does this often—doles out an order and does not listen to the reply before he hangs up.

Before Theo can put his phone back in his pocket, someone is tapping him on the shoulder. He turns to see Marco, lead aerialist. His expression is terse.

"Mr. Crane, I know I've mentioned this to you before, but the group put me up to approaching you about it again."

"The nets and rigging," Theo says, nodding.

Marco sighs. "Yes."

Theo nods more vigorously. "I've been working on this with Mr. Donahue. He understands your concerns, and you know I do, too."

"I know. You've been good, advocating for us. We've figured out a workaround, but you know..."

Yes. Theo knows. The nets are old and fraying in some areas. At a glance they look fine, but it does not take a mechanical engineer to understand they need to be replaced. The 'workaround' Marco speaks of? All of the aerialists have learned to drop away from the weakest area, even the less experienced ones. They don't fall often. Almost never, in fact. But they dismount from the trapeze, the tightrope, sometimes even the platform by dropping down to the net rather than climbing down the ladder.

"Absolutely," Theo agrees. "It's such a liabil–" He stops himself mid word and quickly recovers. "I mean, it's such a safety issue. I've encouraged him several times that we need to invest in new nets. New rigging. I will bring it up again."

"Thanks, Mr. Crane," Marco says as he turns to walk away. "Appreciate it."

Except Theo can't hear the last two words, because a shrill voice comes from behind him.

"Excuse me, is that you, Mr. Crane?"

It is hard to mistake Theo for anyone other than himself. He does not wear the casual jeans and tee-shirts the performers wear between dress rehearsals and shows. Instead he wears Dockers, steel-toed boots that are caked with dried mud from yesterday's rain, and a button-down shirt with the sleeves rolled up to his elbows.

He turns to see the concessions manager rapidly approaching him. “Yes, Brenda. How can I help?”

She does not wait for pleasantries; instead, she breathlessly explains that the concessions generator died overnight. Two coolers full of melted ice cream, spoiled meat. Theo knows the additional load on the other generators means he needs to handle this right away. Putting it off guarantees the lights will go out at the most inopportune moment. Like tonight, in front of a full house.

Theo is already pulling up contacts on his phone before she finishes. As he scrolls, he says to Brenda, “I’ll have a rental generator here within two hours. Hopefully sooner. Are you able to go get replacement food, or do I need to send someone else?”

“I don’t have that kinda money, Mr. Crane,” she says. Her voice is two parts exasperation, one part anger.

“Of course I’ll let you use my card for the shopping. Can you squeeze it in, or do you want me to find someone else?”

She sighs and glances at the time on her phone. “If I can go right now, that would be better than sending one of the counter staff.” Her voice drops lower and he hears her mumble, “They’d probably screw it up anyway.”

Theo’s already got the lot mechanic’s number pulled up; he hopes the man will answer right away. Before calling, he adds, “You’re a gem, Brenda. Let’s get this fixed before the first audience members show up.”

A minute later he is still giving the mechanic instructions when he hears a roar from one of the lions. Without missing a beat of their conversation, he turns to see Charlie gesturing to his assistant and approaching the lions’ enclosures, pointing back and forth between them. Bruno is leaning against the bars at the far end of his cage. Hazel is in hers, pacing. Theo can tell this will also require his attention before he can deal with Liz’s VIP package.

He finishes the call he is on, making sure the mechanic understands he will need to secure a backup generator for the rest of the weekend.

Only then does Theo approach Charlie. The sharp smell of urine hits him some ten feet from the big cats' cages.

"Everybody okay?" he asks, moving his gaze between the two lion handlers. He has to breathe through his mouth to keep his eyes from watering, the odor is so pungent.

"Fine," Charlie spits. His assistant Destiny's face tells another story.

"Charlie." The tone in Destiny's voice tells Theo more than anything he is reading from Charlie, who has a scowl etched into his face.

Theo glances between the lion and lioness, both of which are pacing. He is not sure which one voiced the loud complaint. "Was that Bruno?" he finally asks.

Destiny answers before Charlie. "No, it was Hazel," she says, her dark eyes aimed at Theo and broadcasting her judgment.

Finally, Charlie speaks. "This is highly, highly unusual behavior for her, Mr. Crane. Females only mark territory when they are very stressed. And now Bruno is even more stressed, because Hazel is showing her stress."

Theo already knows Charlie's feelings about the extended season. Normally they would have been back to Corpus Christi by this time, weeks before Thanksgiving, but they still have several more stands before arriving at winter quarters. Plus, almost everyone in the company has reason to be unhappy—whether it is performing through Thanksgiving weekend, or knowing they will only have eight weeks off before next season starts, instead of their usual sixteen weeks.

"Look, Charlie, I hear what you're saying. Stressed lions are unsafe lions."

"It's not just that," Charlie says, his voice rising. "You're right, it's more dangerous than usual. But there's no reason for putting them through this, other than Ace has decided he wants to eke out a few grand more."

From the corner of his eye Theo sees Dr. Block crossing toward the back of the Big Top, and he flags down the skilled veterinarian.

"Dr. Block, do you have a couple minutes to talk with me and Charlie?"

The silver-haired man with dark skin and darker eyes turns toward them. Theo sees he is carrying his emergency kit, probably making sure he's prepped for today's shows.

"Yes?" Dr. Block answers, changing direction and heading toward the lions' cages. Like Theo, he notices the smell from several yards away and worry clouds his expression.

"That was Hazel?" he asks Charlie.

"Yes."

Suddenly there are three pairs of accusing eyes staring at him. In the moment Theo can only think of two options.

He clears his throat and says, "Look, you know I've got every sympathy for all the performers and the animals. This is not the norm, and everyone feels like we should be wintering in Corpus already. But we aren't. We've still got three weeks. I was hoping their break while we were in Colorado would help."

Bruno and Hazel were not able to perform in Colorado due to changes in state law preventing big cats from performing for the public, similar to how elephants have been phased out around the country over the past couple decades.

"Yet here we are," Dr. Block says. He gestures at Bruno, still leaning against the bars, then Hazel. She is still pacing in a tight path.

"So, we can extend that time off for them, and hope that takes the edge off. Or, hear me out, Dr. Block. Is there some kind of therapeutic technique, or an anti-anxiety medicine you could administer short-term? Just to help them through these final few weeks?"

Charlie and Destiny exchange a look, but Dr. Block never takes his eyes off Theo; clearly, he has opinions about the latter option.

Charlie turns to Dr. Block, his eyes pleading, though for which solution Theo is not sure. That is, until Charlie leans closer to the elder veterinarian and Theo hears him say, "We've given them something in the past, before you joined us this year. They do well with it."

Dr. Block snaps his attention to Charlie and asks a single word; it sounds like the name of a medicine.

Charlie nods. Destiny shrugs and rolls her eyes, then walks over to grab a bunch of rags. Dr. Block turns to observe Hazel and Bruno, then turns back to Charlie. Last, he turns to Theo.

"I'm going on the record here, Mr. Crane. My recommendation is for them to be finished performing this season. But if I'm being overruled, I will work with Charlie to administer a mild tranquilizer. Only on Saturdays and Sundays, when they have the double performances. They will need to be monitored, and I will titrate the dose as necessary."

"Of course, Dr. Block," Theo says, hiding his relief. "Your expertise is appreciated."

"And this is only for the last three weeks of this season. It is not a solution for the fatigue and stress they're experiencing purely for financial benefit."

"I agree wholeheartedly. I will make sure Mr. Donahue understands."

The mere mention of Ace's name causes Charlie to bristle. Destiny's lips are pressed tight, and she is busy wiping down the bars of Hazel's cage. She watches the lioness closely for her own safety.

"Hey, Brad?" Theo calls to one of the crew hands who is testing sound equipment. "Grab Anna, and let's get this sawdust over here replaced."

As he departs the area, Theo finally is able to breathe through his nose again.

He heads toward the exit, pulling his phone out again. He is about to text Patty to ask what happened with Liz's tickets when Razzle and Dazzle start up again. It's only eight in the morning, but they are broadcasting to anyone who will listen.

"It's a must-see show today, ladies and gentlemen," they call in perfect unison.

Then, Razzle yells, "Don't miss Donahue's Traveling Circus!"

And Dazzle follows up with an equally loud, "You'll be on the edge of your seat while the trapeze artists defy gravity with grace and artistry!"

They are stationed just outside the tent's entrance flaps wearing their bright costumes and garish makeup. Theo tunes them out completely.

*****

The second show ends at nine-forty and the last audience member clears the lot by ten-fifteen. Theo checks his watch. He's been going since five-thirty this morning and has two more things on his list before he can sleep: the debrief with Ace, and the email.

He walks across the quiet lot, nodding to a couple of crew hands who are sweeping up and bagging sawdust. The Big Top is half-dark—its canvas flanks exude warmth, the lasting byproduct of a full house. Both shows had been clean. Good crowds. Enthusiastic response to the new opening number. He's already identified three small adjustments to recommend before the next stand, but those can wait. The debrief never runs long when Ace is in a good mood. And Saturday double-show revenue always puts Ace in a good mood.

He knocks twice and lets himself in.

Ace has loosened his Ringmaster coat and is sitting in the large leather chair he keeps in the back of his trailer, not at his desk, which is where Theo prefers him. He's learned Ace seated at his desk signals work, whereas the wingback chair signals Ace has already decided nothing he's about to say is relevant.

"There's my boy!" Ace says, his tone generous. He is holding a glass of something amber, and gestures broadly in Theo's direction. "Teddy. Hell of a day. Hell of a show. Both of them."

"Both of them," Theo agrees, and takes his usual seat.

He waits the necessary moment. Gives Ace breathing room. There is a particular rhythm to these debriefs, and interrupting it is never worthwhile. The information Ace retains when asked for it is better than what Theo pushes at him unannounced.

Finally Ace spreads his free hand. "So. How bad was it?"

"Morning had some complications. Nothing that affected the shows."

He begins with the generator—Brenda, the spoiled inventory, the rental unit he'd sourced. Ace nods along in the way that Theo has come to understand means he is registering approximately forty percent of the words. He mentions the lions. Charlie's concerns. Dr. Block's recommendation.

"Doc knows what he's doing," Ace says, with the magnanimous wave of a man who made no decision whatsoever. "Good call letting him handle it."

"Thank you. The protocol Charlie and Dr. Block worked out is only for double-show days, and he'll taper off once we reach winter quarters."

"Right, right." Ace is already elsewhere. "Liz had a wonderful time, by the way. Sent me a message after the first show. Said her kids were practically out of their minds."

"I'm glad it came together. I made sure Patty got them situated before the gates opened."

Ace points at him. Wiggles his bushy gray eyebrows and his finger. "That's exactly what I'm talking about. That's the kind of thing…." He trails off, then continues again, "It's the details, young man. People remember that." He takes a slow sip. "You've got a *feel* for it, Teddy, I'll give you that."

Theo offers a modest smile, then continues. "There's the ongoing concern from the aerialists about replacing the nets and rigging. They really are well past their prime. A liability issue."

Ace tenses and wrinkles his nose, then takes a sip. He is quiet for several seconds before he gripes, "They're never satisfied. They got new costumes, and new platforms and ladders this year."

"True." Theo considers mentioning those were cosmetic and not safety issues, but he knows Ace will not be swayed. He finalizes this topic by telling Ace, "For the sake of our insurance, though, we will need to get the new nets and rigging soon."

"I hear you," Ace grumbles, then pulls a piece of lint off his Ringmaster coat. Drops it off to the side of his chair.

"And last, there were two small decisions I made today that were outside my usual authority. I want to make sure you're aware, so there's no confusion later."

Ace tilts his head with lazy curiosity. This is the moment Theo has calibrated carefully. Most subordinates would bury the information or never volunteer it at all. Theo does the opposite—he surfaces it, frames it as deference, and in doing so positions himself as both unusually capable and unusually trustworthy. The two things that make a man indispensable are the same two things that make him dangerous. Ace has never seemed to understand this.

"Brenda didn't have the funds to replace the inventory on short notice," Theo says. "Rather than lose the concessions revenue or delay the food while we sorted out petty cash, I put the replacement order on my personal card. It wasn't much. I'll submit the receipt to Patty in the morning."

Ace waves his glass. "Of course, of course. We'll get you reimbursed."

"There's no rush." Theo lets the pause breathe. "It was the right call for the operation."

Something flickers across Ace's face. Not quite gratitude—Ace is not built for gratitude—but satisfaction. He is the kind of man who interprets loyalty as a tribute to himself. Theo uses his own money for the circus? That reflects well on Ace. That is how good the operation is, how good the boss is, that a man volunteers his own resources without being asked.

"Then, the other thing," Theo continues. "I'm sure you recall Derek Chavez?"

Ace's blank expression gives no hint of recognition.

"Bongo? The skinny clown?"

Now Ace nods. He tends to refer to the clowns by their stage names, even those who go by their given names outside of the ring. Especially those who go by their given names outside of the ring.

"He asked me a week ago if there's any flexibility on Thanksgiving weekend. We'll be in El Paso then. His home town. And his youngest daughter is having her first real Thanksgiving at her own table. Bongo asked if he could take off Thursday and Friday, so he can be there for it."

Ace's expression shifts by a tiny fraction. He doesn't care about Bongo or Bongo's daughter. But he cares deeply about being consulted before decisions are made, especially ones that touch the performance schedule.

"I told him that since we have enough coverage for both days," Theo says, his voice unhurried, "and since he's given us eleven years and rarely asks for anything, I was comfortable approving it. But I wanted you to hear it from me directly, rather than find out later." He meets Ace's eyes. "If you'd prefer those decisions all come to you, I will make sure they do."

The beat holds.

Ace takes a sip. Sets the glass down. He won't say he wanted to be consulted, because that would require he admit that he would have denied it. And the explanation for denying it would require he explain why Bongo's eleven years of consistency, and this request for a holiday off, are less important than the skinny clown being in ring number one… and the last to tumble out of the clown car on those two days. Instead, Ace does what Ace does.

"Good call," he says.

Theo nods. "I appreciate that."

He finishes the debrief—just a few minor items from the afternoon show, and mention of crowd traffic for the Sunday matinee. Ace asks one question that has nothing to do with anything they've discussed and is already refilling his glass before Theo answers it.

Fifteen minutes after he arrived, Theo lets himself out and heads back to his trailer.

The lot is quiet now. A generator hums from the direction of the concessions stand—the rental unit, doing its job. The Big Top has gone fully dark and the flaps are closed for the night.

After entering his own trailer he locks the door. Sits at his desk. Pulls out his phone and types a message to Patty:

Patty, receipt for concessions resupply attached. Brenda Mitchell can confirm the purchase. Please note in my expense reimbursement that this was a same-day emergency to protect tonight's revenue, and that approval came from me directly. Ace is aware. Let me know if you need anything else to process it. Thanks, TC.

He reviews it once. Sends it. Then he opens his laptop.

The email he composes to Ace is brief. Three short paragraphs. A summary of the generator situation. The need to replace the aerialist nets and rigging. The lion medication protocol, with Dr. Block's conditions spelled out clearly: for double-show Saturdays and Sundays only, titrated dosage, not to extend past this season. Bongo's approved two days off. The expense reimbursement amount.

He signs it simply: *Theo.*

He reads it once more before sending. Not because he's looking for errors—there are none—but because he likes to see the shape of it. Orderly. Documented. The kind of email a careful man sends because a careful man keeps records. Because a careful man understands that things can be misremembered, and misrepresented, and that a paper trail is only as useful as the person who thought to make one.

He hits send.

The trailer is quiet. Somewhere out on the lot, a crow shifts on its perch. But it is dark and he cannot see it, so it doesn't exist.

He closes the laptop and goes to bed.

*****

Three more nights. Just five more shows, three more nights.

Theo is counting down, like everyone else with Donahue's Traveling Circus. Especially the performers. But tonight—their final Friday performance of the season—he is feeling the exhaustion too.

They are in San Antonio, the final venue before they head to winter quarters. Corpus Christi. Where Theo first met Ace and talked his way into this job.

One week from tonight, Theo will be home and able to sleep in his own bed—hopefully next to his wife. She's been juggling her schedule, trying to find a way to spend a few days with him before she travels to attend her company's annual awards celebration. This year Advantra is holding the event in Santa Cruz. He was invited too, but will skip it this time. He has attended every year for a decade, but this year it seems more important to unwind and recalibrate in the comforts of home. Sophia understands.

Earlier in the day, as Theo walked the lot, he saw a familiar sight. Clowns were sitting outside their RVs in the thin November sun, legs stretched out, faces tipped back. The crew hands moved with the particular looseness of people who know this weekend marks the last of the season and then they will have eight weeks off. Half the usual length of time. But still, it is much needed time off.

Even the lions seem to sense it; Hazel has been calmer these last few days, her pacing reduced to something almost meditative.

Theo feels their mix of fatigue and understated excitement for the coming break. He shares his own version of it.

What he does not share, and has not figured out, is Ace's temper.

It has been building the last two weeks. Small things, mostly. A sharper edge to his notes after the evening show, an impatience with Patty over filing details that wouldn't have registered in October, a curtness with performers who approach him directly rather than going through Theo. Last Tuesday he dressed down a lighting technician in front of half the crew over a cue that was off by less than two seconds. The technician—a quiet, competent man who has been with the circus since before Ace bought it—said nothing, absorbed it, and walked away. Theo watched him go and made a mental note.

By any objective measure, this has been the best season in Donahue's recent history. Revenue up. Attendance up. Employee retention the highest it has been since Theo joined. He had expected Ace to be expansive, self-congratulatory, already talking about next season in the grandiose terms he reserves for moments of genuine satisfaction.

Instead there is a low-grade irritability that Theo cannot quite account for. He has been turning it over. Trying to arrange the puzzle pieces.

Ace summons him to the main trailer ninety minutes before the Friday show. When Theo enters he finds the office rearranged. Patty's desk is pushed slightly to one side, and stacked along the far wall sits a row of cardboard boxes. Perhaps twenty of them. Each one is sealed and labeled in Patty's neat block print: *DONAHUE'S TRAVELING CIRCUS—SEASON 6.*

Ace is standing in the center of the room with his arms crossed, watching Theo take it in. He is already in his Ringmaster coat, which means this won't take long.

"Go ahead," Ace says, gesturing proudly toward the boxes. "Open one."

Theo takes a pair of scissors from Patty's desk and slices through the tape on the nearest box. Inside, folded in tissue paper, is a jacket. Dark navy, zip front, the Donahue's Traveling Circus logo embroidered on the left chest. He lifts it out and holds it up.

"One for every single member of the company," Ace announces. "Performers, crew, admin. Every last one."

"That's very generous," Theo says, meeting Ace's gaze. The comment is aimed more at the sentiment than the cost. He turns the jacket over in his hands. The embroidery is good. Clean lines, the logo rendered faithfully. The jacket itself is… adequate. A mid-range blank, the kind a vendor sells in bulk. He knows because he has priced similar items for other purposes and recognizes the weight of the fabric. But the gesture is real, and the employees will receive it as real, and that's what matters.

"Try it on," Ace says.

Theo slides it on over his button-down. It fits well enough. He zips it halfway and looks down at the logo on his chest.

"Thank you, sir." He meets Ace's eyes warmly. "This is a thoughtful way to close the season. They'll remember it."

Ace nods, satisfied. But even in satisfaction there is something underneath… a restlessness that this gesture has not quite resolved. He rolls his neck once, left then right.

"Good season, Teddy."

"An excellent season. By every measure."

"Mm." Ace moves to his desk and picks up his phone, sets it back down without looking at it. "You talked to Block lately? About the cats?"

"The lions are doing well. Dr. Block's protocol worked. After Sunday morning he will discontinue the tranquilizers, and they'll have the full eight weeks to regroup before we start back up."

"Good." A pause. "And the jackass?"

Theo has been waiting for the right moment. This is as good as any.

"Ziti. Yes. Dr. Block has been monitoring his gait for about a week now. The limp is intermittent, but persistent enough that he wrapped the leg yesterday. It seems to be helping, but he's going to monitor and do imaging if it doesn't clear up soon."

Ace absorbs this. His expression is unreadable in the way it sometimes gets. Not blank, exactly, but interior. Processing.

Theo continues, "I'll have more info before we break for winter quarters." He keeps his tone even, informational. "Dr. Block is cautiously optimistic, but he wants to see how Ziti responds to the kinesio tape before he does imaging and makes recommendations."

After a long silence Ace finally waves his hand and says, "I'm sure he'll be fine. Donkeys are tough."

"They are," Theo agrees. And moves on. "So, I heard from Brandon—Zippy—that Bongo just got back."

Something tightens in Ace's jaw. There it is.

"It's good he decided to be here for today's show," Ace says. "Day after Thanksgiving, like I told him."

"Right." Theo had understood otherwise. When he'd approved Bongo's two days off, and Ace agreed this was acceptable, somewhere along the line Ace sent word through the crew he wanted Bongo to perform Friday evening. The show was only at sixty percent capacity to an audience comprised mostly of families working off turkey and nowhere particular to be.

Theo had not intervened. He had weighed it and decided against it. But when he saw Bongo, he filed the look on the clown's face for later consideration.

"I'm sure he'll do fine tonight," Theo offers.

Ace grunts. His phone buzzes and he picks it up, reads something, sets it face-down.

Theo studies him for a moment. The restlessness. The low-grade edge. Twenty boxes of jackets that haven't quite fixed whatever is wrong.

Eight weeks, Theo thinks. Eight weeks of comparative silence. No crowds. No announcements. No one in the seats.

The puzzle pieces are clicking into place and he thinks he understands now. Ace doesn't even know why he's irritable. That's the thing about a man whose entire nervous system runs on external validation; the withdrawal feels like everything else. Feels like ingratitude from the company, or a lighting cue that's two seconds off, or a donkey who developed a limp at an inconvenient time.

It doesn't feel like what it really is: a man already longing for the spotlight, before it's even gone.

Theo zips his jacket the rest of the way up. Files the insight away. There will be a use for it.

"There's one more thing I need to bring to your attention," he says. "Something I've been watching for online, and I found it this morning. It's about next season, though, so if you would rather wait until after the show—"

"No." Ace leans back. "What is it."

Theo takes his usual seat.

"It's about Jubilee Circus."

"Jubilee." Ace says the name like he's tasting something mildly stale. He rolls his eyes and waves a hand. "Those two-bit amateurs down in Louisiana? What about them."

Theo feels a small release of tension he hadn't realized he was holding. *Good. He already sees them for what they are.* Not competition. Not a threat. Just a footnote in the industry that Donahue's has long since outgrown.

"Well, that's what I thought too," Theo says. "And normally I wouldn't even bring it up. But I was looking at their route for next season—just doing my due diligence—and something caught my eye."

He pauses. Not for drama, but for calibration. He wants to read Ace's face as the information lands.

"They've booked into Branson, Springfield, and St. Louis. All three. And in each case, they're a week ahead of us."

Ace's expression doesn't change immediately. There's a half-second where his brain is still running the old software—*two-bit amateurs, nothing to worry about*—and then the update installs.

"They *what*?"

Theo clears his throat softly before he says, "A week ahead. Same venues. I confirmed it this morning."

The color starts at Ace's black silk collar. Theo watches it climb. Past the jaw, past the ears, into the temples where something new appears: a vein, throbbing visibly beneath the skin. Theo has sat across from this man through firings, tirades, and the time Ace threw a walkie-talkie at a tent pole. He has never seen that vein before.

"Those fools," Ace says, and his voice has dropped into a register Theo hasn't heard before; it's low, almost gravelly, stripped of all performance, "took my cities. Took them. I built those markets. I went to those venue managers personally. Shook their hands. Took them to dinner."

Theo blinks. Thirty seconds ago Jubilee was a two-bit amateur operation barely worth mentioning. Now they've *stolen* Ace's cities? Their audiences don't even overlap; Jubilee draws a family-and-petting-zoo crowd, Donahue's pulls spectacle seekers willing to pay three times the ticket price. This isn't a competitive threat. It's a scheduling inconvenience at best.

But that vein is still throbbing. And Ace is just getting started.

Okay, Theo thinks. *Let him run.*

Ace's voice has acquired an edge that is growing sharper by the sentence. "And now some two-bit southern operation with trained dogs and a secondhand tent is pushing into Missouri like they own the place." He shakes his head slowly. "No. No. That is not happening."

Theo lets the silence hold for a moment. He watches Ace's face—the jaw set, the eyes fixed on the middle distance—and recognizes the stillness that follows genuine anger in a man who is used to getting what he wants.

"You're right that it's a provocation," Theo says, carefully crossing the line from neutral to aligned. Not rushing it. Just stepping over. "And the timing isn't accidental. They waited until we'd locked our venues for next season. There's nothing subtle about it."

Ace turns to look at him.

Theo continues. "Honestly? The audacity of it is remarkable. Jubilee has been running the same southeastern loop for thirty years. Respectable little operation. They know their lane." He pauses. "Or they did."

"So, what do we *do* about it." Not a question. A demand for options.

Theo opens his mouth—and something moves across his face that is gone almost before it registers. A calculation completed in less time than it takes to blink.

"Burn 'em to the ground," he says.

Ace blinks. Then something kindles behind his eyes—surprise first, then a slow, almost admiring recognition, like a man hearing his own thoughts spoken aloud by someone else.

Theo raises a hand to hint at caution. "Metaphorically speaking, of course. What I mean is—" he shifts forward, elbows on knees, voice dropping the register he uses for serious strategy, "—we go directly at them. Move our Branson date up. Book Springfield a week earlier. St. Louis too. Beat them into their own bookings. We have the infrastructure to move faster than they do, the vendor relationships, the advance team. They leaned on our schedule because they can't build their own. So we take ours away from them."

He watches Ace consider this.

"We could also contact the venues directly," Theo continues. "We've got longer relationships, and better revenue histories in all three of those markets. A quiet conversation suggesting we'd look favorably on exclusive booking arrangements in future seasons. That's not a threat; that's just business."

But Ace has gone quiet. It's not the processing quiet from earlier. Something else. He is looking somewhere slightly past Theo's shoulder, and in the low light of the trailer a faint warm glow from Ace's desk lamp throws a reflection across his face.

Theo watches it. Says nothing.

After a long moment Ace nods, once, slowly.

"I'll think on it," he says.

It is the most opaque thing Ace has said to him since they've met. Theo files it.

"Of course." He rises. Smooths his jacket—his new Donahue's jacket which is still zipped. "We've got a show coming up soon. We'll pick this back up whenever you're ready. Even during winter quarters, if you prefer. There's no rush, as long as we make some decisions by end of the calendar year."

Ace doesn't respond. He's still looking at that middle distance, as though in a trance. The reflected light moving only slightly as he breathes.

Theo sees himself out.

*****

It's five after eleven and the November darkness bites through Theo's new jacket. He is halfway back to his trailer, having left the Big Top a few minutes ago, where there were only a few crew members still working to break down concessions tables and change out trash bags.

The lot is mostly quiet until Theo's radio crackles only steps before he reaches the steps to his trailer. Ace's voice, unmistakable even through the static: Teddy. Get everyone back in the Big Top. Now.

Theo pulls the radio from his belt. Switches to the all-company channel. "All Donahue's personnel, please return to the Big Top immediately."

When Theo enters the tent flaps he sees Ace standing in the center ring under a single work light. Ringmaster coat still on. Others arrive either in single file or in small groups and head for the stands to await whatever Ace felt was important enough to call them all back. Theo stands between the two main sets of bleachers. The employees' shuffling turns to clomps as they walk up into the first few rows. As people settle, there are a couple of light coughs, and finally heavy silence falls over the space. That is when Ace tears into them.

The sound tech who lost audio for what Theo clocked as maybe one second. Martinez, who was allegedly a full beat slow on his tumbling pass. Bongo, whose giant red smile was twisted into some freak-show frown.

And Cupcake. Poor Cupcake. Ace complains to her, "You smell so bad that even the stupid jackasses were running away from you."

Theo suppresses the urge to sigh audibly. The donkeys run from Cupcake in every single performance. It is choreographed. It is one of the most reliable laughs in the clown act. Ace either doesn't know this, or doesn't care.

"We've got two more nights," Ace booms. His voice is menacing and sounds like a threat. "Four more shows. Make them count."

He leaves. The tent exhales. The company disperses in silence.

Theo waits until the Big Top is nearly empty, then walks back to his trailer. He drafts a short email to the full company—leaving out Ace. He thanks them for a strong night. Acknowledges the long season. Tells them what he always tells them, which happens to be true: that he is working behind the scenes to make things better, and he appreciates their patience and professionalism.

He reads it once, sends it, and goes to bed.

*****

As always when it comes to vacations, Theo's eight days off passed quickly. He is settled into the back seat of a Mercedes S-Class and tells the driver—through an intercom—which terminal his flight leaves from. He is rested for the first time in months. Sophia had picked him up at the airport and informed him she had a bottle of wine waiting for them at home. She also gave strict instructions they would not talk about work until Saturday. They both honored that. They slept in, ate breakfast in bed, and spent an evening at their favorite restaurant. He even managed to get halfway through a novel. He can't remember the last time he read half a novel, though he wonders when or if he will ever finish it.

Now his mind is shifting back. The two semis that need engines or replacement. Ziti's leg. The scheduling conflict with Jubilee. Whether Ace has calmed down or wound tighter in his absence. There's a comfortable rhythm to it—the mental sorting, the quiet prioritizing. He's good at this part. He's missed it, even.

He pulls out his phone and scrolls idly. News, weather, a couple of emails from Patty he'll deal with at the gate. Then a headline stops his thumb.

TOTAL LOSS FOR JUBILEE CIRCUS:
SIXTY YEARS OF HISTORY DESTROYED IN EARLY MORNING FIRE

He stares at it. Reads it again. His hand lowers slightly, the phone resting against his knee.

Burn 'em to the ground.

He'd said it. Hyperbole. A figure of speech followed immediately by practical alternatives—booking strategies, vendor relationships, exclusive arrangements. The kind of aggressive language men in leadership use when they're strategizing, not when they're issuing orders. He'd walked it back within seconds.

Ace had nodded once and said, "I'll think on it."

Theo puts the phone in his coat pocket. Watches the snow for a moment… fat flakes drifting under the streetlights, accumulating on parked cars and store awnings. The wipers thump steadily.

He pulls the phone back out. Opens the article and sits up straight to take it in.

The fire started in the climate-controlled building that housed the boa constrictors. Faulty wiring, according to the preliminary investigation. The blaze moved fast—by the time the volunteer fire department arrived, the main structures were fully engulfed. Vehicles, equipment, gear, costumes, rigging—sixty years of history reduced to debris and ash. Two boa constrictors perished. The large animals, housed in a separate facility on the opposite end of the property, survived.

Jubilee's owner, a seventy-one-year-old woman named Carol Thibodaux who'd inherited the circus from her father, was quoted as saying she did not plan to rebuild.

Theo shakes his head slowly as he reads. When he gets to the end, he scrolls back up and reads it through again. He sighs, locks the phone, and puts it back in his pocket. Watches the snowflakes spiral under another streetlight.

He presses his lips together tightly.

Shakes his head one last time.

I said figuratively, Ace.

The cab slows for a red light. Theo sits with it for a minute. Then he reaches for his phone again and pulls up Ace's number. His thumb hovers over the call button.

He puts the phone down.

He opens a text thread with Ace. The cursor blinks in the empty message field.

He locks the phone. Returns it to his pocket. Leans back in the luxurious bench seat of the Mercedes. Folds his hands.

The light turns green. The cab moves on. The snow keeps falling. And somewhere south of all this white silence, a reckoning is waiting.

*****

The Corpus Christi afternoon sky has a unique quality of light in December. It is pale and flat, as though the sun isn't sure it's worth the effort. Donahue's winter quarters land is just east of the city. It sits on twelve serene acres, and when Theo pulls through the gate he notices the lot has that particular stillness of a machine at rest. RVs are parked in tidy rows. There is a group of crew hands working on one of the semis, and as Theo drives past he sees the engine compartment wide open like a silent scream.

Somewhere behind the storage buildings, Theo hears one of the llamas make a sound that is neither complaint nor greeting. He parks the Tahoe and sits for a moment. When he left his house before dawn this morning it was twelve degrees and snowing, but it is sixty-one degrees here and there is a faint smell of petroleum mixed with the salty air.

A buzz in his back pocket alerts him to a text. He checks it and sees a message from Sophia: "My parents are hosting Christmas at their cabin in Vermont. Hope you can join us. I'll get there on the 24th."

He responds, "I'll let you know," and returns his phone to his pocket.

The walk to Ace's trailer takes him past the animal housing. He slows when he passes the donkey enclosure and sees Ravioli standing near the fence. Ziti is lying down, which is unusual for this time of day. His left front leg is wrapped in bright blue kinesio tape. Dr. Block's handiwork. The ultrasound images are probably already on their way to a specialist.

Ravioli watches Theo with dark, expressive eyes and twitches one of his enormous gray ears. Theo gives a single nod in Ravioli's direction and immediately feels foolish for acknowledging a donkey. He keeps walking and hears both donkeys bray. It sounds like they are arguing. He continues walking to the farthest end of the trailers, well aware Ace does not like being anywhere near the animals.

The green trailer looks the same as always. Buzzer, doorknob, the sign in the window. He is just about to knock when the door swings inward. Ace is wearing his reading glasses and waves Theo in.

"Teddy. Glad you're back. Good week off?"

"Oh, yes," Theo answers from inside Patty's office as Ace closes the door. "Very good, thanks."

Light filters softly through the solitary window, and Theo notes everything looks exactly the same except for two details. The overhead lights are shut off, and Patty is conspicuously absent.

"How about yourself? Everything go okay holding down the fort?"

Ace strides toward his office before stopping at the hidden door handle. "Yes. The week was pretty quiet."

"When does Patty come back?" Theo follows Ace into his dimly lit office. Takes his usual seat.

"January fourth. She's still available if you need her for anything, though."

Ace offers Theo a drink but he declines, and he is mildly surprised when Ace does not pour himself a scotch.

Good, Theo thinks. *Less chance of any misunderstanding.*

Ace sits at his desk and Theo notes he has several folders fanned out in front of him. He removes the glasses and sets them down. "You look rested."

"I am. Sophia sends her regards."

Ace waves this away as though Sophia is a minor weather pattern. "Sit. I want to go over next season's routing. I've been looking at the numbers from this year, and I've got some ideas."

They spend twenty minutes on logistics. Theo guides the conversation with the light touch he's perfected—offering data, letting Ace arrive at conclusions that Theo planted three sentences earlier. The extended season had been profitable by every measure. Ace wants to push it further. Theo counsels patience, knowing Ace will ignore the counsel but appreciate having received it.

When the routing discussion winds down, Theo leans back slightly and allows a pause. Then, as though the thought just occurred to him he mentions, "I saw the news about Jubilee while I was traveling."

Ace's expression doesn't change. "Terrible thing."

"It is. A total loss, too." Theo shakes his head slowly. "I was thinking about it on the plane, actually. Not the fire itself, but… how it might look from the outside. Given the timing."

He watches Ace carefully. Not staring. Just... present.

"I'm not following," Ace says slowly, his voice guarded. Somewhat threatening.

"We had just talked about Jubilee. Their routes overlapping ours. And then, a week later..." Theo opens his hands, palms up, a gesture of mild concern. "I just want to make sure there's no chance anyone could connect those dots. Point a finger in your direction. Even unfairly."

There it is. The question, wrapped in the cotton of loyalty.

Ace leans back. Strokes his chin once. Then, he waves his hand—that familiar, imperious wave—and says, "No. That's not an issue at all."

Interesting, Theo notes. *Not an issue at all?*

He holds his expression perfectly steady. Files the phrasing. The tone. The absence of denial.

"Good," Theo says, his voice warm with relief he does not feel. "That's what I figured. But I wanted to hear it from you."

"Faulty wiring," Ace says. "Old building. Climate-controlled unit for the snakes. Those things are firetraps."

Theo nods. "I read that. The boa constrictors didn't make it."

"No," Ace says. "But the horses were fine. Good thing they kept the large animals on the far end of the property, away from the warehouses."

Theo blinks once. Slowly. The specificity of that detail… *the far end of the property, away from the warehouses*. It's not the kind of thing a man learns from a headline. It's the kind of thing a man knows because he was briefed. Or because he gave the instructions.

"Right," Theo says. "Except the boa constrictors. That's apparently where it started. The climate-controlled building."

"Pity," Ace says.

The word falls into the room and lies there. Neither of them picks it up.

After a moment, Theo shifts forward slightly, as though changing the subject. "You know, I was thinking on my drive back here from the airport. The morning shows—*Today*, *Good Morning America*—they'd probably love to have you right now. 'Circus industry mourns a historic loss'," he gestures into the air to highlight invisible words. "You could express sympathy, talk about the legacy of these family-owned operations, and then pivot to what Donahue's has got planned for next season. New markets, the early start date. It's free advertising wrapped in a public service."

Ace's eyes change. The restlessness Theo had observed in his boss prior to leaving for vacation is suddenly gone. In its place, something brighter. Cameras. Hosts leaning in, eagerly. His name on a chyron.

"That's...." Ace starts, then nods once, firmly. "That's smart. Very smart, Teddy."

"I can start making calls tomorrow morning, if you'd like."

"Do it." Ace is already somewhere else—rehearsing the interviews in his mind, probably. Choosing which coat to wear. Theo gives him a few seconds to live there before continuing.

"There's one other thing I want to bring up," Theo says. His voice drops half a register. Not dramatically. Just enough to signal a shift. "And this one stays between us."

Ace's attention returns. His eyes narrow slightly, the way they do when he's trying to decide if he should be interested or alarmed.

"I've talked with Roger a few times since you set up our meeting in September," Theo begins. "Going through the books. Understanding the financial architecture."

He pauses. Watches.

"Roger is exceptionally good at what he does," Theo continues. "The structure he's built. The routing, the entities, the way cash moves through the operation. It's genuinely…" He pauses very briefly, then nods decisively when he continues, "Impressive. I've seen a lot of financial systems in my career, Ace. This one is..." He searches for the word, as though finding it in real time. "Elegant."

Ace has gone very still. The kind of still that could tip in either direction. Several long seconds later, his words emerge slowly. "What exactly are you telling me, Teddy?"

Theo sees the danger in Ace's expression and does the opposite of what it demands. He settles back in his chair. "I'm telling you that I understand the full scope of what Roger manages on your behalf. All of it." Theo holds the pause for exactly two beats. "And I'm telling you I'm impressed. And that your secret is safe with me."

The silence stretches. Ace's jaw works once, twice. His fingers, which had been resting on the desk, curl slowly inward.

"How long have you known?"

Theo can hear the accusation in Ace's tone. He answers simply, "A few months."

"And you didn't say anything."

"I didn't need to. It wasn't relevant to my work until now." Theo meets his eyes. Steady. Open. "But we've reached a point where I think it's better for both of us, if there are no blind spots between us. I'd rather you know what I know. And, I know that I'm not going anywhere."

Ace processes this. Theo can see it happening—the calculations, the risk assessments, the weighing of a man who has spent his entire life deciding whether people are useful or dangerous. The mathematics of trust in a man who doesn't trust anyone.

"How?" Ace finally asks. "Roger wouldn't just... he knows better than to..."

Theo smiles. Not wide, not smug. Just the faintest warmth at the corners of his mouth.

"The same way I know about most things, sir. I pay attention. And I learn."

The words settle into the space between them. Ace stares at Theo for a long moment. Whatever he sees in Theo's face—the calm, the competence, the absence of threat—it shifts something behind his eyes. Not softening, exactly. More like recalculation. A man rearranging the furniture in his mind to accommodate a piece he hadn't planned for.

"Well," Ace says. He leans back. Strokes his chin again, and this time there is something almost like admiration in the gesture. "Well, well."

Theo waits.

Ace studies him for a long moment, then leans forward. "So. What do you want?"

The question hangs in the air. Theo knows what Ace is really asking. A man who discovers a money laundering operation and brings it to the boss's attention is a man who expects to be compensated for his discretion. That's how Ace's world works. Everything has a price. Everyone has an angle.

"Nothing," Theo says.

Ace blinks. His expression shifts through several phases—suspicion, confusion, and something that might be the faintest edge of alarm. A man who doesn't want a cut is a man Ace doesn't know how to read.

"Honestly, Ace, I'd rather not have anything traceable to me. I'm already in deep enough just knowing about it." He holds Ace's gaze and lets the faintest self-deprecating smile cross his face. "Let me earn my keep the old-fashioned way—by making this circus the most profitable show on the road."

Ace is quiet. Processing. Then something settles in his expression. The alarm fades. What replaces it is a warmth Theo has not seen directed at him before—the particular warmth of a man who has just discovered that the person sitting across from him is not only capable and loyal, but incorruptible. Which, in Ace's calculus, makes him the most valuable person in the room.

"You know, Teddy, I've been thinking," Ace starts. "This operation has gotten bigger than one man can oversee. Even me." He pauses to let the weight of that concession register. For Ace, admitting he cannot do something alone is roughly equivalent to a Cardinal renouncing his faith. "I need someone I can trust with... all of it. The whole picture. Not just the day-to-day."

Theo says nothing. Lets Ace arrive.

"How would you feel about a promotion? With a raise to match. Second in command."

"I'd be honored, sir," Theo says, gratitude in his voice. "Would you mind if I keep my title though? Operations Manager is more accessible, in my humble opinion."

Ace looks at Theo with a whisper of curiosity, then replies. "That's up to you. In this new role, though, you'll have full authority when I'm not available. Access to everything. Financials, contracts, personnel. The board will need to be informed, of course. But that's a formality."

"Of course. I truly appreciate it."

Ace extends his hand across the desk. Theo takes it. The grip is still firm—still the dominance ritual—but this time Ace holds it for a fraction longer than usual, and when he lets go there's something new in his expression.

Satisfaction, certainly. But Theo also sees a flicker of relief. The relief of a man who has been carrying something heavy and has finally found a second pair of hands he believes are strong enough to share the load.

Theo rises. Smooths his tie.

"I'll touch base with Patty tomorrow. She and I will coordinate things with the morning shows," he says. "And I'll set up a proper review with Roger before the new year. Make sure everything is tight for the season."

"Good man," Ace says. "Good man."

Theo lets himself out through Patty's silent office. Outside, the December sun sits low over the Gulf. The lot is still quiet. The crew hands have closed the semi's engine compartment and moved on.

He walks back toward his trailer and stops when he hears the sound. A familiar, indignant bray from the direction of the animal enclosures. Ziti, probably, complaining about his leg wrap. Or Ravioli, complaining on principle. Or both of them, complaining at each other, the way brothers do.

A flash of black moves through Theo's peripheral vision. He turns to see a crow that's just landed on the corner post of the enclosure for the llamas, who are inside their barn eating their evening meal. Hay, or whatever it is that llamas eat.

The crow settles its glossy feathers and looks at Theo from an ebony eye. That is when he sees the white scar across its beak. For a moment Theo thinks he is imagining things. *That can't be the same crow I saw in Omaha. Can it?* He makes a mental note to look up whether crows migrate.

Theo regards the bird for a moment.

"Are you following me?" he inquires.

The crow says nothing, but neither does it leave.

Theo turns toward his trailer. Behind him, the donkeys are quiet now. The afternoon light is already beginning to fade, and somewhere inside the green trailer, a man in a red coat is practicing what he'll say to a morning show host about the terrible tragedy that befell a beloved competitor.

There is no sawdust on the ground in the winter quarters, something Theo is only realizing in this moment. He is surprised by the fact he misses it.

* * * * *

The first Monday of the new year arrives with a sky so blue it looks manufactured. Theo has been back in Corpus Christi since the twenty-eighth. Most of the company is still scattered. A handful of crew hands trickle in and out of winter quarters to work on equipment maintenance, but the lot is largely empty. Dr. Block is still on vacation, but between a few circus employees and contractors, the animals are tended to daily. The performers must be back by the twentieth, but Theo learned from Patty they could start filtering in up to a week before then.

Most of the days and nights are peaceful, which Theo has come to appreciate. It is during these stretches that he does his best thinking, his best planning. No interruptions. No fires to put out. Just the work.

Theo happens to be looking out his trailer kitchen window when he sees Ace pull through the gate. It is just before noon and he is driving the black Lincoln Town Car he keeps garaged in Corpus Christi. Ace's trailer is not far from Theo's, and when he parks and exits the vehicle the tan is impossible not to see. Wherever he spent the holidays, there was sun.

Twenty minutes later, Ace texts him. *Walk the lot with me. I've got some energy to burn.*

They meet near the main trailer and head south along the gravel road that runs the length of the property. Ace is in a good mood—better than Theo has seen in weeks. The tan suits him. He looks at least five years younger than he did in San Antonio.

"You know what everyone told me, Teddy? Everyone. My attorney. Patty. Even Dazzle." He shakes his head, walking with his hands clasped behind his back, chin lifted, surveying the property as though he's inspecting a kingdom. "They all said it was too risky. Going on the morning shows so soon after the Jubilee fire. 'People will ask questions, Ace. It'll look opportunistic, Ace.' Every single one of them tried to talk me out of it."

Even Dazzle, Theo thinks. He's heard rumors, and apparently they are true. Because Ace just mentioned her along with his attorney and Patty, close confidants.

"And you did it anyway," Theo says.

"Damn right I did. And what happened? Dakota from *Rise and* Shine called it the most emotional interview she's ever conducted. The *Today* segment? They want me back in March, once the season is underway. Carol from Jubilee even sent me a personal note. Said she appreciated my kind words." Ace shakes his head with what he probably believes is humility. "Sometimes you just have to trust your instincts, Teddy. That's what separates the men from the boys. Vision. Courage."

"They simply can't fathom your genius, sir," Theo says, and before the words are even fully out of his mouth he recognizes there was more sarcasm in his tone than he intended. He is already formulating a follow-up comment, but clearly Ace did not hear anything other than the praise he so desperately needs.

"Exactly, son." He claps Theo on the back with the palm of his hand in a gesture that is probably as close as Ace ever comes to expressing gratitude.

They keep walking.

They pass the row of storage buildings where most of the rigging, set pieces, and costumes are kept during the offseason. Ace gestures toward one of the smaller structures. “That one needs a new roof before the season starts. I noticed a leak in November.”

“Already on the list,” Theo says. “I’ve got a contractor coming Wednesday.”

Ace gives a satisfied grunt.

“So,” Theo says, keeping his tone conversational, “I’ve gotten a few calls since Jubilee went under. Performers looking for work. A couple of clowns, a horse trainer, a rigger.” Ace doesn’t break stride.

“No.”

“That’s what I figured. But I wanted to run it past you.”

“We’re not a charity, Teddy. We’ve got a full roster. Besides….” He waves his hand. “Their training, their style, it’s all wrong. Jubilee was a family petting zoo with a tent. Our operation is a different caliber entirely.”

“Understood.” Theo lets a beat pass. “I’ll let them know we wish them well.”

After a brief silence Ace says, “Sure.”

They round the corner past the storage buildings, and the animal housing comes into view. The three llamas—Mocha, Chai, and Toddy—are outside their paddock standing in a loose cluster. They are making their soft humming sounds as if communicating secrets; Theo has never quite figured out if there is a deeper purpose to these contemplative sounds they make.

The lion enclosures are farther back, strategically located downwind so the other animals are not stressed by their scent. Bruno and Hazel are not within sight, which means they are inside and probably sleeping.

Theo and Ace continue their walk, passing a utility shed.

"Oh," Theo says, a memory surfacing. "I meant to ask—did Patty finalize the insurance renewal, or is that still pending?"

Ace's chin tilts up. He squints against the sun as he tries to recall. "I think she... hmm. I'll have to check with her on that."

It is in this brief pause—Ace frowning, trying to retrieve a detail that has already slipped away—that the sound erupts. Both donkeys. At once. A sustained, full-throated, ear-splitting duet that bounces off the storage buildings and seems to come from every direction. Ravioli's bray is the deeper of the two, a resonant foghorn of complaint. Ziti's is higher, more staccato, almost indignant. Together they create a sound that no reasonable person could ignore… and no unreasonable person could tolerate.

Ace's jaw tightens. His hands drop from behind his back and clench at his sides. The pleasant mood, the tan, the morning show triumph, the blue January sky—all of it evaporates in the span of two seconds. "Those goddamn animals," he says.

The braying continues. If anything, it intensifies. One of them—Ravioli, probably—kicks something metallic and it clangs.

"I cannot—" Ace starts, then stops. Breathes. The braying subsides slightly, then surges again, as though they've found a second wind. "Every single time," Ace says, his voice dropping. "Every single time I set foot on this lot, those jackasses lose their minds."

"They do tend to get vocal," Theo offers.

Ace turns to look at Theo, and there is something in his expression that Theo has not seen before. Not performative anger. Not the strategic displeasure he wields to keep people off balance. This is older. More personal. The resentment of a man who believes two animals have been mocking him for years and has finally reached the end of his patience.

"What did Block say about the lame one?"

"Ziti. Suspensory ligament strain. The specialist reviewed the ultrasound and confirmed it. Eight to twelve weeks of rest. No performing." Theo pauses, then adds, "Dr. Block also recommends that Ravioli not perform during that time. They don't do well when they're separated."

"Eight to twelve weeks," Ace repeats. He is still looking toward the enclosure, though the donkeys are not visible from where they stand. The braying has tapered off into intermittent complaints. "That puts us into March."

"At the earliest. Could be April if healing is slower than expected."

Ace is quiet. Then he turns and starts walking again, away from the animal housing. Theo matches his pace. They walk in silence for perhaps thirty seconds—a long time, when walking with Ace.

"I want them gone, Teddy." His voice is low.

Theo says nothing, but glances casually around to see if anyone is within earshot. It is just the two of them.

Keeping his tone at a quiet register, Ace continues. "Not relocated. Not retired. Not sent to some farm to stand around eating hay." He stops walking and faces Theo directly. The morning's good humor is entirely absent now. What remains is flat and ice cold.

"I mean permanently. I'll sleep better knowing those creatures no longer roam the earth."

Theo silently contemplates for perhaps three seconds. Then meets Ace's gaze and nods once. His voice is confident when he says, "I'll take care of it, sir."

Ace exhales. His shoulders drop by a fraction. "Good man." He claps Theo on the shoulder—that same rare gesture of what Theo thinks might be gratitude—and resumes walking. His stride is slightly looser now, as though something that had been wound tight inside his chest has been released.

They walk in silence back toward the trailers. As they pass the donkey enclosure, Theo glances through the fence. Ravioli is standing at the far end, ears forward, watching them. Ziti is beside him, still lying down, the blue tape vivid against his brown coat.

Ravioli shifts his weight and one enormous ear swivels forward while the other tilts back.

Theo turns his gaze to the road ahead and falls in step with Ace who is softly whistling a tune he does not recognize.

* * * * *

The concessions storage building smells of cardboard and stale popcorn. Theo has been at it for nearly two hours, working methodically through the inventory boxes that Brenda keeps organized by product type. He is grateful for her fastidiousness; it has made this task far more efficient than it might have been.

He pulls the last plush donkey from a box labeled STUFFED ANIMALS—ASST and drops it into the black garbage bag at his feet. Sixteen total—eleven Zitis, five Raviolis. He knows this because in addition to being different colors, each toy has a tag on its ear with the name printed in a bold red font. The Raviolis outsold the Zitis, which tracks—Ravioli was always the more animated of the two, the one kids gravitated toward.

A waste. He'd told Ace as much. These are revenue, not reminders. People buy them because their children love them. You retire the animals, fine—but you don't retire the merchandise. If anything, you lean into it. One final production run. Maybe add a small clover embroidered on the shoulder—a nod to the sanctuary story. Parents eat that up. It practically sells itself, and every plush donkey with a clover on it reinforces the narrative that these animals are grazing somewhere, living a life of luxury now.

Ace had not even let him finish. "I want every trace of those jackasses gone, Teddy. Every last one. I've got something better coming, and I don't want the old garbage cluttering up the new merchandise."

Something better. Theo still doesn't know what Ace has planned, only that it involves a purchase Ace has been unusually secretive about. He'd asked twice. The first time, Ace waved him off. The second time, Ace said, "You'll see," with the self-satisfied grin of a man who believes surprise is a management strategy.

So here he is. Six in the morning, pulling plush donkeys out of boxes and dropping them into garbage bags. Following an order he argued against, executing a task he considers wasteful, because the man who gives the orders does not distinguish between counsel and insubordination.

He ties the bag and sets it beside the other two. One contains every program from this season and last—because they include the donkeys in the performer lineup. The other holds their trading cards, a handful of bumper stickers, and a half dozen miniature red felt sombreros—replicas of the ones the real donkeys wore during their act. The sombreros had been strong sellers at the southern stands.

He moves to the posters. Three rolled tubes of promotional material, tucked vertically in a crate near the back wall. He unrolls the first one far enough to confirm—yes, there they are, cartoon Ravioli and cartoon Ziti flanking the Donahue's logo, wearing their red sombreros at jaunty angles. The artwork is charming. Lively. He rolls it back up and drops all three tubes into a fourth bag.

Now he stands in the middle of the building and turns a slow circle. Shelves, boxes, crates. Donahue's branded cups, pennants, glow sticks, snow globes, keychains. He checks each product line for any trace of the donkeys. The keychains feature only the lion and the Big Top. The snow globes contain a generic circus tent with falling glitter. He gathers the last remaining items. Sighs. Drops them in the bag.

The sky outside is the particular gray that precedes a Gulf Coast winter sunrise—not dark, not light, just suspended. He has not slept.

At four a.m. he had stood in the gravel road between the storage buildings and the animal housing, hands in his jacket pockets, watching a veterinary transport back up to the enclosure gate. The whole thing had struck him as unnecessary. Not the logistics—those he'd handled cleanly. But the act itself. Ziti's injury was treatable. Eight to twelve weeks and the animal would have been fine. The clowns could have reworked the act around Ravioli alone for a couple of months, or folded in a new bit with the llamas.

There were options. Practical ones. But Ace didn't want options. Ace wanted silence. Wanted to never again hear the sound that he was convinced, against all reason, was two animals laughing at him. And so here they were.

The veterinarian—not Dr. Block, who would have balked—had been professional, efficient, and entirely uncurious. A mild sedative for each animal, administered without difficulty. Ravioli went first. He stood calmly in the predawn chill. Cooperative even. Ziti required more coaxing. The injured leg made the ramp difficult, and for a long moment the vet struggled to guide him forward while the animal's dark eyes rolled and searched for his brother, who was already inside. Theo watched from thirty feet away, his breath visible in the January air, and said nothing.

It could have been a sanctuary. A real one. He had looked into it, briefly, in the days between Ace's order and this morning. There were facilities all over the country. Even a few in Texas. The cost would have been minimal—a transport fee, a modest monthly boarding rate. The animals would have lived. The narrative would have been true. And the outcome for the company would have been identical.

But a sanctuary leaves a trail. Boarding invoices. A location someone could visit. A place where a curious clown or a diligent vet could show up unannounced and yes, prove the story true, but also prove the animals still accessible. Which means Ace would know they still existed, somewhere, braying into someone else's morning. And Ace did not say retire them. He said make them disappear. Forever.

So, Theo had found someone who accepts large sums of cash and asks no questions. The cost was considerably more than a lifetime at a sanctuary. But it purchased something a sanctuary could not: permanence.

What had irritated him was the truck. GULF COAST VETERINARY SERVICES was stenciled in dark blue across both doors, and the trailer bore the same name along its aluminum flank. He had specifically requested an unmarked vehicle. The dispatcher had assured him one would be available. It wasn't. And so a truck with a veterinary company's name emblazoned on it had pulled through the winter quarters gate at three-fifty this morning, sat idling for twenty minutes while two donkeys were sedated and loaded, and then pulled back through that same gate with its blue letters catching the security lights for anyone who might have been watching.

No one had been watching. He'd made certain. The skeleton crew that remained during winter quarters—four hands, not counting himself—were housed on the opposite end of the property. At four in the morning in early January, none of them were awake.

Still. The signage bothered him. It was the single variable he had not controlled, and it nagged at him the way an unclosed parenthetical nags at a careful writer. If someone had seen that truck, the name on the door would become a detail. Details become questions. Questions become conversations. Conversations become problems.

But no one had seen it.

He had watched the trailer's taillights shrink down the access road until they turned onto the county highway and disappeared. Then he stood for another minute, listening. The lot was silent in a way it almost never was. No braying. No hooves on packed earth. Just the hum of the utility generator and, somewhere far off, the low moan of a ship's horn from the port.

He had walked to the enclosure. Stood at the fence where he'd once nodded at Ravioli and felt foolish for acknowledging a donkey. The gate was open. The water trough was full. Two piles of hay sat untouched in the feeding station. A roll of bright blue kinesio tape sat on a shelf inside the barn—Dr. Block's, left there because he'd planned to come back in a week to check on Ziti's progress. Theo picked it up and turned it over in his hands. There was no reason to take it. He put it in the jacket pocket anyway and told himself he would give it to Dr. Block when he returned.

Now, back in the concessions building, he surveys the shelves one final time to ensure he has been thorough. Then, he hoists two of the garbage bags and carries them to the dumpster behind the building. Returns for the other two. The first time he drops a bag in and lets the lid fall, it bangs closed. He winces in the murky twilight and waits several long seconds, making sure the noise did not bring unwanted attention. For the remaining three bags he closes the lid as quietly as possible.

He removes his work gloves, takes one last look around, and shuts off the lights.

The sky has shifted from gray to pale rose along the eastern horizon. He checks his watch. Six-twenty. There is time for a shower and coffee before he sits down at his desk. There are two communications to write, and each one requires a different version of the same lie.

He walks back to his trailer without looking in the direction of the empty enclosure.

*****

Theo's hair is still damp from the shower when he opens his laptop. A mug of black coffee steams at his right hand. He starts a new email, addresses it to Ace, and types the subject line: Donkey Matter—Resolved.

He reads it. Deletes the subject line. Types instead: Update—Asset Retirement, January 7.

Better. Clinical. The kind of language that means nothing to anyone who isn't looking for something.

Ace—

I'm writing to confirm that I've handled the matter with the donkeys, exactly as you instructed during our conversation on Monday.

Within a few minutes of getting this email, you will receive a second email addressed to the entire company, in which I explain that the donkeys have been retired to a sanctuary. I am sending you this email first, so it is clear that I executed your directive as discussed.

As I had already noted, I do think there was still revenue in the merchandise, and I would have recommended a final production run to commemorate their retirement. But I understand your decision to clear the inventory entirely, and it's done.

Roger assisted with the funds required to arrange the transport. I will follow up with him to ensure the books are reconciled. If you have any questions, I'm happy to discuss in person at your convenience.

—Theo

He reads it through once. Reads it again. His eyes settle on "exactly as you instructed" and "your directive as discussed." Two phrases performing the same function. Redundant—unless the purpose is documentation. The paragraph about the merchandise does the same work from a different angle: I counseled against this, you overruled me, and I want that in writing too. He considers softening it. Leaves it.

He hits send.

Then he opens a new message. This one he composes more slowly, choosing each word the way a mortician chooses foundation—to make something lifeless look peaceful.

To: All Donahue's Traveling Circus Staff

From: Theodore Crane, Operations Manager

Re: Update About Our Beloved Donkeys

Dear Donahue's Family,

I hope everyone is enjoying a well-deserved winter break. I'm writing with news about Ravioli and Ziti.

As many of you know, Ziti has been recovering from a leg injury that required extended rest. After lengthy deliberation, Ace made the difficult but compassionate decision to retire both donkeys from performing life. They have been relocated to a sanctuary that specializes in providing permanent homes for retired working animals. They will spend their remaining years on open pasture with shelter, veterinary care, and—I was assured—more clover than two donkeys could eat in a lifetime.

This was not an easy decision. Ravioli and Ziti have been part of this circus family their entire lives, and their contributions to the clown act and to the joy of our audiences cannot be overstated. We are grateful for every performance, every bray, and every stolen sombrero.

We will share details about next season's clown act in the coming weeks. In the meantime, please know that this decision was made with the animals' well-being as our foremost priority. As such, Ace requests that we respect the donkeys' privacy in their retirement.

Enjoy the rest of your break.

Warm regards, Theo

He reads it once more. The sanctuary does not exist. The clover is invention. The phrase "their remaining years" is doing more work than any reader will ever know. He is satisfied with the construction and considers, briefly, whether "every stolen sombrero" is too much. It is sentimental in a way that Theo typically avoids. But sentiment, applied correctly, is a tool. It tells the reader—the grieving clown, the skeptical crew hand, the little girl who will hear this news from her father—that the author of this email cares. That he, too, will miss them.

He leaves it and hits send, knowing he will be answering questions for weeks. Especially from the clowns. He is prepared to answer those questions, calmly and with compassion.

He picks up his phone. Opens the text thread with Sophia. The last message is hers, from two days ago: *Miss you. Boston is freezing.*

He types: *Hope yesterday was good and glad you're able to hunker down in boardrooms instead of traveling again today. I've had to deal with a difficult issue at work the last couple of days, but it's fully resolved now. Talk soon.*

He reads it once. Sends it. Sets the phone face down on the desk. Although his coffee has gone lukewarm, he gulps down the last of it.

Outside, the pale rose sky has brightened into a clear blue. Somewhere on a county highway, a truck with blue letters on its doors is carrying two donkeys toward a destination from which nothing returns.

Theo rinses his mug in the small sink, dries it, and places it back in the cabinet. He closes his laptop. Checks his watch.

It is seven-fifteen in the morning on January seventh. The winter quarters lot is quiet. The enclosure is empty. The dumpster is full. The emails are sent. The spreadsheets will be revised.

He wonders if he can get a couple hours of sleep before Ace makes new demands. Decides to silence his phone so he can at least try to get a nap.

When a steady buzz pulls him from a dream he cannot remember, Theo is disoriented at first. But a quick look at his phone on his nightstand resolves the date and time, and he remembers he set an alarm so he wouldn't sleep more than three hours. It's been going off for eleven minutes, however, and he can also see from the home screen that he's received numerous emails, texts, and phone calls while he slept.

Before he gets a chance to review any of them his phone buzzes in his hand. Ace. He rubs sleep from his eyes and inhales deeply before taking the call.

"I fired Block. Find me a new vet."

No greeting. No preamble. Theo holds the phone slightly away from his ear and waits for more, but that appears to be the entire message.

"Okay," Theo says, keeping his voice even. "Can I ask what happened?"

"What happened is the vet *you* hired decided to call me directly and start asking questions. Where were the donkeys sent. Why wasn't he consulted. Wants to forward their veterinary records." A sharp exhale. "As if I owe an explanation to an employee about how I manage my own property."

As he listens to Ace complain, he scrolls through apps on his phone. Sees nothing from Dr. Block. Which means he skipped over Theo and went directly to Ace. He grumbles internally: *Why, Block.*

He exhales silently before saying, "If he'd come to me first, Ace, I would have handled it."

"Well, he didn't come to you. He came to me. And now he's history." Ace's voice drops half a register. "Find someone who does their job without thinking they're in charge. Someone younger. And this time I want to see the résumés before you make any calls."

This time. There is more than a hint of blame in Ace's voice. Dr. Block was Theo's hire. Theo's recommendation. Theo was the one who'd winnowed dozens of résumés down to three excellent candidates and then offered to let Ace conduct the interviews himself. Ace had waved him off. *You've got a good eye, Teddy. Just pick the best one.* And now, seven months later, the best one asked the wrong person a reasonable question, and the trust that came with "just pick the best one" has been quietly revised.

"Of course. I'll have candidates for you within forty-eight hours."

"Sooner."

The line goes dead.

Theo sets the phone on the desk and presses his fingers against the bridge of his nose. This is what working for Ace Donahue produces. Not problems—Theo can handle problems. But *messes*. Avoidable, self-inflicted messes born from a man who cannot tolerate being questioned and does not think two moves ahead. Firing a competent veterinarian over the phone for following up on his own patients. Without consulting Theo first. Without considering what Block might do next.

Because Block *will* do something next. He has Charlie's number. Probably half the company's numbers. He is a principled man with decades of professional standing and, as of ten minutes ago, nothing left to lose.

Theo picks the phone back up and dials Block's number.

It rings four times. When Block answers, his voice is clipped and tight. "Mr. Crane."

"Dr. Block. I just got off the phone with Ace. I want you to know that I was not consulted, and I would have handled this very differently."

Silence.

"He fired me because I asked about my patients."

"I know. And I'm sorry. Ace reacts. You know that. He doesn't think things through, and the people around him pay the price." He lets that sit for a moment. "Here's what I'd like to do. I'm going to process a three-month severance. And I'll write you a personal reference letter. I know a couple of practice owners in the region, and I'm happy to make calls on your behalf."

The pause on Block's end is long. Theo can hear him recalibrating. Anger competing with something more practical.

"I appreciate that," Block says, still guarded.

"I also think the cleanest thing for both of us is to let this settle quietly. I'll send word out to the company today. Simple, professional. I won't get into what happened because frankly, the details don't reflect well on Ace, and airing that doesn't help anyone." A pause. "Including you. The less noise around a departure, the stronger the reference reads."

"That makes sense."

"Good. You'll receive the severance paperwork by end of this week. And Dr. Block—I meant what I said. This one's on Ace, not on you."

Brief, professional goodbyes. Theo sets the phone down, opens his laptop, and composes a short email to the company. Dr. Block will not be returning. He has asked that we respect his privacy. We are grateful for his care. A new vet will be in place before the season begins. Twelve lines. He hits send.

Now, the replacement.

Over the next day and a half Theo makes a series of calls. Casual, exploratory. The kind of conversation a young veterinarian fresh out of school would find flattering. A respected traveling operation reaching out directly. No headhunter. No impersonal job listing. Just a warm voice saying, *Your credentials caught my eye.*

In each call he listens more than he talks. And carefully woven into the conversation, the questions that actually matter. How do they handle disagreements with management? How do they feel about environments where decisions come from the top?

By the end of the second day he has three names. All women. All under thirty. All qualified, all hungry for an opportunity that would take years to find through normal channels.

None of them asked about the previous vet.

He prepares a brief email to Ace with the three résumés attached. Graduation dates that speak for themselves. He reads it once and hits send.

A headache has started to form. He closes his eyes and gently massages his temples for a minute. Then he takes in a series of slow, deep breaths through his nose. Exhales them even slower through his mouth.

He stands, stretches, and reaches for his Donahue's jacket hanging by the door. As he slides it on, it is heavier than usual. He reaches inside a pocket and pulls out the roll of bright blue kinesio tape. Stares at it for a long moment. Then crosses to the kitchen and slams it into the garbage can.

He zips the jacket and opens the door of his trailer. On the ground a few feet ahead of him is a single black feather. He steps over it and keeps walking.

*****

The three rings are alive with organized chaos, the way they always are on setup day.

In ring one, the aerialists are warming up. Marco is on the platform, chalking his hands, while Helena stretches on the mat below. They've been working on a new trick for weeks—a double-twisting layout release, in which Helena launches from one trapeze, completes two full rotations with a half twist, and is caught mid-air by Marco hanging from the catch bar by his knees. It's the kind of trick that separates a good aerial act from a great one. They've landed it dozens of times in rehearsal. Helena makes it look effortless, which is the hallmark of a woman who's been on a trapeze since before she could read. Fourth generation. Her great-grandmother performed with Trentini's original troupe. Her grandmother trained her mother. Her mother trained her. The circus is not Helena's career; it's her bloodline.

In ring two, the llama handlers are running all three animals through their paces. The act has become one of the more reliable crowd-pleasers since it debuted in February, and the llamas themselves have an unflappable quality that Theo finds almost meditative to watch. Mocha—the smallest, a dark chocolate color—is the audience favorite. She has a habit of stopping mid-routine to stare directly at someone in the front row, which the handlers have learned to incorporate rather than correct. Pip had been standing at the ring barrier a few minutes ago, stroking Mocha's neck and whispering something into the llama's fuzzy pointed ear. Now she's back in ring three with the clowns.

In ring three, the clown troupe is rehearsing their revised act. It has taken months to get here. After the donkeys were retired, Ace had presented the clowns with what he called a gift—two Lipizzan mares. Stunning animals—white as marble—with graceful necks and flowing manes and feathery tails held high. They'd cost far more than the new safety nets Ace still hadn't ordered.

The clowns had tried. They'd genuinely given it their best. Patches spent two days attempting to teach a dressage-trained horse to steal his hat. The elegant mare had regarded him with aristocratic disdain and refused to move. Cupcake was the only one who could get near either horse without being nipped, and even she couldn't make a Lipizzan do physical comedy. Bongo took one look at them and said nothing, which was louder than anything he could have said.

After four days, Ace—who'd been receiving daily updates from Theo on the clowns' progress—or lack thereof—pivoted. The Lipizzans, Moondancer and Jeté, would have their own act. Two acrobatic showgirls arrived within the week—Shelby and Katrina—with costumes. A full set arrived the next morning. The speed of it was remarkable, and if anyone noticed that a plan this elaborate couldn't have been assembled in four days, no one said so out loud. Theo noticed. He filed it and moved on.

The clowns, for their part, built something new from the wreckage. Without Ravioli and Ziti, the physical comedy had to carry the entire act. Brandon choreographed new sequences. Patches developed a bit involving an increasingly enormous stack of suitcases that collapses on him in stages. Pip—who had cried for three days straight when she returned to winter quarters in January and found the enclosure empty—had gradually channeled her grief into her work with a focus that startled even Brandon. She'd developed a solo bit involving a tiny bicycle and an oversized pair of shoes that reliably brought the house down. She performed it with Ravioli's plush donkey tucked into the front pocket of her coveralls for the first month. Then intermittently. Now Theo only sees the plush peeking out of her pocket a couple of times a week. She seems to be moving on, which is good.

The act isn't the same. It will never be the same. But it works, and the audiences don't know what they're missing because they never saw what came before.

Theo is standing at the edge of ring two, watching Chai execute a surprisingly graceful turn, when Pip skips past him. She's just come from the ring barrier where she was visiting Mocha, and she flashes Theo a gap-toothed grin as she runs back toward ring three. He catches a glimpse of fluffy gray ears sticking out of her coveralls pocket and feels a small tug he doesn't bother to examine.

He turns his attention back to the llamas. Mocha has stopped again, staring at an empty seat in the third row as though she's spotted someone who owes her money.

A sound erupts from ring one that Theo can't process immediately. It is not a scream, but a gasp—the collective intake of breath from eight aerialists who all see the same thing at the same time. Then a sound that is harder to describe. The fibrous groan of netting under sudden violent stress. A ripping. And then screams.

Theo's head snaps left. He is running before his brain assembles the image. The aerialists are converging beneath the rigging. Marco is… where? Marco is still on the catch bar as its swaying slows. He is hanging by his knees, arms extended downward… hands open, showing his chalk-white palms.

Helena is in the net. Not on it. *In* it. Her body crashed through the frayed section—the section every aerialist learned to avoid, the workaround that Marco briefed Theo about months ago—but her head caught in the mesh as her body weight tore through. She is suspended at an angle that the human body was never designed to hold. Her neck is wrong. Everything about the angle of her neck is wrong and it hurts to look at her.

"Call 911!" Theo shouts at the nearest crew hand. The man freezes. "Now!" The man runs.

"Everyone out. Everyone out of the tent." He points at two more crew hands. "Get them outside. Everyone who is not an aerialist, outside now."

The three most experienced aerialists have already gone under the net. They are supporting the mesh around Helena's body, trying to distribute her weight, trying to prevent her from slipping further. They aren't moving her. They know not to move her. They're just holding the net and looking up at her face and knowing what the angle of her neck already tells them. Tears stream down each of their faces. The other three younger aerialists are huddled together near the base of the ladder. One cannot look away from Helena; the other two cannot look up from the floor.

Marco is still on the catch bar. Someone is yelling at him to come down. He doesn't come down. He hangs there with his empty hands open, staring at the space between his palms where Helena was two minutes ago.

Theo turns to the center ring. The llama handlers are frozen in place. Brandon is cradling Pip against his chest, his hand over her eyes, and he is guiding her quickly toward the exit. The other clowns are following. Cupcake's face is almost as white as the makeup she wears for performances. Charlie, who had been passing through on his way to the lion cages, stands motionless near the bleachers, staring at ring one with an expression Theo cannot read.

"Everyone. Out. Now."

The tent empties. Theo stays.

He hears sirens before the last person clears the flaps and wonders how that's possible—it's been less than three minutes. Then realizes someone must have called before he gave the order. One of the aerialists, probably. On the ground with a phone to their ear before Theo even started running.

The EMTs enter. A man and a woman. They take one look at Helena—the angle, the net, the stillness—and the woman EMT reaches for her radio. It's clear they will need backup to get her released and to the ground with as little movement of her neck as possible.

And while they do this, Theo takes the opportunity to move away from everyone. Position himself behind one of the enormous speakers where no one can see him.

He takes out his phone. Opens his email and enters a keyword, then hits search. Scrolls through the dates. Five emails to Ace about the nets, the first one last August, and the latest one from only a few weeks ago.

He steps out from behind the speaker and sees Helena is already strapped to a backboard on the ground, an EMT performing CPR.

Marco has managed to climb down and is standing near the ambulance. Svetlana supports him from his left, Diego supports from his right. Because without them, he would have collapsed to the ground.

The EMTs are loading Helena onto a stretcher. The EMT climbs onto the stretcher and straddles Helena. He is compressing her chest in quick, rhythmic pushes that Theo can hear from thirty feet away, and the sound is worse than the silence.

He approaches and hands one of them his business card. “Theodore Crane. Operations Manager. I’ll be your primary contact.”

He turns to see Svetlana and Diego. They are leading Marco toward the back of the ambulance; his eyes are vacant yet haunted.

The aerialists help Marco into the ambulance and Theo hears a sound he has never heard from an adult male. It is small and high and it does not stop until the doors are shut by one of the uniformed EMT’s, who then runs to the driver’s seat and climbs in.

The siren starts. The lot goes quiet.

*

Heart hammering, Theo calls Ace. Ace answers on the first ring, which has never happened. Theo tells him. There is a silence on the line that stretches past three seconds, past five. When Ace speaks, his voice is smaller than Theo has ever heard it. “How?” Theo tells him. The net. The frayed section. A fall when the pair did not make the connection on the double-twisting layout release they’d landed dozens of times before. Ace says nothing. When Theo checks his phone to make sure the call hasn’t dropped, the timer is still running. Finally Ace says, “I’m coming over.” Not *I’m on my way.* Not the commanding voice of a man who owns the lot. *I’m coming over.* Like a man steeling himself to enter a room he does not want to enter.

*

Ace arrives looking five years older than he did this morning. Something behind his eyes has retreated.

*

The call from the hospital comes at two-fifty-five. Helena Danforth did not survive. Cervical spine fracture, sustained during a fall through a safety net that failed under impact. She was thirty-one years old.

*

Ace calls everyone back to the Big Top at three-forty. He stands in the center ring under a single work light. Ring one is dark, the net barely visible. Nobody wants to look in that direction, but they all steal involuntary glances.

He tells them Helena is gone. His voice cracks on her name. Theo watches from the bleachers and catalogs this: he has never heard Ace's voice crack before.

Ace tells them the doctor assured him that Helena did not suffer. The injury was catastrophic and immediate. She did not feel anything in her final minutes.

Marco is standing in the front row. He has not changed clothes. There is chalk on his pants from the catch bar. His eyes are red but dry. He has moved past tears into something deeper, something that has no moisture left in it. He says, "She slipped. She's never slipped. I had her and then I didn't."

Ace points at Marco. "This is not your fault. You hear me? This was a tragic accident. Nobody is to blame. These things happen."

Theo watches the aerialists. They are glancing at each other. Quick, subtle looks—the kind exchanged by people who share knowledge they have agreed not to speak aloud. They know what happened. The trick didn't fail. Marco didn't fail. Helena didn't fail. The net failed. The net that Marco requested be replaced. The net that Theo requested be replaced. The net that five emails and seven months of asking could not convince Ace Donahue to spend money on, because the aerialists got new costumes and platforms last year and what more could they possibly want.

These things happen. The aerialists hear those words and their faces say everything their mouths don't.

*

Ace says the aerialist act will not be performed tonight, out of respect for Helena and the aerial team. The rest of the show will proceed, if the company is willing. Full refunds will be offered to any guest who wants one. The performance will be dedicated to Helena's memory, with a minute of silence before the opening number.

The tent is quiet. Theo watches faces. The clowns look at Brandon. Brandon looks at the torn net. Charlie stares at the ground. The crew hands wait for someone else to go first.

Finally Vincent, one of the ground acrobats, stands up. "She'd want us to perform."

A murmur moves through the bleachers. Nods. A few tears. Cupcake blows her nose loudly.

*

The show starts at seven. The tent was three-quarters full at five-thirty. By six-forty-five every seat is taken. Word has spread through Amarillo. Not morbid curiosity, or at least not entirely. Something else. The town heard a young woman died at the circus and the circus decided to perform anyway, in her honor, and some-thing about that moved people off their couches and into their cars.

*

Razzle and Dazzle are subdued for the first and only time in their careers. Their patter is quieter. Stationed at the opening of the Big Top, like always, they are wearing their usual sequined costumes. Their usual colorful makeup and hairstyles are toned down to fit the somber occasion. As audience members file in, the two women hand out programs. They repeat the same phrase over and over, sometimes in unison, sometimes taking turns: *Tonight's performance is dedicated to the memory of Helena Danforth, aerialist, whose family performed with Trentini's for four generations.*

It is the only time anyone has said the name Trentini under this tent since Ace bought the circus.

*

The minute of silence before the opening number is the longest sixty seconds of Theo's life. Fifteen hundred people and not a cough, not a whisper, not a child's fidgeting. Just stillness. Ring one is dark. The rigging overhead, empty. The torn net is still there; nobody removed it because there wasn't time… or because removing it felt wrong… or because leaving it there said something that words couldn't.

*

The show is extraordinary. Every performer gives something they didn't know they had left. The clowns are transcendent. Pip lands a tumble she's never landed in rehearsal, and for one pure second the tent erupts in the kind of joy that exists only because grief cleared the space for it. Brandon catches her as she finishes and lifts her onto his shoulders, and his painted smile is real.

*

After the show, the lot clears slowly. Theo stands near the exit, thanking audience members as they leave. He has never done this before and will never do it again. A woman stops and squeezes his hand and says, "That was beautiful." He nods. Says thank you. Means it, he thinks.

*

The Big Top empties. The lights go down. Above ring one, a torn net hangs in the darkness like a mouth that opened and swallowed something it can never give back.

*

It is nearly eleven when Theo knocks on the green trailer door. He does not wait for an answer. He lets himself in, passes through Patty's dark office, and pushes open the inner door.

Ace is at his desk. Scotch in hand. The wingback chair has been pulled back to its usual spot, but Ace is at the desk, which surprises Theo. What surprises him more is Ace's demeanor. The man who looked five years older this afternoon, whose voice cracked on Helena's name, who stood in the center ring and told the company it was a tragic accident—that man is gone. In his place is the Ace that Theo knows best. Settled. Expansive. Almost relaxed.

"Teddy. Sit down. Helluva night. Those performers really stepped up."

Theo chooses not to sit. "We need to talk about what happens next, Ace. There will be an investigation. OSHA will be on this lot within forty-eight hours. Possibly sooner, depending on when the hospital files its report. They have the authority to suspend operations. We are not talking days. It could be weeks. Potentially indefinitely, if they determine—"

Ace waves his hand. That familiar, imperious wave. The one that has dismissed generator failures and insurance renewals and donkeys and a veterinarian's career. He takes a sip of his scotch.

"Don't worry about it. I've got connections. People who owe me favors." He sets the glass down. "There will not be an investigation beyond the local level."

Theo stops.

He has been in this room hundreds of times. He has sat across from this man through firings, tirades, the Jubilee fire, the money laundering reveal. He has cataloged Ace's tells, his patterns, his vulnerabilities. He has mapped the interior architecture of Ace Donahue's mind with the precision of a surveyor.

And he did not know this.

Connections. People who owe favors. The ability to suppress a federal safety investigation into a workplace death. This is not the same as knowing a morning show producer or having a vendor relationship. This is an entirely different category of power. The kind that doesn't show up in financial records or Roger's ledgers. The kind that exists in phone calls that are never logged and conversations that never happened.

Theo recalibrates. Quickly. Files it. Moves on.

"Regardless of whether there's a federal investigation, we need to get the nets replaced immediately. I would do it myself but I don't have the authority for such a large purchase. You need to order them tonight. Back date the invoice. It has to be rush delivery. If the manufacturer can't—"

"I'll handle it."

"With respect, Ace, I'd like your okay to coordinate this myself. The vendor I've been in contact with since July has the specs on file. I can have the order confirmed by morning and delivery within—"

"Don't tell me how to run my business, Teddy."

The words land with the casual authority of a man who has been telling people what to do for fifty years and has never once been told otherwise. Ace picks up his scotch again. Takes a sip. Sets it down. Looks at Theo with an expression that is closer to boredom than anything else.

A woman died today. Fell through a net that Theo asked to be replaced five times in nine months. And Ace is sitting behind his desk drinking scotch, waving away federal investigations, and telling Theo not to tell him how to run his business. As if the nets are a scheduling inconvenience. As if Helena is a line item. As if today was a bad day at the office and not the preventable death of a thirty-one-year-old woman whose family built this circus.

Something shifts in Theo's chest. It is not strategic. It is not calibrated. It is not the product of any calculation he has ever made in this room.

"Tonight, I will tell you how to run your business." His voice is quiet. Level. But stripped of every layer of performance he has worn in this room since the day he walked in and shook Ace's hand. "Because your carelessness cost a life."

Ace's glass pauses halfway to his mouth.

Theo continues. "The nets will be ordered tonight. The rigging will be replaced by Friday. You will authorize a full safety audit of every piece of equipment on this lot—conducted by an independent firm, not our people. And the results will be documented and filed before we leave Amarillo."

He holds Ace's gaze.

"And going forward, I'd prefer you call me Theo."

The room changes. For over a year, he's been Teddy, or kid, or son, or boy. Thirteen months of the bland smile, the practiced deference, the careful architecture of a man who let himself be made small because being small kept him invisible. And now, standing in this office with a dead woman's name in the air and scotch catching the lamplight, Theo has pulled all of it back in a single sentence.

Ace sets the glass down. The casualness is gone. What replaces it is something older and harder—the reflex of a man who has never in his life allowed someone to dictate terms to him. Not his board. Not his attorneys. Not the federal government, apparently. And certainly not the man he hired to make him look good.

"I'll call you whatever the hell I want to, Teddy." Ace's words come out hard. Final. The voice of a Ringmaster who will not be told what to do in his own trailer, in his own circus, by his own employee.

Theo holds his gaze for three seconds. Four. Five.

Then he turns. Walks to the door. Opens it.

He pauses in the doorframe without turning around.

"Order the nets, Ace."

He walks out. Through Patty's office. Through the outer door. Into the cool night, where the air smells of popcorn and diesel and something faintly metallic that might be the rigging or might be his own adrenaline.

He is halfway to his trailer when he realizes his hands are shaking. He stops. Looks down at them. Opens and closes his fists twice, and the tremor subsides.

He has never spoken to Ace Donahue like that. Not once. Not during all these months of absorbing insults and swallowing corrections and performing deference as though it were oxygen. He has never raised his voice, never issued an ultimatum, never stood over that desk and let a man see even a fraction of what lives behind the careful, calibrated surface.

And then there is also this new thing. Ace has connections that can suppress a federal investigation. Ace has people who owe him favors at a level Theo had not accounted for. This is information he did not have an hour ago, and it rearranges several things he thought he understood about the man he works for.

He files it. Not with alarm. With interest.

Tomorrow he will need to repair this. Apologize. Restore the dynamic. Slide back into the deferential posture that keeps Ace manageable and keeps Theo invisible. He is already composing the language—*I was out of line, sir. The stress of losing Helena... it got to me. It won't happen again.*

But tonight, walking across a dark lot in Amarillo, Texas, with his hands still tingling and a dead woman's name echoing through the tent behind him, Theo allows himself to feel something he rarely permits.

Anger. Clean, unproductive, entirely human anger.

By morning it will be gone. Folded up and filed and replaced with the careful machinery that has gotten him this far. But for thirty seconds, walking in the dark, Theo is just a man who is furious at another man for letting a woman die.

He reaches his trailer. Unlocks the door. Steps inside.

On the counter, where he left it this morning, is a navy blue Donahue's mug filled with cold coffee. He picks it up, empties it, rinses it, dries it. Places it back in the cabinet.

Tomorrow, the machine starts again.

ACT III

Four weeks later, end of March, Joplin, Missouri.

The performers' entrance behind the center ring is where Theo stands, and from here he detects the familiar mixture of smells: sawdust, diesel, chalk dust, hairspray. Even hot grease from the concessions fryers. There is a particular electricity that precedes a full house.

Theo is aware that compared to this time last season, ticket sales over the past month have increased dramatically. He has had to walk a fine line between honoring Helena's loss and capitalizing on it.

In the sparse light of the wings Theo waits with his hands in his pockets, watching the crew hands make their final adjustments to the ring barriers. It is fourteen minutes before the Sunday matinee. Through the canvas he can hear the chatter of audience members looking for seats and leafing through their programs. They sound animated and eager, and the bleachers are nearly full.

Razzle and Dazzle are in fine form outside the entrance flaps, their voices cutting through the afternoon heat.

"You won't believe your eyes, ladies and gentlemen!"

"Donahue's Traveling Circus presents an afternoon of wonder!"

"Thrills!"

"Chills!"

"Don't forget to visit the concessions stand—today's special is the Big Top Sundae!"

Ace emerges from the corridor between the back lot and the performers' staging area. He is already in his Ringmaster's coat—buttoned, brushed, lapels sharp. His color is better today, though his energy is still not what it was last season, Theo notes. The coat fits him well, and the stiffness in his shoulders is not quite as noticeable as it was yesterday.

"Impeccable timing, as always, sir," Theo says.

"Teddy." Ace is rolling his neck, loosening up. Left, right. Both crack. "Good crowd?"

"Sold out. Families, mostly. A few groups from the hotels."

"Good, good." Ace flexes his hands, interlacing his fingers and pushing his palms outward. A stretch he picked up from Marco last season. "You hear from Marco lately?"

"I checked in with him about a week ago," Theo says. He keeps his tone neutral. "He's not ready. Still isn't sure if he's coming back at all."

Ace stops stretching. His jaw shifts slightly, the way it does when a piece of information lands somewhere between disappointment and annoyance. "He's been gone a month now."

"Yes."

"The man needs to make a decision. We can't hold that spot indefinitely."

"We can't," Theo agrees.

"Start looking. For both spots." Ace resumes his stretching, pulling one arm across his chest. "Helena's and Marco's. We need fresh talent A-S-A-P."

Theo lets a beat pass. "I think we should be careful with Helena's replacement. The aerialists have restructured the act, and it's working. If we bring someone in too soon, before the team has fully stabilized, it could backfire. They're still grieving."

"Grieving," Ace repeats, as though the word is mildly foreign.

"As for Marco… I'd like one more shot at getting him back before we go outside. I have an idea that might appeal to him. If I can offer him final say in who we hire as his new partner, that gives him some ownership. Some control. After what happened, I think that's what he needs to feel before he's willing to walk back into this tent."

Ace grunts. It is the sound of a man who wants a swift decision and is being counseled on patience instead. However, Theo believes Ace has learned over the past year that patience tends to produce results.

Ace drops his arms and straightens the coat. "Fine. But don't drag it out. If he's not committed by the end of the month, we move on."

"Understood."

A crew hand approaches and tells Ace they're ready for him. Ace places his hand on his top hat to keep it in place when he dips his head in a nod once—a sharp, downward motion, almost military—then strides toward the ring entrance. Theo watches him go. The coat brushes against the edge of the nearest work light and the red fabric takes on a warm glow.

Ace steps through the curtain and into the center ring. The spotlights find him instantly. Two thousand watts of focused light on the red coat, the silver hair, the broad shoulders. The crowd responds with applause, genuine and enthusiastic. The sound has the particular warmth a Sunday matinee audience brings because they chose to be here on a day off, with their children, spending money they could have spent elsewhere. From the wings, Theo watches Ace open his arms and receive it.

"Ladies and gentlemen," he begins. His voice fills the tent the way it always does, louder than the microphone requires, as though the amplification is merely confirming what his vocal cords already accomplished. "Welcome to Donahue's Traveling Circus."

More applause. He lets it wash over him. The timing is good. The posture is good. Theo relaxes half a degree.

"Before we begin this afternoon's spectacular program, I want to take a moment." Ace's voice drops to a register that signals sincerity, or what he believes is sincerity. "A moment to reflect on what you're about to experience."

Theo's relaxation retreats.

"When I first saw this operation—years ago now—it was on life support. Old man Trentini, God rest his soul, he'd given everything he had. Heart and soul. No doubt blood, sweat, and tears. But heart and soul don't pay the bills, and his circus was hemorrhaging money. The banks had walked away. The performers were jumping ship. The animals…." Ace shakes his head slowly. From behind, Theo can see the practiced quality of the gesture in the way Ace's shoulders roll with it—choreographed gravity. "The animals were in rough shape."

The tent is quiet now. Not the engaged quiet of an audience leaning forward, but the uncertain quiet of people who came to see acrobats and are being given a keynote address.

"Nobody believed this circus could be saved," Ace continues, his voice gaining momentum. "Nobody. The industry experts wrote it off. The media said it was finished. But I saw something they didn't. I saw potential. I saw an opportunity that no one else had the courage to take. And I said, 'I'm going to buy this circus, and I'm going to make it the greatest show in America."

A smattering of applause from a few seats near the front. Theo watches Ace's chin lift, his shoulders pull back, his spine straighten by a full inch. The applause is landing on Ace's nervous system like a hit of something chemical. Whatever he's hearing from inside that spotlight, it isn't the polite, scattered quality of what Theo hears from the wings. Ace is hearing a roar.

"And that's exactly what I did. I brought in the best talent. I invested in the infrastructure. I expanded the season, brought the show to cities it had never reached before. And now—now—Donahue's Traveling Circus is the premier touring operation in this country. Bar none."

More quiet. A child somewhere in the upper rows turns to ask his mother a question. A few audience members shift in their seats. The energy in the tent has gone from anticipation to something flatter, something patient in the way people are patient when they are waiting for the thing they paid for.

Ace doesn't feel any of it. He is in the spotlight and the spotlight is where he lives, and from inside that white circle the world beyond the first three rows is just darkness and warmth and the sound of his own voice returning to him from the canvas walls.

"The vision it took. The stamina. The sacrifice…"

Theo catches the eye of one of the crew hands near the ring barrier. The man looks back at him with an expression that asks a question without words. Theo holds up one finger. Wait.

"…and I'll tell you something else. When the other circuses started copying my model—the extended season, the premium pricing, the multimedia marketing—I wasn't flattered. I was…"

Theo turns to Danny, who runs lights and audio from a board in the wings, four steps to his left. The young man's headset is around his neck and his eyebrows are at his hairline.

"Bring up the opening number," Theo says quietly.

Danny's eyes flick toward the ring. "He's still—"

"I know. And he shouldn't be. Start the intro music for the first act."

Danny hesitates for one second, maybe two. Then his hands move across the board. The opening bars fill the tent—bright, percussive, impossible to talk over.

Ace's head turns a fraction toward the speakers. Something crosses his face that is visible even from the wings—a flash of irritation so brief it could be mistaken for a blink.

But he is Ace Donahue, and he is in the center ring, and there is an audience, and whatever else he is, the man knows how to land. He pivots on his heel, extends one arm toward ring number one, and raises his voice over the music. "And without further ado—the act you've been waiting for—I give you the astonishing, the breathtaking, the incomparable Tumbling Tropiques!"

The crowd erupts. Not for Ace, but for the nine ground acrobats who cartwheel into ring one wearing electric blue and gold, their bodies already in motion before the audience fully registers their arrival. The energy in the tent jumps by a factor of ten in only three seconds, and Ace walks out of the spotlight and toward the wings. His eyes find Theo immediately.

"What the hell was that." His voice is low and tight, a coiled thing. But there is something else in it too, something that surprises Theo: genuine confusion. As though Ace cannot fathom why the music started when he was clearly in the middle of something important.

Theo steps closer. Drops his own voice to match Ace's register, but keeps it warm.

"Sir, they already know. Everyone in this tent knows what you've built. You don't have to convince them—they already bought the ticket." Ace's jaw works once. Twice. "You're the reason they're here," Theo continues. "But right now, in the ring, they need you to be the Ringmaster. They need you to show them what's next. That's what they came for—to be guided through the show by the man who built it. And that's a role nobody else can fill."

The knot in Ace's expression begins to loosen. Not because the irritation is gone, but because something in Theo's words has found the frequency that Ace's ego tunes to. He built this. They came because of him. The Ringmaster is the role only he can play.

"If you want to talk about the business, the vision, the legacy—and you should, because it's a hell of a story—I can set up another round on the morning shows. Dakota Landry on *Rise and Shine* loved you last time. Those audiences tune in specifically to hear that story. But in here?" Theo points toward the bleachers beyond the center ring. "In here, they're on the edge of their seats waiting for you to tell them who's performing next. That's the power of the Ringmaster. Every act lands because you introduce it."

Ace is quiet for a long moment. Behind them, the Tumbling Tropiques are in full flight—flips, lifts, human pyramids—and the crowd's cheers rise and recede with the daring of their moves.

"Dakota would probably want another segment," Ace says. "I'll make the call tomorrow." Ace straightens his coat. Rolls his neck once. When he looks back at Theo, the irritation has been fully replaced by something warmer. The expression of a man who has been reminded of his own importance by someone who understands it.

"Good man, Teddy."

He turns and walks back toward the corridor, no doubt already composing what he'll say when he returns to the ring to introduce the next act.

Theo watches him go. When Ace is out of earshot, he glances back at Danny. The young man looks up at Theo and shakes his head. Contorts his mouth into a stretched grimace and bares his teeth which are clenched tightly. It is the expression of a man who just watched something he wishes he hadn't. Theo offers a small shrug.

"It's getting worse," Danny whispers.

Theo turns back to the show.

*****

The matinee earns a standing ovation. Theo watches from the wings as Ace takes his final bow—arms wide, chin high, the red coat catching the light the way it always does. Whatever happened during the opening, the show recovered. The Tumbling Tropiques were electric. The clowns had the crowd howling. And the aerialists—Svetlana and Diego running the act as a duo now, with two of the younger flyers filling the formation—delivered a routine that earned a gasp so unified it sounded rehearsed.

Ace strides through the curtain with the energy of a man who believes the ovation was for him. His color is high and his eyes are bright and he is, for this moment, the version of himself that Theo finds easiest to work with.

"Tremendous show, sir. Sold out, and they got every penny's worth."

Ace tugs at the cuffs of his coat. "Damn right they did."

"I've been thinking about what we were talking about earlier. The morning shows." Theo falls into step beside him as they walk toward the back corridor. "Dakota would love to have you back. But I had another thought, and I want to run it by you. I'm not sure how you'll feel about it, so just hear me out before you make a decision."

Ace glances at him. The request to withhold judgment has the intended effect; it slows him down. He stops walking and turns to face Theo fully, arms crossed over the red coat.

"I'm listening."

"What if you didn't just talk about the circus on the morning shows? What if you gave them something to talk about?"

"Meaning what."

"A performance. Your own act." Theo pauses long enough for the words to land but not long enough for Ace to dismiss them. "The tightrope."

Ace's expression doesn't change, but his arms uncross by a fraction of an inch.

"I know it's not something a man your age would typically consider," Theo says. "But that's exactly why it's such a brilliant idea." He lowers his voice and takes on a conspiratorial tone as he begins gesturing to emphasize his words. "Think about it. Ace Donahue—the man who saved the American circus, the man who resurrected a dying business model—is now going to thrill audiences with a feat no ringmaster has ever attempted. Not as a gimmick…. but as a grand finale."

For dramatic effect, Theo takes a step back and holds his hands up to form a square with his thumbs and fingers before he adds, "Ace Donahue, Ringmaster as performer. The man who runs the show, stepping into the show himself."

Ace is quiet.

Theo drops his arms back down to his sides and waits to see how his idea will be received.

Ace's jaw works once, the way it does when he is turning something over rather than rejecting it. Theo reads the silence accurately. This is not a no. This is a man calculating how much attention it would generate.

"Imagine the coverage," Theo continues. "Every local affiliate in every city we visit. National press. 'Seventy-two-year-old circus owner walks the tightrope in his own show.' That's not a segment. That's a *headline*. That's a *week* of headlines."

"I'm not seventy-two," Ace says. "I'm seventy."

"Of course," Theo demurs, though he knows very well Ace will turn seventy-three in August. "You start training now? You can probably debut before your birthday. The audiences, the media, the critics? They'll lose their minds."

Something shifts behind Ace's eyes. Not quite excitement. Something more cautious than that… and more hungry. The look of a man who wants to say yes but has not yet found a reason that allows him to.

"It would need to be kept quiet," Ace finally says. "Until I'm ready."

"Completely. No one outside the training team. You try it for a few weeks, see how it feels. There's no commitment. If it's not for you, nobody ever knows. And of course we would take every precaution. The new nets. A balancing pole. A harness." Theo says this with the easy confidence of a man listing items on a grocery list. "No need to risk breaking a hip. You learn the fundamentals, get comfortable, build your confidence. And after a few weeks, if you're enjoying it, you train in earnest."

"Who trains me?"

"Well, that's the other thing I wanted to mention. I think this could be the piece that brings Marco back." Theo lets that sit for a beat. "I've been trying to find the right thing to offer him. Something that gives him a reason to walk back into this tent. If I can tell him that you—the owner, the man who built this operation—wants to learn the tightrope, and that you specifically want the best in the business to teach you? That's not a job offer. That's an honor. Marco's pride won't let him say no to that."

Ace lifts and tilts his head, no doubt pondering the magnificence of his act. The last of his hesitation is dissolving into something that looks very much like the expression he wears when he steps into the spotlight. He is already seeing it. The wire. The lights. Two thousand people holding their breath. And him at the center of all of it—not introducing someone else's act, but performing his own.

"Get Marco on the phone," Ace says. "But Teddy. Not a word of this to anyone, until I say so."

"Understood, sir."

Ace smooths the front of his coat, rolls his neck once, and walks toward his trailer. His stride has a quality Theo has not seen in weeks.

Theo watches him go. When Ace rounds the corner and disappears from view, Theo allows himself a brief moment of self-congratulation.

He heads toward his trailer and exhales slowly, thinking: *That didn't take as much work as I was expecting.* If the training goes well, Theo knows Ace will be in a better mood than he's been in months. And a man with a new obsession is a man who's not looking for problems to create.

Before he's even arrived at his trailer door, he's already mentally composed the message he's about to send to Marco.

*****

Second week of April, Springfield, Missouri.

Marco arrives on a Tuesday evening, driving a rented sedan. He's got a duffel bag in the back seat and nothing else. Theo meets him at the lot entrance, shakes his hand, and walks him to the trailer the company has offered. It is a significant upgrade from the RV he and Helena used to share. "You're the senior aerialist, and you should have more comfortable accommodations than the RV," Theo had explained on the phone. When they arrive at the door,

Theo cannot tell whether Marco is pleased with the new accommodations.

Understandable, Theo thinks, *under the circumstances.*

The two men do not discuss Helena. Not yet. Theo tells him that breakfast is at seven in the tent adjacent to the practice area, and that they can talk properly in the morning. Marco nods once and closes his trailer door.

At seven-fifteen the next morning, the breakfast tent smells of bacon grease and fresh coffee. It holds the warmth of a space that has become, over the past several weeks, something more than a meal. Brenda Mitchell and her assistant, a young woman named Cassie who was promoted from ticket sales, have turned Theo's cost-saving measure into one of the most popular perks the company has ever offered. The scrambled eggs are made to order. The pancakes come out in batches. There is fresh fruit, cartons of milk, and pitchers of orange juice and cranberry juice… and everything gets refilled without anyone having to ask.

Theo is already seated at one of the folding tables when Marco enters. A few heads turn. Word has traveled, as it always does on the lot, and the reception is warm—handshakes, shoulder claps, a couple of the younger crew members nodding with visible relief. Marco accepts the attention with the quiet grace of a man who is not yet sure he made the right decision.

He sits across from Theo with a plate he has barely touched. A single pancake. Black coffee. He looks thinner than when he left, and older in a way that has nothing to do with the weeks that have passed.

"Jasmine Hawke accepted," Theo says. "She's leaving Toronto and flying into St. Louis on Monday. From there she joins us in Sullivan."

Marco's fork pauses over the pancake. "Helena knew Jasmine."

"I know."

"She said Jasmine was the most talented flyer she'd ever seen. That if she could build a team from scratch, Jasmine would be the first call she made."

Theo lets that sit. He does not rush past it, does not redirect.

Marco sets the fork down. He looks at Theo with an expression that is not guarded, exactly, but careful. The expression of a man who has decided to say something he has not said to anyone else.

"I was going to ask her to marry me, Theo. Did you know that?"

The tent noise continues around them—silverware on plates, Cassie calling out that a fresh batch of pancakes is ready, someone laughing near the coffee station. None of it reaches the two men at the table.

"I knew you were in love," Theo says softly. "Hell, everyone knew." He pauses. "But I didn't know you were going to propose."

Marco exhales. It is a long, slow breath—the kind that carries something out of the body that has been stored there for too long. He picks up his coffee and takes a drink and does not say anything else about it. He doesn't need to.

"When does Jasmine arrive?" Marco asks. His voice has shifted. Still quiet, but the register has changed. He is talking about work now. He is a professional again, and the transition happens so cleanly that Theo understands something about Marco that he had not fully appreciated: this man survives by compartmentalizing. The grief goes in one room. The work goes in another. The door between them is very thin, but it holds.

"Monday afternoon. I've arranged for her to have an RV next to Svetlana. I figured you'd want her close to the aerial team from day one."

"Good." Marco glances toward the far end of the tent, where a section has been cordoned off with portable barriers. A narrow strip of webbing, perhaps fifteen feet long, is stretched between two low posts no more than a foot off the ground. Remy is standing to one side, hands ready, while Ace moves along the webbing in slow, deliberate steps. His arms are extended for balance. His focus is absolute.

"He's been at it for about a week," Theo says. "Remy's been working with him on the basics. Balance, posture, foot placement. Just the fundamentals."

Marco watches without speaking. Ace reaches the end of the webbing, steps off, and shakes out his legs. Even from across the tent, the concentration on his face is visible. He is not performing for anyone. He is genuinely trying.

"He's not bad," Marco says. There is no enthusiasm in it, but there is no dismissal either. It is the honest assessment of a man who has spent his life on the wire and can tell the difference between natural balance and the absence of it. Ace has the former.

"Strong core," Marco adds. "Good center of gravity for his age. Low and stable." He takes another sip of coffee. "Who chose the webbing width?"

"Remy. Two inches."

Marco nods. "That's right for a beginner. You start narrow, you build bad habits."

Theo does not respond to this. He lets Marco talk, lets him settle into the role of expert, lets the professional identity reassert itself over the grief. This is what Marco needs. Not sympathy. Not patience. A reason to be the best at something again.

Ace spots them from across the tent. His face opens into an expression of genuine pleasure—the broad, unguarded smile of a man who is happy to see someone, uncomplicated by strategy or agenda. He crosses the tent with his hand already extended.

"Marco." He grips Marco's hand with both of his own. "Welcome back. Truly."

"Thank you, sir." Marco stands for the handshake. It is brief but real.

"Did you see?" Ace gestures toward the webbing with a kind of boyish pride that Theo has never seen from him before. Not the preening, performative pride of the center ring. Something smaller and more honest. The pride of a man who is learning something difficult and knows he is not yet good at it.

"I did. You've got a feel for it."

"Remy's been a good teacher," Ace says, glancing at the young aerialist who is coiling the webbing near the posts. "But I'm ready for the real thing. I want to put a feather in this cap, Marco. A real one."

"We'll get you there."

Ace claps Marco on the shoulder once—a firm, downward motion—and turns to head toward the exit. Remy falls into step behind him, and the two disappear through the tent flap into the morning light.

Marco sits back down. Picks up his coffee. Looks at Theo.

"He means it," Marco says.

"He does."

Marco nods slowly. He wraps both hands around the mug and stares at the space where Ace was standing. Whatever he is thinking, he keeps it behind the thin door.

"Monday," he says, "I'll be ready for Jasmine."

*****

Third week of April, Sullivan, Missouri.

Jasmine Hawke arrives at the Meramec Community Fairgrounds just after 3:00 PM. The exotic-looking twenty-six year-old woman exits the cab holding a small equipment case. She is seventy miles away from the Lambert Airport in St. Louis where she climbed into the cab, and a world away from her home city of Toronto.

The young, earnest cabby trots to the back of the vehicle and removes two suitcases from the trunk. He sets them on the ground next to her, accepts a cash tip, and bows his head to bid farewell.

Theo is approaching, but she has not spotted him yet. Instead, she stands for a moment with her hand shading her eyes, taking in the scene with the focused assessment of someone who has spent her entire life reading performance spaces.

Theo arrives at her side. They shake hands, he picks up her suitcases, and she follows him toward the aerial team's corner of the lot. Svetlana is already waiting outside her RV with her arms crossed and an expression that is not unfriendly but is not warm either. It is the expression of a woman who loved Helena and is looking at the person standing in Helena's absence and does not yet know what to do with that.

Jasmine looks back at her steadily. She does not fill the silence with reassurance or apology. She simply meets Svetlana's eyes and waits.

Something in Svetlana's posture shifts by a fraction. She unfolds her arms. Extends her hand.

Theo leaves them to it, and texts Marco to let him know Jasmine has arrived.

Early the next morning is the first opportunity Jasmine has to work with Marco. They only have two performances scheduled in Sullivan, and the first is tomorrow. Though Jasmine will not perform with Donahue's for at least a week, she is eager to learn some of the routine.

Theo keeps glancing at them from the top row of the bleachers closest to the center ring, ostensibly reviewing vendor invoices on his phone.

They start on the ground. Not the trapeze, not even the low practice rig—just the mat, running through connection drills. Timing exercises. The fundamental vocabulary of two people learning how the other moves.

Twenty minutes later they transition to the air. Marco calls a sequence and Jasmine follows, then Jasmine calls and Marco follows, and within just another twenty minutes there is something happening between them that Theo recognizes without being able to name. Not chemistry exactly. More like fluency in a language that has no alphabet; it is all weight and counterweight, the grammar of momentum, and trust measured in milliseconds and inches.

Theo is watching them from his seat. Marco calls out something as he is swinging from a trapeze bar and Jasmine is standing on one of the platforms. He cannot make out their exchange but Jasmine listens, nods, leaps… and Marco catches her easily.

After glancing back down at his phone, Theo puts it in his pocket and gives his full attention to their session.

*****

Early June, Fort Wayne, Indiana

Theo hears a soft knock on his trailer door, which is propped open because it's a mild afternoon. When he turns toward the door he sees Brandon; he is standing on the metal landing, leaning against the railing and holding an envelope.

"Got a minute?"

"Of course. Come in."

Brandon does not come in, and for that matter does not move other than to bend his elbow and display the white envelope he is holding between his index and middle fingers. It is small—the kind sold in packs of fifty at the drugstore. Pip's handwriting is on the front in purple marker. TO RAVIOLI AND ZITI, it says. She has included a red heart sticker under each name, and also made a passable attempt at drawing the two donkeys… one gray, one brown… all four ears standing tall.

"Another letter," Brandon says.

"I see that." Theo reaches for it. Brandon holds onto it for a half-second longer than necessary before releasing it. The delay is so brief it could be accidental. Theo senses it is not.

"She's been working on it all week," Brandon says. "Every morning after breakfast. She keeps asking me if I think they'll write back."

“Kids,” Theo says, and offers a smile.

Brandon does not return it. Instead he crosses his arms and looks out across the lot. The late afternoon light is catching the tops of the trailers and turning them the color of warm copper. Somewhere behind the main tent, a crew hand is running a pressure washer, and the rhythmic pulse of it fills the silence between the two men.

“I was wondering,” Brandon says, still looking at the lot rather than at Theo, “if you think anyone from the sanctuary will ever write back to Pip.”

The question lands in the space between them with the weight of something so heavy, Brandon could no longer carry it.

“It sure would mean the world to her.” He turns to meet Theo’s gaze before he adds, “Something. Anything.”

Theo hears what is underneath the words. It is not a question. Not even a request, really. It is closer to a telepathic dare. *If you need to write the letter yourself, then write the letter yourself.* Brandon is not accusing him. He is offering Theo an out—a way to maintain the lie more convincingly—and in doing so, he is telling Theo that the lie as it currently stands is not holding. Not with Brandon. Not anymore.

Theo adjusts his tone to its warmest register.

“I’ll talk to them again, Brandon. I’m doing my best. They’re probably really busy there, but I will ask.” He waits a beat before adding, “Again.”

The two men regard each other. Brandon’s face is composed, looking very much like a man who has heard exactly what he expected and is choosing not to push further. Not because he believes Theo. But because his daughter drew two donkeys on the front of that envelope, and there is nothing to be gained from tearing down the only wall standing between Pip and the truth.

“Thanks so much,” Brandon says. It is the most precisely wielded sentence Theo has heard in months, and he has made a career of wielding sentences precisely.

He dips his head once, turns, and walks down the steps and onto the gravel road that runs between the trailers. His stride is unhurried. His hands are in his pockets. He does not look back.

Theo watches him until he rounds the curve past the generator shed and disappears from view. Then he looks down at the envelope in his hand. The purple marker. The lopsided donkeys. The hearts.

He steps out of the trailer and walks to his Tahoe, parked in the narrow strip of shade between his trailer and the storage building. Opens the driver's door and sits down, but does not pull his left foot inside.

The door is open and the engine is off, and for a moment he simply holds the envelope on his thigh and looks at it.

He glances to his left. The utility pole at the edge of the lot, the one that carries the power lines from the road to the main tent—the crow with the white scar on its beak is there. Perched on the crossbar. One eye visible, dark and unblinking, angled down toward the Tahoe.

Theo holds up the envelope.

"You don't approve."

The crow turns its head… slowly, deliberately… and looks the other direction.

Theo lowers the envelope to his lap.

He opens the glove box. The registration. The insurance card. The owner's manual he has never read. And beneath all of it are two white envelopes. Same drugstore stock. Same purple marker. The first one is slightly crumpled at the corner. The second is pristine.

He does not open the third letter. He learned that lesson with the first one.

The memory arrives without permission. A few months back, perhaps a week into the start of the new season, Brandon had tapped Theo on the shoulder. Handed him the first envelope with just a quick, "Pip wrote to the donkeys, can you mail this to the sanctuary?" Theo had taken it, and later that night he drove off the lot. Pulled into a gas station a few miles down the road with plans to throw it away. Instead, he'd opened it.

Dear Ravioli and Ziti,

I didn't get the chance to say goodbye—

That was as far as he got. His hands moved before his mind caught up. Hastily folding the letter back into its creases, jamming it into the envelope, fumbling with the glove box latch. He buried it beneath the registration and insurance cards and every other piece of paper he could find, as though the depth of the burial could undo the reading. He closed the glove box and gripped the steering wheel with both hands.

His right hand had trembled as he moved it toward the steering wheel. Faintly. Just enough that he'd noticed.

With that first letter, he'd sat there in a gas station parking lot for a solid fifteen minutes with his hands tight on the wheel before he'd started the engine and drove back to the lot.

He never opened the second letter.

Now he places the third envelope at the bottom. Beneath the other two. Beneath the paperwork. He closes the glove box with a quiet click.

He starts the engine. Pulls his left foot inside. Closes the door. And drives.

When he returns thirty minutes later, he parks in the same spot. Opens the glove box one more time. Looks at the three envelopes, stacked neatly at the bottom. Closes it.

The crow is gone from the utility pole.

Theo walks back to his trailer and does not think about the letters again for the rest of the evening. Tries not to, anyway. Which is not the same thing.

*****

Mid June, Decatur, Illinois.

The morning is already warm when Theo crosses the lot toward the breakfast tent. June has settled over the fairgrounds with the particular heaviness of the rural Midwest—the kind of heat that starts early and has no intention of leaving. The crew has propped the tent flaps open on both sides to let whatever breeze exists pass through, and the smell of coffee and something sweet drifts out across the gravel.

He is halfway there when he sees Pip.

She is on the far side of the llama pen astride Mocha, the smaller of the two females. Her legs hang well below the animal's belly and her sneakers—the same pink ones she always wears, the ones that look too small for her now—nearly brush the ground on either side. She is holding a fistful of Mocha's wool near the base of the neck, not a proper grip but the instinctive clutch of a child who has figured out a thing on her own. Her face carries an expression of total concentration.

He is not sure she is allowed to ride the llamas. He is fairly certain no one gave her permission, and equally certain no one told her not to. Theo is certain that in Pip's moral framework, this is the same as a yes. He is about to call out to her when Mocha decides she is finished.

It happens fast. Something spooks the llama—a sound, a scent, or possibly just the indignation of an animal who did not agree to be ridden. Whatever the impetus, Mocha lurches sideways and bolts three strides toward the fence. Pip holds on for the first stride, loses her grip on the second, and is on the ground by the third.

She lands on her knees and the heels of both hands. The gravel in the pen is loose and dry and it does exactly what gravel does to the knees of a child in June.

Theo takes two quick steps forward before he stops himself. A crew hand is already jogging over. Pip is sitting up, examining her palms. Her face is cycling through the phases that every skinned knee produces: surprise, inspection, the dawning realization that it stings, and then the decision about whether or not to cry.

Pip decides not to cry. She wipes her hands on her shorts, looks at the blood beading on both kneecaps, and says something to the crew hand that Theo cannot hear. Whatever it is, the crew hand laughs. Pip gets to her feet and walks over to Mocha, who has stopped at the fence and is watching her with the flat, unrepentant gaze of a llama who has done nothing wrong. Pip reaches up and strokes her neck.

Theo does not move.

Seeing the gravel… her knees… the way she went down fast and unexpected. The animal pulling her forward before she could react. The blood coming through in small bright dots on skin that was clean a moment ago.

Witnessing this chain of events allows a vivid memory to surge and encase him.

He is eight years old, being pulled along the sidewalk of Hickory Drive just two blocks from his grandmother's house. Her Saint Bernard's name is Digby and he is a hundred and forty pounds of amiable stupidity. Every day after school Theo walks him for a quarter. His grandmother had her doubts. "That dog outweighs you by sixty pounds, sweetheart. What happens if he sees a cat?" But Theo had worked with Digby. Trained him, as much as a boy can train a Saint Bernard. To heel, to stop at curbs, to not pull. He carried treats in his jacket pocket—the small liver ones that came in a yellow box. And Digby was, on most days, a gentle giant.

The squirrel bolted through a hedge at full speed.

Digby went from walking to running in less than a second. The leash snapped taut and Theo's feet left the ground. Not metaphorically. His shoes left the pavement entirely and he landed, knees first, in a driveway with a sound he would not forget—the grinding scrape of skin and gravel meeting at speed.

He let go of the leash. Digby was already twenty yards down the street, his blue leash bouncing behind him, the squirrel long gone up a tree.

Theo looked at his knees. The blood was coming through where the rough pebbles had taken the skin cleanly off. There was grit embedded in both kneecaps and it stung enough to make his eyes water.

He got up and ran after the dog.

Not because he was brave. Because he could not go back to his grandmother's house without Digby. Because the quarter depended on it. Because Digby was his responsibility, and responsibilities did not end when your knees were bleeding and you were fighting back tears.

He found Digby two blocks away sitting at the base of the tree. Looking up, panting hard. His leash was tangled around a fire hydrant. The dog turned to look at him with an expression of pure, uncomplicated joy, as if the last sixty seconds hadn't happened.

Theo untangled the leash, put a liver treat in his palm, and walked Digby home. His grandmother cleaned the gravel out of his knees with peroxide and a washcloth and told him he was the toughest boy on Hickory Drive. He did not feel tough. He felt like a boy who had held on as long as he could, and then got up and kept going because there was no other option.

Pip is scratching Mocha behind the ear. Her knees are bleeding in the same small, bright way, and she does not seem to notice or care.

The memory releases him. It does not fade so much as step back, retreating to whatever room it lives in. The door closes behind it and leaves Theo standing in the middle of a dusty lot watching a nine-year-old girl forgive a llama.

He walks into the breakfast tent.

The morning rush is underway. Brenda and Cassie are working the serving line with the efficient choreography of two people who have done this enough times to stop talking about it. The griddle is producing a steady rotation of pancakes—plain, blueberry, and the chocolate chip ones that Pip requests and Brenda always makes regardless of whether Pip has appeared yet. A tray of scrambled eggs sits beside a tray of bacon, and the coffee station at the far end has a line three deep.

Theo pours himself a cup of coffee and moves toward the back of the tent. He has inventory to check; Brenda mentioned they were low on the bulk syrup and the napkin stock was running thin, and he wants to verify before placing the next supply order. The storage area is behind a partition of stacked boxes near the rear flap, and he settles into the narrow space between a column of paper goods and a pallet of canned fruit with his coffee and his phone.

He is scrolling through the vendor catalog when the conversation at the nearest table reaches him. When he glances up, he notices there is a narrow gap between the two boxes in front of him. Peeking one eye through the opening, he can see several people seated at one of the tables.

"—honestly can't believe how much time she spends with those horses."

Theo recognizes the voice as Shorty's. He is seven-feet-nothing and one of the veteran clowns. "Every morning she's over there before breakfast. Brushing them, talking to them, checking their hooves."

"Dr. Ellie?" Another voice. Diego, one of the younger aerialists.

"Who else. She acts like they're her personal pets. You'd think they were golden retrievers instead of thousand-pound divas."

A snort of laughter from someone Theo cannot see. Then Virginia's voice, warm and knowing: "I told her my secret. Apple slices. Cut thin, not thick. She's been slipping them apple slices every visit and now those Lipizzans follow her around the paddock like puppies."

"Of course our sweet Cupcake figured it out," Shorty says. "You're the only person on this lot those horses don't look down their noses at."

"Literally," Diego says, and the table laughs.

The conversation drifts. Someone mentions the heat. Someone else complains about the parking situation at the next fairground. And then, with the natural inevitability of a topic that has been simmering in every backstage conversation for weeks, someone brings up Ace.

"So how's our tightrope walker doing?" This is from Patches, the oldest clown. His tone carries the dryness of a man who has worked for the circus long enough to find everything both amusing and exhausting.

"Remy says he's actually not terrible." Diego again. "Good balance. Takes direction."

"Sure, on the practice wire twelve inches off the ground," Shorty says. "Wait till he's forty feet up and his prostate kicks in."

Laughter. The easy, careless laughter of people who are eating breakfast and roasting their boss and have no idea anyone is listening.

"I could teach him the trapeze," Diego offers. "Get him up there in a sequined leotard. The crowd would love it."

"Maybe Katrina and Shelby could teach him to ride the Lipizzans," Virginia says. She is referring to the two showgirls who joined Donahue's right after the fancy horses—who refused to learn even one amusing trick—got their own act. "Put him in one of those sparkly dressage outfits." More laughter, then she insists, "He'd go for it, too. You know he would."

"Chainsaw juggling," Patches says. "In full clown makeup. We'll bill it as the grand finale."

The table is laughing steadily now, the kind of laughter that builds on itself, each new suggestion more absurd than the last. Theo remains motionless behind the boxes. His coffee is going cold. He does not reach for it.

Then Charlie speaks.

Charlie, who has said perhaps forty words in Theo's presence since the day Theo arrived. Charlie, who trains Bruno and Hazel with quiet competence and infinite patience, and never complains about anything. He's got twenty years' worth of scars from working with big cats. On his hands, his arms. Even a thin raggedy scar below his left cheek.

"I could teach him to get Bruno to jump through a flaming hoop," Charlie offers without a trace of humor.

The table goes quiet. Not because the joke is offensive but because it's Charlie. Charlie doesn't do this.

He takes a bite of his pancake. Chews. Swallows. The table is watching him.

"And I would rub raw meat all over his Ringmaster coat before he does the act."

It's quiet for a beat, then Virginia gasps, "Charlie!"

Whether it's Charlie's joke or Virginia's shocked exclamation—maybe the combination—everyone breaks. The laughter that erupts is different from what came before—louder, less controlled, tinged with the shock of hearing the quietest man in the room say the darkest thing anyone has said all morning.

The moment things start to die down, Charlie offers one more zinger. "Maybe it's not a coincidence that my assistant's name is Destiny."

Another raucous outburst. Diego puts his head down on the table. Virginia claps both hands over her mouth. Even Patches, who is not easily surprised, is shaking his head with his eyes closed.

Charlie displays a small, private smile… the smile of a man who has been thinking about this for a while and is satisfied with how well it landed. He picks up his fork and takes another bite of his blueberry pancakes.

The laughter subsides into the warm, scattered hum of a table that has just shared something it will reference for weeks. Shorty reaches over and claps Charlie on the back. Charlie accepts this with a nod and continues eating.

Behind the boxes, Theo shifts so he is no longer able to see the group. His coffee is cold. His phone screen has gone dark.

Even Charlie, is all he can think.

He sets the coffee down on top of a box of napkins. Picks up his phone. Opens the vendor catalog again.

The breakfast tent goes on without him.

*****

Late June, Champaign, Illinois

Three months in, and Ace Donahue can walk a tightrope.

Not beautifully. Not with the fluid, weightless grace of Svetlana or the mechanical precision of Diego. But he can cross forty feet of braided steel cable at a height of thirty-five feet, with a balancing pole and a harness, without falling. He does it three days a week. He has not missed a session since Marco took over from Remy. And the compliments he receives from the company are, for perhaps the first time in his tenure as owner, genuine.

Not universally generous. Some are begrudging—the tight nod from Patches, the measured "looking good, sir" from Shorty that carries just enough warmth to pass as sincerity. But others are real. Remy, who laid the groundwork, watches Ace's progress with the quiet pride of a teacher whose student has outgrown the first lesson. Cassie, who serves Ace his breakfast every morning, told him last week that she'd watched him practice and thought he was brave. Ace had carried that compliment around for two days like a coin in his pocket. One morning Patty sauntered over from Ace's trailer just to grab the last bagel and ooh and ahh over Ace's improvements.

Marco says little. He corrects Ace's posture, adjusts his grip on the pole, reminds him to breathe. When Ace does something well, Marco nods once. When Ace does something poorly, Marco explains why without raising his voice. The relationship between them has settled into something functional and almost warm—the elder student and the patient master, working together inside a discipline that does not care about money or ownership or whose name is on the tent.

Ace has told Theo he is ready to perform in front of an audience.

Theo is in his trailer when he tells him. It is early evening, after a matinee that went well, and Ace is in that light mood that follows a good show and a good practice session—expansive, talkative, sitting in the chair across from Theo's desk with one ankle crossed over the opposite knee, the red coat draped over the armrest.

"I want to debut it in Wisconsin. Probably La Crosse," Ace says. "That's a mid-sized market."

"I think that's the right call," Theo says. "Not too big, not too small."

Ace has a satisfied expression and nods his approval.

"Also," Theo continues, "I have something for you."

He opens the bottom drawer of his desk and lifts out a flat box—white cardboard, no label, the kind that might contain a winter coat. He sets it on the desk and pushes it toward Ace.

Ace looks at the box, then at Theo, then back at the box. He opens it with the careful curiosity of a man who is not accustomed to receiving gifts and does not entirely trust them.

Inside, folded neatly in tissue paper, are two items.

First, a harness. It is not the standard-issue safety harness that Ace has been training in—the white nylon webbing with industrial buckles that is visible from the back row, the one Ace has complained about since his first week on the wire because it makes him look, in his words, like a man being lowered from a helicopter.

This is something else entirely.

At first glance it appears to be a vest—red and black plaid, heavy cloth, cut close to the body and tailored to sit cleanly beneath the Ringmaster's coat. The kind of thing a man might wear for warmth, or style, or both. The harness itself lives underneath the fabric, invisible. The buckles and straps that will do the actual work of keeping Ace from falling are entirely concealed beneath the plaid exterior, their hardware secured to a single reinforced loop centered between the shoulder blades—the attachment point, camouflaged so thoroughly into the pattern of the material that even knowing it is there, the eye struggles to find it.

Ace lifts the vest out. Holds it up, turns it, runs his thumb along the back until he finds the loop. He looks at Theo.

"What about my Ringmaster coat?"

Theo lifts out the second item and holds it up. "A duplicate. Identical in every way except for this." He turns the coat around and shows Ace the hidden slit in the back panel. "Your coat is untouched. Montreal made this one from your measurements and a fabric swatch." He sets it on the desk between them. "Shelby gets up on the platform with you. She pulls the loop embedded in the harness through the slit, clips the safety cable to the harness, smooths the coat back into place." He pauses. "From the audience, nothing is visible. From the wings, nothing is visible. From thirty-five feet below on the sawdust floor, nothing is visible."

Ace is quiet, his fingers moving over the titanium loop. "Shelby," he says, nodding slowly. "She's the taller of the two."

"Yes. Good thinking."

"Then she hands me the pole." He looks up at Theo. "This could all become part of the act."

"Yes," Theo agrees. "It already is, in a way. During these months of training, either Marco or one of the riggers has been attaching the safety cable. Functional, but hardly theatrical. With the custom harness, Shelby could clip you in while she's still in costume. The safety aspect? That just becomes a showy part of the performance."

A long silence. Ace looks back and forth between the two pieces. When he finally looks up, his eyes are shiny and his voice, when it comes, is quieter than Theo has ever heard it.

"How did you know?" He shakes his head slowly. "How did you know exactly what I needed?"

Theo holds his gaze. "The same way I know most things, sir. I pay attention."

Ace does not say anything for a long moment. His jaw is working, but not in the way it works when he is angry or calculating. This is something else entirely.

"Teddy," he says. "This is… this is really something."

"You've earned it, sir. You've worked hard. And when you walk out on that wire in La Crosse, the audience should see the Ringmaster. Not a man in safety equipment."

Ace sets the harness down on the desk. He looks at it the way he looks at the spotlight—with hunger, but also with something rarer. Gratitude. Not the transactional gratitude of a man who has been given something useful. The deeper, less guarded gratitude of a man who has been seen.

"You know," Ace says, "my kids… they've never once come to see a show. Not once. I've invited them. Every season. They don't come."

Theo waits. He can see the shape of what's coming but does not reach for it.

"You're more like a son to me than either of them ever were."

The words land in the trailer with a weight that neither man was fully prepared for. Ace's eyes are bright. Not wet, exactly, but bright. Like the eyes of a man who has said something he means, and is surprised by how much he means it.

Theo allows the silence to hold for three seconds. Then he speaks, and when he does, his voice carries a slight roughness that was not there a moment ago.

"My father left when I was five," Theo says. "I don't even remember what he looked like. Just the sound of the front door closing." He pauses. Looks down at his hands, then back up at Ace. His eyes are damp. "You've been more of a father to me in the last year than he was in my entire life. I hope you know that."

Ace reaches across the desk and grips Theo's forearm. The grip is firm and it lingers. Two men in a trailer, holding onto something that feels, from the outside, like the most honest moment they've shared.

Theo's tears are real. His father did leave when he was five. He does not remember his face. The front door did close. Everything he said is true. He just chooses particular moments when he allows himself to feel it.

"Now," Theo says, clearing his throat with the practiced ease of a man returning to business after a moment of vulnerability, "let's talk about Fort Wayne. I want to make sure we've got the rigging exactly right."

Ace nods, releasing Theo's arm. He picks up the harness again, lighter this time, with the possessive tenderness of a man holding something he intends to keep.

"You know," Ace says, turning the harness over in his hands, "the only time I didn't wear the harness—you remember, maybe two months ago—I slipped about three-quarters of the way across. Fell to the net. Twisted my ankle."

"I remember."

"The net caught me fine. New net, strong as hell. But the fall." Ace shakes his head. "Thirty-five feet. Your stomach leaves your body before you do. I decided right then—harness every time. No exceptions."

"That's exactly right," Theo says. "And now you've got one nobody will even see."

Ace smiles. It is the private, satisfied smile of a man who has solved a problem he didn't know how to articulate. The harness was the problem, not the danger. Ace has never been truly afraid of falling, because Ace has never truly believed he will fall. The problem was the aesthetics. The indignity of visible safety. And Theo has removed that obstacle with a white box and a fabric swatch and a phone call to Montreal.

Ace tucks the harness under his arm, picks up the red coat from the armrest, and stands.

“La Crosse,” he says.

“La Crosse,” Theo says.

Theo sits at his desk. He looks at the empty white box, the tissue paper, the indentation where the harness had been folded. He picks up the box, folds it flat, and drops it in the wastebasket.

Then he opens his laptop and begins drafting the press release for La Crosse.

Ace walks out of the trailer with the harness under one arm and the coat over the other. His footsteps on the metal stairs have a sound that Theo has come to recognize—heavier than when he arrived, and more sure.

* * * * *

Early July, Peoria, Illinois.

Theo passes Patty’s desk on his way into Ace’s trailer and stops.

There is a plant on her desk. A pothos, in a small ceramic pot the color of cream. Its leaves are glossy and boast contrasting shades of dark and pale green. They are spilling over the rim in loose tendrils that trail over the edge of her desk, as if testing the distance to the floor.

Hundreds of times Theo has walked past this desk, and there has never been anything on it that did not serve a direct operational purpose. No photographs. No coffee mug with a slogan. No calendar with pictures of sunsets or golden retrievers. Patty’s desk has always been a surface, not a space—the workspace of a woman who does not confuse where she works with who she is.

And now there is a plant.

Patty is gone for the day. But the pothos is there, alive and indifferent to his observation, and Theo looks at it for a moment longer than is warranted before continuing through to Ace’s office.

Ace is behind his desk in his shirtsleeves. The red coat is hanging on the stand in the corner—the same stand it has occupied since the day Theo first walked into this room and cataloged every surface and shadow. Ace's sleeves are rolled to the elbows and he has the look of a man who has been sitting with something for a while and has finally decided to say it.

"Sit down, Teddy. I want to talk to you about something."

Theo sits. He reads the room the way he always reads rooms—the posture, the tone, the objects on the desk. There is a bulky manila envelope near Ace's right hand. It sports a white label that takes up half the front and is addressed to Ace Raymond Donahue. The return address is Duncan, Calhoun, Parks, Weisburg & Associates out of Century City, California. Theo has never heard of this law firm, but he knows no one has lawyers in Century City unless they've got the assets to pay for them.

"The numbers this season," Ace begins. "Best we've ever done. You know that."

"I do. Fourteen percent over last year's gross. And the tightrope act has been—"

"It's not just the numbers." Ace waves a hand. "The numbers are the numbers. It's the whole operation. The way things run now. The way the crew looks when they come in for breakfast. The way the tent feels before a show." He pauses. "That's you, Theo. That's what you've built here."

Theo notes the use of his actual name. Not Teddy. Theo. It's happened three times in sixteen months, and each time it has preceded something significant.

"I've been thinking about what happens after I'm gone," Ace says. He taps the fat manila envelope once. "Not tomorrow. Not next year. But eventually. When I head to that giant Big Top in the sky." He smiles at his own phrase with the satisfied amusement of a man who believes he has coined something clever.

"I had my attorneys update my estate documents last month. My kids are taken care of. They've got the houses, the investment accounts, the whole portfolio. They'll be fine. Better than fine. They'll be wealthy, and they'll never have to think about this circus or the work it took to build it."

He opens the metal tabs on the envelope, removes a set of documents, turns them around to face Theo, and lays them on the desk. Theo does not reach for them.

"When I retire—or when I'm gone, whichever comes first—the circus goes to you."

The trailer is quiet. Outside, someone is running a generator, and its low hum vibrates faintly through the floor. Theo's hands are resting on the arms of the chair. He does not move them.

"Sir."

"It's already done. My attorney filed the amendments last week. Donahue's Traveling Circus—all assets, all contracts, all intellectual property, all equipment—transfers to you upon my retirement or my death. Whichever comes first."

Ace is watching him. Not with the usual hunger for validation, but with something steadier. The expression of a man who has made a decision he is proud of and wants to see its effect on the person it was made for.

"I don't know what to say," Theo says. And for once, this may be true. Not because the words are unavailable but because the distance between what is happening and what he expected to happen today is large enough that even Theo's machinery needs a moment to calibrate.

"You don't have to say anything," Ace says. "You've earned it. Every morning you're the first one on the lot. Every night you're the last one to leave. You built that breakfast thing. You brought Marco back. You got me on the goddamn tightrope." He laughs—the short, percussive laugh of a man delighted by his own trajectory. "My kids couldn't run a lemonade stand, Theo. This place needs someone who gives a damn. That's you."

Theo reaches for the folder. He opens it. Inside are legal documents—dense paragraphs, formal headings with Roman numerals, and notarized signatures. He does not read them. He closes the folder and holds it on his lap.

"Thank you, sir. I'll spend the rest of my career making sure you never regret this."

"I know you will." Ace stands. The meeting is over. When Ace decides something is finished, it is finished, and there is no room for lingering. He retrieves his coat from the stand, shrugs it on, and adjusts the collar. "Now get out of here. I've got a call with the Fort Wayne promoter in ten minutes."

Theo stands. He tucks the folder under his arm. At the door, he turns back.

"I meant what I said, sir. About what you mean to me."

Ace nods once, already reaching for the phone. "I know, Teddy."

Teddy. The name restored in the same breath. The moment of Theo has passed. He is Teddy again—the loyal son, the reliable second, the man whose real name surfaces only when it serves the father's emotional needs and is retracted the moment business resumes.

Theo shuts Ace's office door when he leaves. He barely glances at the pothos on Patty's desk as he walks past and exits the trailer.

In his own trailer, Theo sets the folder on his desk and sits with it for several minutes. He does not open it again. The generator hum is quieter here, replaced by the ambient noise of the lot settling into evening—voices, a truck backing up, someone's radio playing country music at a distance that turns the lyrics into texture.

He picks up his phone and calls Sophia.

She answers on the second ring. "Hey, you." Her voice has the particular warmth of a woman who is in a comfortable room doing something undemanding and is happy to be interrupted by her husband.

"Hey. How was your day?"

"Good. Long. The Hendersons' dog got into their garden again, so Margaret was at the door for twenty minutes explaining, like I could do something about it." She laughs. "How was yours?"

"Good. Really good, actually. I wanted to—"

He stops. The words he intended to say—*Ace wants me to take over the circus when he retires, and he's already changed his will—are* right there, fully formed, waiting. He can feel their gravitas on his tongue.

"You wanted to what?"

"I wanted to ask about the sunroom. Did the painter finish?"

"Yesterday. It looks amazing, hon. He matched the color perfectly. After all those swatches, I was nervous, but he got exactly the shade we wanted."

"I can't even remember what we picked, we looked at so many color swatches."

"I know! I saved the final one though. It's on the fridge. Mountain Sage. Or Mesa Sage. Something sage."

"Be sure to thank the neighbor for the recommendation. He did a great job."

"Already did. I brought Linda a lemon loaf this morning."

"That's nice. That's really nice."

They talk for a few more minutes. Sophia tells him about a farmer's market she found on Saturday and a book she started that she's not sure about yet. Theo asks the right questions. He laughs in the right places. He is present in the conversation in the way a man is present when he is talking to the person he is most comfortable with in the world—not performing, not strategizing, just existing inside the ordinary rhythm of a marriage that works.

When they hang up, he says "I love you" and she says it back and the phone screen goes dark.

Theo sits in the silence of his trailer. The folder is on the desk. The phone is in his hand. The evening is settling around him like water.

He reaches for a scrap of paper. It is the back of a supply requisition form—Brenda's neat handwriting on one side, the other side blank. He picks up a pen.

Dear Pip,

We are getting big bellies from all the clover. The pasture has lots of room to run and there is a nice lady who brings us carrots every morning.

He pauses. Looks at what he has written. The handwriting is not his usual precise, controlled script. It is looser. Rounder. As though the hand holding the pen belongs to someone younger, or someone trying to write the way a donkey might if a donkey could hold a pen.

Sending you all our love, Ravioli and Ziti

He reads it once. The supply requisition form sits on his desk with Brenda's inventory requests on one side and a letter from two dead donkeys on the other.

He picks it up. Holds it for a moment.

Tears it in half. Then in half again. Drops the pieces in the wastebasket, on top of the folded white box from the harness that he threw away the other day.

He sits back in his chair. Looks at the wastebasket.

Gets up. Goes back to work.

*****

Mid July, La Crosse, Wisconsin.

The press release went out ten days ago. *Donahue's Traveling Circus—One Night Only Special Event—Ringmaster Ace Donahue Makes His Tightrope Debut.* Theo wrote it himself. Three tight paragraphs, the right balance of biographical context and forward momentum. The La Crosse Tribune ran a preview piece on Wednesday.

The tent is nearly at capacity when the show begins, and the crowd is a mix of people who bought their tickets without knowing Ace would be performing, and people who bought their tickets because they wanted to see the host of that old game show walk the tightwire.

During Ace's opening intro for the show, he mentions that tonight he will debut an act he's been working on for months. Behind the scenes, he and Theo have discussed how best to incorporate his tightrope act, and both men agree. Ace will take over the finale from the Lipizzans tonight. If it goes well, then Ace will close the show through the remainder of the season.

Theo is relieved Ace kept the mention of his act brief, then quickly pivots to introducing the Tumbling Tropiques with impeccable timing. He works the crowd between acts with the ease of someone who has spent fifty years in rooms like this and knows every frequency. When he introduces the clowns he crouches down to talk to a small boy in the front row who has been watching everything with enormous eyes, and the exchange is warm and unrehearsed and the boy's mother looks like she might cry.

Even Pip, tumbling out of ring three with her too-big clown costume and neon orange wig, gets a special introduction.

"Ladies and gentlemen, our youngest performer—and possibly our bravest—Miss Piper Hodges, better known as Pip!"

On hearing this Pip stops dead in the center of ring three, hands on her hips, utterly delighted, and takes a bow so elaborate it nearly topples her forward. The audience loves it. Ace loves it. For ten seconds the tent belongs to a nine-year-old girl in vibrant face paint and a spongy red nose, and no one minds at all.

The aerialists perform a four-person act—Svetlana, Diego, and two of the younger flyers. Jasmine appears in three numbers tonight; she is fluid and precise, already moving with the confidence of someone who has found her footing. Marco watches from the wings with his arms crossed and something that is almost but not quite a smile.

In the second-to-last act, Katrina and Shelby work the beautiful Lipizzan mares through their paces. Both women wear silver-and-gold sequined leotards with gold shoes, and display the practiced elegance of women who have made their peace sharing the spotlight with thousand-pound divas. When the snowy-white horses take their final bow—a genuine bow, front legs folding, heads dropping—the crowd applauds with the warmth reserved for something they didn't expect to find this moving.

Ace steps back into the center ring as the Lipizzans exit.

"Ladies and gentlemen," he says. His voice carries in the register of a man who is about to say something that matters. The tent settles. "In just a few moments, we are going to attempt something that has never been done in this tent." He pauses. Lets it sit. "Actually… this is something that's never been done by *any* ringmaster, in the entire history of the American circus." Another pause. The silence is doing exactly what silence does when a man who knows how to use it lets it work.

He projects his voice even more now, enough that the crowd is hanging on his every word when he says, "So, don't try to sneak out early." He gestures toward the audience and sweeps his arm from one end of the bleachers to the other before he adds, "Because I *will* see you. And I *will* be offended." His grin is easy and—for this moment—completely unguarded.

The audience laughs. Warm, genuine, the laugh of thirty-eight hundred people who just decided they love this man.

Ace takes his bow and exits. The lights dim to a working glow. The tightrope rig descends into position—forty feet of braided steel cable between two platforms, catching the light. The rigging crew moves with quiet efficiency. The audience watches.

Then a single spotlight finds the center ring. And Theo walks into it.

He is wearing a red blazer. Not the Ringmaster's coat—that belongs to one man and everyone in this tent knows it. Just a red blazer, open at the collar, the operations manager doing his job in the best clothes he owns for the occasion. He holds a small wireless microphone. He looks, if anything, slightly uncomfortable with the spotlight, which is entirely intentional and entirely effective.

"Good evening," he says. His voice is warm and measured, the voice of a man who is not a performer and knows it and is fine with that. "My name is Theo Crane. I'm the Operations Manager for Donahue's Traveling Circus, which means I handle the parts of this operation that happen when the spotlight is off." A small laugh from the audience. "Scheduling. Logistics. Making sure the elephants—well, we don't have elephants, but if we did—making sure they show up on time."

More laughter. Theo nods once, acknowledging it without milking it.

"I stand before you tonight to introduce a man who, approximately four months ago, walked into my office and told me he wanted to learn to walk a tightrope." He pauses. "I want to be honest with you. My first thought was: this is going to be a problem." Laughter. "My second thought was: this man has surprised me before." He lets that land.

A spotlight finds the far platform in ring one. Ace is already there, in his Ringmaster coat and top hat, silver hair catching the light. Shelby is standing beside him in her metallic sequins, holding the master safety clip in her hands, ready.

Ace's voice booms across the tent without a microphone, carrying the way it always carries. He feigns exasperation when he bellows, "I'm right here, Teddy, I can hear you."

The tent erupts. Not polite laughter—the real thing, loud and surprised and delighted, the laughter of nearly four thousand people who just watched the most dignified man in the room get caught talking about someone standing ten feet away.

Theo laughs. It is a real laugh and catches him slightly off guard. He holds up a hand in surrender.

"I can't get anything past this man," he says into the microphone. More laughter. He takes a small bow—modest, self-deprecating, exactly right. Then he straightens and his voice settles back into something quieter and more serious. The laughter fades with it.

"Suffice it to say, ladies and gentlemen, this man is full of surprises. Because what has happened over the last four months was, frankly, one of the most remarkable things I have witnessed in my professional life. The speed at which he learned. The discipline." He shakes his head slightly, as though still mildly astonished.

Ace clears his throat loudly and the audience cracks up again.

"And so… without further ado…." Theo extends his arm toward the platform where Ace stands and Shelby moves into position beside him. He turns his back to her and she attaches the industrial clip to the equally strong loop embedded deep within the harness material. "It is my genuine honor to present to you the owner, the visionary, the Ringmaster of Donahue's Traveling Circus—" (he pauses one final beat) "—Mr. Ace Donahue. On the tightrope."

Theo exits the spotlight. It extinguishes behind him. The tent falls dark except for the platform spot.

Shelby smooths Ace's coat over the attachment point of the harness. Except for the cable that extends above him, the safety mechanism is invisible on Ace's person. Shelby then extends the balancing pole to Ace. He takes it in both hands. She steps away so she is no longer in the spotlight.

The music begins. It is low and cinematic, something that makes the tent feel larger than it is. It builds for sixteen bars and then, as Ace steps to the edge of the platform and looks out, it fades to nothing.

Silence.

The wire catches the light.

Ace steps onto it.

His first steps are what they are—careful, deliberate, real. Not graceful in the way Svetlana is graceful, not precise in the way Diego is precise. But sure. The sureness of a man who has fallen from this wire and gotten back up and kept going because he decided, at some point in the last four months, that this was worth doing. The balancing pole tilts slightly left. Corrects. His chin comes up.

He keeps walking.

At the one-quarter mark something shifts in the tent. It starts in the lower rows, barely audible, more felt than heard—a rhythm emerging from the silence the way rhythms sometimes emerge from crowds without anyone deciding to start them.

Donahue. Donahue.

Soft at first. Tentative. As though the people saying it aren't sure it will catch. But it catches. Row by row, section by section, the way fire moves through dry grass when the conditions are right.

Donahue. Donahue.

Ace is at the midpoint now. He does not look down. He looks straight ahead at the far platform, at Shelby waiting there in her sequins, at the fixed point Marco told him to always seek. But something in his posture changes—a fractional straightening, an almost imperceptible lift of the chin—and Theo, watching from the wings, understands that Ace can hear it. Hearing his name is landing on his nervous system the way applause always lands, like a hit of something chemical, but cleaner. More earned.

Donahue. Donahue.

The chant grows. The tent is fully inside it now, thousands of people in rhythm, the sound rising and tightening as Ace moves through the final third of the wire. His steps do not change. His grip on the pole does not change. But the air in the tent has changed—charged with something that is not quite circus magic, because circus magic is manufactured and this is not. This is real and everyone in the building can feel the difference.

He is ten feet from the platform.

Five.

His foot touches the platform and the Big Top detonates.

Not applause—something bigger than applause. The sound of thousands of people jumping to their feet simultaneously and cheering as though they had all been holding their breath and now they can exhale and scream their relief.

Katrina is beside him, beaming. She accepts the pole from Ace and ducks out of the light. Ace glances behind himself, as if to remind himself of what he just accomplished, then turns to face the crowd again.

He opens his arms. The red coat. The silver hair. The spotlight. And the sound washing over him from thirty-eight hundred people who came to a circus on a Friday night in La Crosse, Wisconsin, and got something they were not expecting and will not forget.

Below, in the wings, Marco unfolds his arms.

He does not clap. He stands with his arms at his sides and watches Ace take his bow on the platform with the expression he wore at the breakfast table in Lexington—the expression of a man who has done the same math and is watching the equation complete itself. Whatever is behind the thin door, it stays there. But the door is thinner tonight than it has been since Amarillo.

Theo does not move from the wings. The sound is rolling over him and he observes the standing ovation the way he observes everything—with the precise, cataloging attention of a man who needs to know exactly what has happened here tonight.

What has happened here tonight is that Ace Donahue walked forty feet of tightrope in La Crosse, Wisconsin, and thirty-eight hundred people chanted his name, and the look on his face when he heard it was the look of a man who has finally, irrevocably, been given the thing he has wanted his entire life.

Pleased with how well this went, Theo smiles and applauds from the wings.

* * * * *

Mid July, Minneapolis, Minnesota.

Three sold-out shows down. Two more tomorrow.

Theo enters the office at ten-fifty. Ace is already out of the Ringmaster's coat and has put away the harness. He pours a scotch over ice and offers it to Theo, who politely declines. Ace pushes the sleeves of his dress shirt up and sits in his wingback chair with the looseness of a man who is quite pleased with himself. He takes a sip of the scotch. Grimaces, then chuckles.

"Helluva show, eh, Teddy?"

"Very strong," Theo agrees. "On every count."

"Twenty-two thousand five hundred people this weekend."

"Five shows at full capacity, yes."

"Twenty-two thousand, five hundred people in this city…" Ace swirls his glass before finishing his sentence, "cannot be wrong."

The debrief is brief tonight because there is very little to debrief. The show was clean. The aerialists were extraordinary. The Lipizzans were flawless. Jasmine drew an audible gasp in ring one during the second number that Theo suspects people in the Twin Cities are still talking about. Charlie's lions were magnificent. Even the clowns pulled off a couple of epic skits that the audience loved.

Ace is quiet for a moment. With Ace, quiet usually means something is forming.

"The wire," he says.

"Yes."

"The far ends." He pauses. "The people sitting at the far ends of the bleachers—they're seeing me sideways. They paid the same ticket price as everyone else."

Theo understands exactly what he is saying. "The expression is lost."

"The expression. The hands. The—" Ace makes a gesture that encompasses everything a forty-foot wire at altitude communicates to the man walking it. "They should see my face."

"Big screens," Theo says.

Ace points at him. "Two of them. One each side of center ring. Suspended. And large enough that the kids in the farthest end bleacher seats can see exactly what I look like when I step onto that wire."

Theo is already doing the math. Rental in each market. Camera operators—three minimum, Danny on the switcher. The logistics are manageable. The cost is justified.

"I'll have something for you by Denver," he says.

Ace raises his glass. "Denver," he agrees.

Theo makes a note. Closes his notebook. Outside, the summer night is warm and filled with the faint trill of crickets.

Denver. He has his work cut out for him.

*****

Late August, Mankato, Minnesota.

Theo stares at a stack of folders resting on his dining table. He's been reviewing performer contracts from last fall, knowing Ace wants changes incorporated for next season. All of September will be a bonanza of reviews. Last year he only handled the performers' reviews and contracts; this year Ace wants him to take on the crew and admin reviews as well.

Morning sunlight is spilling through a transom window in his kitchen. Specks of dust are suspended in the beam of light crossing his field of vision and he is momentarily distracted by the phenomenon. He lifts his hand into the stream of dusty sunlight, and when he wiggles his fingers he casts a shadow on the wall.

When his phone buzzes, his fingers stop abruptly and he glances at the screen. A text from Ace. Never a good sign. Ace only appears in doorways or issues a summons through Patty. A text from Ace means something has unsettled him enough that he couldn't wait for a more dignified form of communication.

Come to the office.

He sighs before responding: *Be right there*.

Scoops up the pile of folders, slips them into a filing cabinet. Locks his trailer on the way out.

Stifling heat this early in the day means tonight's show will be sticky. Theo makes a mental note to have the crew set up the extra large fans in the Big Top.

He finds Ace in his office, behind the hidden door. He has a laptop open on his desk, reading glasses on. He turns the screen toward Theo without preamble.

It is a comment on the Minneapolis Star Tribune's online coverage of the shows. The article itself is glowing—four paragraphs, a photograph of Ace mid-wire, the kind of regional press coverage that generates ticket inquiries. But below the article, in the comments section, someone going by the handle YaketyYak495 has written: *Ringmaster walks a tightrope while wearing a safety harness. Big whoop. Anyone could do that LOL.*

Theo reads it twice. Then he looks at Ace over the top of the screen.

Ace has removed his reading glasses and is pinching the bridge of his nose with two fingers. "Who is this person."

"I don't know."

"Find out."

"I can't find out."

Ace opens his eyes. "What do you mean you can't find out."

"YaketyYak495 is not a real name. It's an anonymous handle. This person could be anyone. Anywhere." Theo pauses. "In all likelihood, sir, this is what's called a troll."

Ace stares at him. "A what?"

"A troll. Someone who posts inflammatory or provocative comments online specifically to generate a reaction. They are not a professional critic or a disgruntled audience member. They almost certainly didn't attend the show. Whoever it is, they saw this article about you and decided to be unpleasant. Because they can. With no consequences."

Ace is quiet for a moment, processing this.

"So... this person," he says slowly, "has never seen me perform."

"I'm sure not."

"Has never seen me on the wire."

"Correct."

"And yet felt entitled to suggest my skill is unimpressive. Unworthy."

Theo chooses his words carefully. "They felt entitled to be unpleasant in a forum where unpleasantness costs them nothing. It is not a reflection of your performance, your ability, or your reception in Minneapolis. It is a reflection of the internet."

Ace picks up the unopened bottle of water on his desk. Sets it back down. "How many people saw this."

"Fewer than saw the article. Comment sections are read by a fraction of the people who read the piece itself. And—" Theo turns the laptop back toward himself and scrolls, "—this comment has two likes. Whereas this one—" he turns the screen back, "—has forty-seven."

He reads aloud.

Just got back from Saturday night's show. When the crowd started chanting his name I actually got chills. My son is ten years old and he hasn't stopped talking about it. We'll be back next year.

Ace is listening.

Theo scrolls again.

Say what you want about Donahue's but that man on the wire was something I genuinely did not expect to see. Bought tickets for the Sunday matinee on the spot.

And again.

Forty feet. Seventy years old. I dare any of you keyboard warriors to try it.

Ace is quiet for a long moment. Then he picks up the bottled water again. Cracks open the seal. Sets the cap on his desk and takes a swig.

"Dakota Landry," he says.

"Yes. First Wednesday in September," Theo confirms. "The segment is locked."

Ace nods slowly. The reading glasses go back in their case. The laptop gets closed.

"Delete that comment," he says.

Theo has to stifle a smile. "I can't delete it. It's not our platform."

Ace waves a hand. "Then ignore it."

"That's what I'd recommend, yes."

"I wasn't asking for your recommendation, Teddy."

"I know," Theo says. "Will you be at the breakfast tent at some point this morning, sir?"

"Doubtful." He takes another swig of the water.

"I'm going to head over. Brenda said they will have an omelet station set up today."

Ace makes a noise that sounds like *hmph*, and Theo lets himself out the way he came in.

*****

Mid September, Des Moines, Iowa.

Advance press for the weekend has been good. The Des Moines Register ran a feature on Thursday featuring Ace on the wire in Minneapolis, the crowd on their feet, four column inches and a pull quote. The Friday night and Saturday matinee shows sold well. Saturday night is near capacity.

Theo is in the wings when it happens.

Ace is working the crowd between a clown act and an aerialist act, the easy back-and-forth of a man who has done this ten thousand times. The audience is warm and generous, the kind of crowd that arrived ready to be delighted. Theo is keeping his eye on ring three where Pip and Shorty are clearing props to make way for the next act. Pip is struggling with something heavy that is not collapsing the way it should, and Shorty takes three strides to cross the ring and assist her. Because he is making sure they have things under control, he almost misses the moment Ace's tone shifts.

Almost.

"Ladies and gentlemen, before I bring out our extraordinary aerial company tonight, I want to say a few words." Ace's voice drops into the register he uses for sincerity. The crowd settles. "Earlier this season we lost one of our own. A young woman who had been with this company for over ten years. Helena Danforth." He pauses. The tent is very quiet. "Helena's family has been in the aerial arts for four generations. She knew the risks. She accepted them. And she died doing what she loved."

Theo has gone very still.

"I think about Helena every time I climb that ladder," Ace continues, and his voice is beginning to lift now, finding its performance register… the register that fills a tent. "And I think—if that beautiful, talented young woman had the courage to go up there every night, then by God, so do I." He spreads his arms. "Because nothing worth doing comes without risk, ladies and gentlemen. Nothing. Worth. Doing."

The crowd begins to applaud. They think this is a tribute. They think they have just witnessed something moving.

Ace leans into the microphone.

"Now I want to be honest with you." The conspiratorial warmth, the voice of a man sharing something he probably shouldn't. "When Helena fell, there were people—people within this very organization—who thought we should ground the entire aerial program. Just… shut it down entirely." He shakes his head with the slow gravity of a man who has carried a burden alone. "Let fear win. Let one tragedy define what this company is." He pauses. "I said no. Because Helena Danforth would not have wanted that. She was willing to take risks. And I respected that about her, about all our aerialists of course." His voice is rising now, the audience being carried toward something and not quite knowing how they got there. "Of course I wanted to do everything I could to protect these brave performers—"

Theo steps out of the wings carrying his own microphone.

He does not run. He does not raise his voice. He walks into the light at the edge of ring one with the measured, deliberate pace of a man who has made a decision and is entirely at peace with it. He is still holding his clipboard. To the audience, Theo is certain he looks like a man who has received important information that cannot wait.

Ace sees him. His eyes move through surprise, irritation, and calculation in approximately one second.

When Theo is a few feet from Ace he begins talking. Addresses the crowd with a small apologetic nod, speaking into the mike in his left hand. He keeps his tone lighthearted but contrite. "Ladies and gentlemen, I do beg your pardon—we have a brief rigging matter to attend to before the aerial act. We'll have our aerialists in the air for you in just two minutes." He looks at Ace. His expression is entirely neutral and entirely immovable. "Sir."

The crowd murmurs indulgently. Someone near the front starts a small round of applause. Ace catches it, pivots to them with the practiced ease of fifty years in rooms like this, grins like a man who has never been caught off guard in his life.

"Two minutes," he says into the microphone. "Try not to miss me too much."

Laughter. Warm, genuine. Ace hands the microphone to a nearby crew member and walks into the wings with the unhurried dignity of a man who is choosing, for the moment, to let this happen.

Danny wisely starts a short and jaunty song to fill the void.

The moment they are past the curtain Ace's hand closes around Theo's arm. Not hard. But not gently.

"Ten seconds," Ace says quietly. "You have ten seconds to tell me what you just did and why."

Theo does not look at the hand on his arm.

"The audience was beginning to shift," he says. "But that is the smaller problem." He keeps his voice low and even. "Your aerialists are standing thirty feet from where we are having this conversation. What you consider a moving tribute, they are hearing as brutally insensitive. These are the people who trained and worked with Helena. Loved her. And watched her fall. They have performed in every show since Amarillo." He pauses. "You are traumatizing them all over again, in front of four thousand strangers."

Ace releases his arm. Something moves across his face that is not quite anger and not quite shame; Theo thinks it is perhaps the collision of the two.

"I was honoring that girl," he says.

"I know you were." Theo holds his gaze. "They don't hear it that way."

The silence between them is brief and very full.

"One of the reasons you wanted to walk that wire," Theo says quietly, "was to show them something. That you understand what they do up there. That you respect what it costs." He lets that sit for exactly one beat. "Don't throw that away in a Saturday night speech."

Ace looks at him for a long moment. His jaw is tight. His eyes are doing the calculation they always do, weighing what is true against what is useful against what he is willing to accept.

Then he straightens. The red coat settles across his shoulders. His chin comes up.

"Get me the microphone," he says.

Theo nods once and steps away.

Danny's timing with dialing back the music coincides perfectly with Ace walking back into the light. There is a warm ripple of applause when he raises his right arm high above his head and waves, as if the audience might have forgotten him in the short time he was not in the center ring. His voice is infused with the generous, illuminated warmth of a man who means every word as he names each aerialist. He talks about what they do as though he understands it from the inside, which—Theo reflects, watching from the wings—he now does, in his way.

The audience loves it. The aerialists perform.

In the wings, Theo exhales slowly.

He does not know, standing there, whether he has just protected the aerialists from Ace or protected Ace from himself. Perhaps both. Perhaps neither.

He files the moment and watches Jasmine climb.

After the show, Theo is standing at the edge of the wings. The crowd is filing out and the company is dispersing, and there is just enough noise to make a quiet conversation private. That is when Ace finds him.

"Don't ever pull me out of the center ring during a show again." His voice is low and completely level. "Do you understand me? I don't care what the reason is. You do not pull me out of my ring." He holds Theo's gaze. "Or you won't have a job here anymore."

Theo looks at him.

"Understood," he says.

Ace holds the look for one more beat. Then he turns and walks toward his trailer, the red coat catching the last of the light.

Theo watches him go.

He thinks: *That is the second time he has threatened to fire me.*

He thinks: *He won't.*

He closes his notebook and goes to find the aerialists.

An hour later, the rigging tent is empty; Theo has asked Danny to make sure of this. At half past eleven, the aerialists arrive in ones and twos. Svetlana first, then Diego, then the younger flyers, then Jasmine. Marco enters last and closes the tent flap behind him. He stands with his arms at his sides and says nothing, but Theo can see accusation in his eyes.

He briefly rests his gaze on each of them for a moment. Eight people. The ones who go up.

"You heard what was said tonight," Theo says. It is not a question.

No one speaks.

"I want to be clear about something." He keeps his voice low and even. "What was said about Helena tonight was not said with this company's blessing. And it will not be said again. I will see to that personally." He pauses. "That is the first thing I want you to know."

Svetlana's jaw is tight. Diego is looking at the ground.

"The second thing." He looks at each of them in turn. "There will come a moment... I cannot tell you when… I cannot tell you exactly what it will look like. But when that moment comes, I will need each of you to act quickly and without question. I will ask something of you, and in the moment I ask it, I need you to act without hesitation, and without asking me to explain myself first."

Marco has not moved.

"I am not asking you to do anything tonight or tomorrow. It could be weeks. It could be months. But when I do ask, I need you to be ready to follow through. I am asking for your trust." He looks at Svetlana. "Can you do that?"

A long pause.

"Yes," she says.

He looks at the others. One by one, quietly, they give him the same answer.

Marco gives him nothing. He simply holds Theo's gaze across the rigging tent with the expression of a man who has already answered this question and has been waiting for Theo to catch up.

Theo nods once.

"Get some rest," he says. "Two more shows tomorrow, then we move on to Omaha."

*****

Mid October, Denver, Colorado.

As Theo had arranged, the vendor's truck arrives Tuesday morning with two sixteen-foot-wide screens. Unfortunately, one of the screens arrives with a hairline fracture across the lower left panel. When powered up, the bottom third of that screen makes the image look like a shattered car windshield.

He stands in the parking lot of the National Western Complex, looking at it for a long moment. The driver apologizes with the energy of a man who knows his company has failed a client… and is hoping the client is not the kind of person who makes calls to supervisors.

Theo is not that kind of person.

"Get me your manager," is all he says. "Not to complain. To problem-solve."

By noon the vendor has located a replacement screen—in Salt Lake City. By two o'clock it is clear the replacement will not reach

Denver before Sunday, and Saturday happens to be their last day of the stand.

At three o'clock Theo accepts the comp on the functioning screen, thanks the vendor's manager with genuine courtesy, and is standing outside Ace's trailer working out exactly how to frame the conversation he's about to have.

Ace takes the news with the controlled displeasure of a man who has learned, over half a dozen decades, that certain frustrations are beneath open expression.

"One screen," he says.

"One screen. Fully functional, positioned stage left of center ring." Theo pauses. "I want to be honest with you about my reservations."

"When are you not."

"One screen creates an asymmetry. The stage right bleachers will have the full experience you envisioned. The stage left bleachers will have what they've always had. The imbalance will be visible and it will be felt." He keeps his voice even. "Two screens or no screens are both cleaner than one."

Ace looks at him over his reading glasses for a long moment.

"Put up the one screen."

"Yes, sir."

"And find me two screens for Santa Fe that arrive in one piece."

"Already working on it."

He does not mention that Charlie's lions have been grounded since Fort Collins. Ace already knows. The whole company knows. It is a bruise that does not need pressing.

The Denver shows are good. Not Minneapolis good, and not La Crosse good—Charlie's absence for these shows in Colorado leaves a gap in the program that Theo has partially filled by extending the clown segment, which Pip has treated as a personal opportunity, and

Brandon has treated as a professional obligation. Audiences are receiving them warmly without knowing what they are missing.

Ace's tightrope act yields its breath-holding silence and its standing ovation and its aftermath of people in the concession line telling each other what they had just seen. The stage right bleachers have been electric at each show; the stage left bleachers, warm.

Ace feels the difference. Has felt it at every show.

After the final performance Theo heads to Ace's trailer and finds him in his dimly lit office, laptop open, footage from the single camera playing on the screen. The scotch is poured and this time he has not set it down. He watches himself step onto the wire, the balancing pole leveling, the first careful steps. He stops the footage. Rewinds. Watches it again.

Theo sits. He waits.

"You were right," Ace says.

Theo says nothing in spite of the rarity of this occasion.

"About Denver. One screen." He shakes his head, then closes the laptop without looking up. "You were right. It was worse than none."

"I appreciate you saying so."

"I'm not saying it for your benefit."

Theo has no response to this. He simply waits for Ace to continue.

Finally he picks up the scotch, ice tinkling against the glass as he takes a gulp. "Santa Fe."

"Two screens," Theo says. "I have a vendor in Albuquerque who comes highly recommended. Both screens arrive on Wednesday, two days before opening night. I'll inspect them personally when they come off the truck." He opens his notebook. "And, I've already confirmed hardware and staffing for the full setup through the remainder of the season. Santa Fe, Albuquerque, Socorro, Las Cruces, Roswell, and then we go back into Texas."

Ace nods slowly, listening.

"For Colorado Springs and Pueblo I'd recommend we run without screens. The logistics are tighter in those markets and..." Theo pauses briefly before adding, "we will also have the *Rise and Shine* segment while we're in Colorado Springs. We don't want to be juggling too much at once." He allows himself the smallest latitude. "After all, we're not clowns."

Ace looks at him with an expression that is completely flat.

Theo moves on without acknowledging it.

"The segment in Colorado Springs gives us something better than screens in that market anyway. Dakota Landry. Her audience is national. If we do this right—"

"How do we do it right," Ace cuts him off. The flatness has shifted. He is listening now in the particular way he listens when something interests him against his will.

"We don't put you in a chair. Instead of being stuck in one spot…." Theo leans forward slightly. Allows excitement to creep into his voice. "We put you in your world. The camera crew gets footage of our setup… they could move through the wings, get footage in the last looks tent where the clowns are touching up wigs and makeup… maybe even a quick zoom on Razzle and Dazzle—"

"The audience loves Razzle and Dazzle."

"Everyone loves Razzle and Dazzle," Theo agrees, and becomes more animated as he describes what he's envisioning. "Then, Danny waves at the camera from the sound board. The riggers are checking lines overhead. And then? Then, the camera finds *you*. In the middle of all of it. The man who owns it, manages it, emcees it, and…" Theo holds his pause for exactly the right length before adding, "has his own tightrope act in it." He sits back. "The circus is you. You are the machine that makes this circus work. *That's* the segment."

Ace is quiet for a long moment. He swirls the scotch. Sets it down.

Theo can tell this idea is about to come in for a beautiful landing.

"If I go to New York," Ace says slowly, measuring his words, "it would just be a chair."

"Yes."

"Colorado Springs… it would be the whole tent."

"Yes."

Ace picks up the scotch again. Something in his posture has shifted—the disappointment of the one-screen stand giving way to something more like the man who sold out five nights in Minneapolis without breaking a sweat. He is, Theo knows, already composing the segment in his head. Already deciding which version of himself Dakota Landry's audience is going to meet.

"Colorado Springs," Ace says. As though it was his idea. "Remote. The full production."

"I'll arrange it."

The silence that follows is comfortable in the way their silences sometimes are—two men who have spent two years in close proximity and have arrived at a functional fluency that neither of them would describe as friendship.

Ace looks at the closed laptop. Then out the small window of the trailer at the dark lot beyond.

"La Crosse," he says.

Theo waits.

"It's too bad we can't bottle up the spontaneity of the crowd chanting like that during my act." He shakes his head slowly, something almost wistful moving across his face. "But I get it. Sometimes all the conditions fall into just the right place, at just the right moment." A pause. "Never to be repeated."

Theo looks at him for a moment.

"Yes, Ace." His voice is quiet and even. "I completely agree. It was magical, and unlikely to ever happen in that perfect way again."

Ace nods once. Raises his glass slightly, as though toasting something.

Theo closes his notebook.

Outside, the National Western Complex lot is dark and quiet, the crew long finished with load-out, the tent already coming down.

Theo runs through the next couple of months in his mind: *Two more stands in Colorado sans lions, then we push into New Mexico, and then—finally—we return to finish out the season in Texas.*

*****

Late October, Pueblo, Colorado.

The Colorado State Fairgrounds sit on the west side of Pueblo. The land is exceptionally flat, as though it has been used hard for generations and makes no apologies for it.

The stand runs clean—four shows, solid crowds.

Bruno and Hazel are still not allowed to perform, same as the other stands in Colorado, and Charlie has stopped mentioning it. New Mexico will come soon enough and then Charlie, Destiny, and the lions will be back to work.

For this last show in Colorado, Ace's act is the finale, as it has been since they added it in La Crosse. Theo always introduces him, and tonight is no different. As soon as Theo announces the last act, the audience cheers and then the spotlight moves off Theo and onto the starting platform.

With the quiet efficiency of ritual, Shelby attaches the safety cable to the harness. Then, she smooths down the red panel on his Ringmaster coat, and finally she offers and he accepts the balancing pole. He always pauses dramatically before he steps tentatively onto the wire.

And like every show since they've added Ace's finale, he receives a standing ovation that continues after the lights come up… while Ace descends the ladder… while all of the other performers return to the rings to take their bows.

After this final Colorado show, Theo walks the back lot alone as he always does after the last performance of a stand. Checking. Cataloging.

The night is crisp but not cold. The air surrounding him smells of dust and something dry and mineral that is specific to this part of Colorado. Between the Big Top and the distant mountains on the western horizon, the desert is wide open.

He stops at the equipment bay and checks his clipboard against the load-out list. Everything is where it should be. The trucks are staged correctly. The crew is moving with the quiet competence of a team that's been working together all season.

He makes a note. Shuts the clipboard.

* * * * *

Early November, Santa Fe, New Mexico.

The Sangre de Cristo Mountains are invisible in the dark but their presence is felt. There is a unique quality to the air at this high desert altitude. It is thin and cold and carrying the smell of piñon from somewhere beyond the lot. November in Santa Fe offers fickle weather, and today the crew has been working in jackets all day.

It is a sold-out show. It has been a sold-out show since the press release went out three weeks ago—*Donahue's Traveling Circus, Santa Fe's Finest Outdoor Venue, One Night Only*—and the advance press has been the best of the season. Two features in the Santa Fe New Mexican. A segment on the Albuquerque affiliate that ran statewide. There are photographers with press credentials in the audience tonight, seated in the reserved section along the stage-left bleachers. Theo arranged it.

Both screens arrived yesterday from the Albuquerque vendor. Theo inspected them personally when they came off the truck, the way he said he would. They are working perfectly.

It is Saturday, the morning of their single show in Santa Fe. Theo has been up since before sunrise, running through the show tonight and the rest of their New Mexico run. After walking the lot in the brisk air and warm sunlight, Theo texts Ace to ask if he may stop by his trailer for a few minutes. Ace's reply is brief: "Yes, now is good."

Being Saturday, Patty's office is unoccupied and the only light in the room is filtering through the paper covering the window. Theo notices her pothos looks robust; its variegated leaves are now touching the floor.

He raps lightly on the hidden door and realizes it is already cracked open.

"Come in."

"Good morning, Ace." For a change, there is not a fog of cigar smoke in the room, for which Theo is thankful. "Several performers have commented on the thin air. I know it's the altitude. They're fine, but I wanted to ask if it's bothering you at all."

Ace glances up from his laptop and looks at Theo with an expression he can't quite read. *Not annoyed. Not confused. Perhaps something in between.* Ace drums his fingertips lightly on his desk before answering, "I'm fine."

Theo can tell something is off; he'd noticed it the day after they'd arrived in Santa Fe. This is the real reason he wants to stop by in person… body language and tone of voice can't be discerned in a text.

"Good," Theo offers. "I've been testing the big screens this morning. I think they are positioned at optimal angles for the audience members in those outermost seats."

"Hmm," is Ace's only response. He's returned his attention to his laptop, and Theo is fairly sure he knows what Ace is watching on the screen.

"Denver?" Theo asks, his voice low and gentle.

Ace shoots him a look that lasts only a fraction of a second, which confirms Theo's suspicion.

Theo gestures at the chair and asks, "May I?"

Without taking his eyes off the screen Ace turns his neck left, then right, a crack resulting from each move. "Yes."

He wheels the chair over to the side of Ace's desk so he can see the screen himself. *Sure enough.*

Ace clicks the pause button, freezing the video at a point where the vertical cable coming from his back is visible. Very visible. The angle the camera operator used, the spotlight trained on him, his face steeled in concentration… Theo knows what has been bothering him.

Ace sighs, then leans back in his chair. Almost to himself he says, "There's just no avoiding it. Unless…"

"Unless you don't attach to the safety cable," Theo finishes his sentence.

Ace frowns. "Right. Which isn't an option. I know."

Theo looks at him steadily. "Audiences love your performance," Theo continues, his voice even. "They understand why you use the harness. It's absolutely necessary."

Silence.

"I've watched you walk that wire dozens of times," Theo continues. "More than a hundred, probably. It's been weeks without a single wobble that wasn't part of the act." He pauses. "Personally? I know you could do it. But it's completely understandable if you're not ready."

Ace gives him a wry look. The look of a man who has just been told something that sounds like a compliment and feels like a dare.

Ace is still staring at the paused footage. The cable… bright as a silver beam.

"I know I can do it," Ace says. There is a soft defiance in his tone.

Theo studies him for a long moment. Then, quietly: "I know you can too, Ace. Maybe… maybe tonight is the night you take the training wheels off. Show everyone you're every bit as talented as the other aerialists."

Ace clicks the play button again but remains quiet.

"If you do decide that you're ready… tonight… here's what we do." Ace turns his attention to Theo now, his expression cautious yet curious.

"When you get to the platform and Shelby moves to take the harness clip out, you turn to her. Tell her you don't want the cable. She will probably be surprised, but she's not going to argue." Theo knows this is true. There is no way she would second guess Ace refusing to be clipped in. "I'll be watching, and if I see that happen… I tell the audience that it looks like you're going to walk the tightrope without the harness. There may be gasps, or applause. I'll ask you if that is correct, and you can give a thumbs up. Or just use that Ringmaster voice of yours to say yes. And I will ask the audience for complete silence, so you can put your full concentration on the wire."

There is a gleam in Ace's eyes. He is envisioning it, savoring it.

"But again, sir," Theo counsels. "No one will ever know anything different if you follow the normal routine. Let Shelby clip the cable to the harness. Smooth your coat. Hand you the balancing bar. You're still a pro, doing something amazing. Magnificent, even."

"Magnificent," he murmurs, and then he starts the video over again.

"Yes. Either way. Magnificent."

Suddenly Ace turns his head toward Theo, as if coming out of a trance. "Yes. I'm thinking… yes. And if I skip the harness… you'll see it, and you'll announce it?"

"Of course."

"Very good." Ace glances at his phone; the time reads eight-fifteen. "I've got a meeting, so unless there's anything else?"

"Uh, no. I just wanted to mention the thin air. Make sure you're doing all right."

"Never been better," Ace says with a firm nod. "If Svetlana is in Patty's waiting area, send her in."

"Will do."

When Theo exits Ace's office he realizes the door is still cracked open, which gives him a moment's pause. He swings the door wide open. "Good morning, Svetlana," he says to the aerialist. "Ace says you can go right in."

She turns to look up at Theo from the chair and he can see a question mark in her eyes. She smiles, tilts her head just a tiny bit to one side and says, "Good morning. And thank you."

How much of that did she hear? he wonders. Svetlana stands up as he passes her on the way out. "What's for breakfast today?" he asks.

Svetlana's is already walking toward Ace's office but she turns to respond. "Brenda and Cassie made breakfast burritos. Along with the usual fare."

"Great," Theo says, keeping his tone light. "Thanks."

He exits the trailer and turns to make sure he latches the door. When he turns back, the crow is sitting atop the stair railing—less than two feet away from him. He stops moving. Stands perfectly still.

"Well, hello there, friend," he says softly.

The crow shifts positions, turning its head more to the side, and that is when Theo sees the white scar on its beak.

"So… it *is* you."

Before he puts thought into it, he lifts his hand and reaches out to touch the bird. Just as his fingertips are about to brush its wing, the bird takes flight. Theo watches it fly down the road a ways and land on top of the cab of one of their semis.

He shakes his head and chuckles to himself. Smooths his tie. When he starts down the stairs to head for the breakfast tent, he thinks, *You might be losing your marbles, Theo... you're talking to a bird.*

*****

The show is extraordinary from the first act. The Tumbling Tropiques open with a new sequence that brings two volunteers down from the crowd to allow the athletes to leap over their heads with the help of springboards and coordinated hands and momentum. The audience shrieks with delight several times and they earn a standing ovation before the last song is even finished.

The clowns are electric—Pip hits every mark and lands her bicycle bit to the biggest laugh of the season, and Brandon sweeps her up afterward with the ease of a man who has watched his daughter become something remarkable.

Charlie's lions are back, rested and majestic. Bruno and Hazel each take a turn leaping through the flaming hoop. Near the end of their act, Destiny gives a subtle signal and Bruno lets out a ferocious roar. The audience goes wild, thinking they've just witnessed a spontaneous roar from the king of the jungle. Theo and Ace and all the other performers know it only takes a slight flick of the whip against one of the blue pedestals to cue Bruno's declaration. Charlie smiles proudly in spite of himself.

The Lipizzans are flawless. Katrina and Shelby move through their paces with the unhurried elegance of women who have fully inhabited their act, and the horses—white as the moon and twice as imperious—take their final bow to a sound that fills the tent and spills out into the cold New Mexico night.

Ace steps back into the center ring.

The tent settles. Even the photographers lower their cameras.

Theo is in the wings. He has been in the wings for every performance of this act since La Crosse. He knows the shape of what comes next the way he knows the shape of everything he and Ace have built over the past two years.

Tonight, however, the shape will be different.

Ace tells the audience there's a special finale coming up next, and that his associate, Mr. Theodore Crane, will take over the mike for the next few minutes. Most of the audience knows what's coming, so there are hoots and cheers as Theo makes his entrance and accepts the microphone from Ace.

"Thank you, Mr. Donahue, and break a leg," Theo offers, his tone hearty and generous, as always.

Ace disappears out of the spotlight for the moment and Theo takes over. Begins with his usual introduction.

"Good evening, ladies and gentlemen. I'm going to take this moment to tell you a little more about a man who has many talents, Mr. Ace Donahue. Tonight you will bear witness to something never done before in Santa Fe. Mr. Donahue, owner of this marvelous business… Ringmaster of this magnificent show… is going to perform his own special act. Trained by one of the finest tightrope walkers in the world—and our very own aerialist, Mr. Marco Mura."

There is a round of applause for Marco, though he is not within sight. He and the other aerialists are in the wings near ring one.

Another spotlight starts circling around the tent which is Theo's cue to lay it on thick for Ace.

"Without further ado, please turn your attention to the ladder in ring one…." The spotlight instantly directs its beam on Ace and follows him as he ascends. "Where Mr. Ace Donahue, a man who has proven to be a natural on a one-inch-wide cable that is forty feet high… a man who impressed everyone in our company when he said he wanted his own act, a man who has put his heart and soul into everything he has ever built, including this performance…." Theo pauses. He is acutely aware the spotlight is still on him, though it will dim when Ace steps onto the wire.

The Ringmaster arrives on the platform where Shelby is already waiting for him, clip in hand, ready to connect him to the safety cable.

"Mr. Donahue will be assisted tonight by Shelby who will make sure he has the necessary tools to ensure you enjoy the flawless performance you've come to see."

She smiles and waves broadly to the full spectrum of the bleachers. Ace waves also, and Theo sees him glance toward both of the big screens below and to his left. He is unable to see himself on them, but he knows from the murmurs and gasps of the audience they are working and he is on full display.

The camera operators are following their cues perfectly, zooming in occasionally, then zooming back out so the crowd can see everything from the confidence in Ace's expression, to his custom black leather slippers with black suede soles.

Shelby reaches for the back of Ace's jacket and he leans away, turns to her, and says something no one can hear except for the two of them. Theo sees the surprise on Shelby's face.

He looks up at Ace. Then at Shelby. Then back at Ace.

"Ladies and gentlemen," Theo says, and something has shifted in his voice. The warmth is still there but underneath it is something that sounds like concern. "I… forgive me, I need a moment."

He looks directly up at Ace on the platform. When he speaks again his voice carries the full tent.

"Mr. Donahue. Are you… are you refusing to use the safety harness tonight, sir?"

Ace spreads both arms wide. Two thumbs up. The grin of a man who has made up his mind and is enjoying every second of it.

A wave of sound moves through the audience—gasps, murmurs, a few startled laughs.

"Mr. Donahue." Theo's voice is measured but the concern in it is unmistakable. "I want to ask you—respectfully, sir—to reconsider. The harness is there for a reason. Shelby has it right there."

Ace waves his hand. The dismissive, magnanimous wave of a king declining a suggestion from a well-meaning subject. He is already reaching for the balancing pole.

“Sir.” Theo’s voice drops slightly, the way it does when something is important. “For your own safety. Please.”

Ace takes the balancing pole from Shelby. Turns it horizontal. Grins at the audience. Forty-five hundred people are completely, utterly his.

Theo looks at him for a long moment.

Then he turns back to the audience. His wears the expression of a man who has done what he can and must now accept what he cannot change.

“Ladies and gentlemen,” he says quietly. “It appears Mr. Donahue has made his decision.” A beat. “What I ask of you—what I *must* ask of you—is absolute silence. Give him everything he needs to get safely to the other side.” His voice drops to almost a whisper. “Please.”

A stillness starts settling inside the Big Top, and as that happens Theo’s gaze moves briefly to the wings near ring one. A figure steps forward into the faint edge of the light. Svetlana. He sees her expression and remembers the question he’d asked himself this morning when he saw her sitting in Patty’s waiting area. He has an answer now.

She heard something.

How much, and what exactly she heard, Theo is uncertain. But he is certain that what she heard was not nothing.

Less than a second later, he sees another figure emerge from the dark behind her. Marco arrives by her side, reaches for her hand, gently closes his fingers around hers, and pulls her back. Slowly, without urgency. The way you close a door that was left open by accident. Theo notices that Marco’s expression, in the brief moment it is visible, is resolved.

A drumroll starts, thanks to Danny’s perfect timing, and Theo returns his attention to the platform. Shelby has placed the cable and clip over a rung of the ladder, and she is now holding the balancing pole out for Ace.

He grasps it firmly in both hands and turns it horizontal. Shelby steps away and begins her descent. The spotlight stays on Ace while he adjusts the pole, turning and positioning both hands to get the pole perfectly balanced. It is all a well-choreographed repeat, with the exception of Shelby having to find someplace to set the clip down.

From the center ring, Theo has a view of both of the big screens, although they are at an angle intended for the audience. The spotlight that was on him is now very dim compared to the one shining on the tightwire platform.

Ace perches at the edge, a sight to behold in his Ringmaster coat. Theo glances at the screen between himself and Ace, and the safety cable is conspicuously absent. He hopes Ace will be pleased with the video he is sure to watch after tonight's show.

As has occurred in all of his prior performances of this act, when Ace lifts his right foot to step onto the tightwire the drumroll goes quiet. He tentatively feels the wire with his right foot, finds the ideal placement, and shifts his weight onto his right leg.

If Ace is worried about not being clipped to the safety cable, his expression does not show it. He is staring straight ahead, attention focused on the opposite platform where Katrina stands. He brings his left foot onto the wire now, ahead of the right. The balancing pole is level, Ace's muscle memory has become so finely tuned with doing his act. Murmurs of appreciation ripple through the audience.

Step after step, Ace makes progress. Theo is facing ring one and glancing back and forth between watching Ace forty feet high, and seeing him on screen—either a close-up of his feet, or showing him twelve feet tall. The latter view captures the determination in his eyes as he continues slowly but steadily.

When Ace reaches the halfway point, as always, he looks down. Since Minneapolis he has been executing a performative fake-out to "goose the crowd" as Ace calls it; this involves looking down, acting as if he's spooked by the sight of the sawdust-covered concrete thirty-five or forty feet below him, and performing a near loss of balance. This always produces gasps, and then he always recovers with some minor maneuvering of the pole, and he makes his way to the other platform to tremendous applause.

Theo is watching the big screen when it happens. The camera crew has zoomed in on Ace from his chest up, and when Ace looks down there is the familiar look of fear in his eyes. But tonight, Theo sees that his fear is not performative. He looks toward Ace on the tightrope and sees him leaning differently… not to the right, as he usually does. Not even to the left. Ace is leaning forward. The balancing pole tilts precariously; it does not look like a small movement intended to right his balance.

The pole slips from Ace's hands, and Theo switches back to looking at the big screen. Which is now showing only darkness. Because Ace is no longer in the camera's frame—he is falling, falling—his red Ringmaster's coat billowing out to the sides. There is a collective gasp, followed by the sound of a muffled rip, and then a heavy thud where the Ringmaster lands in the thin layer of sawdust.

And then the screaming starts.

*

Something moves through Theo that he does not stop to examine. He is already moving in long, even strides—not running, because running is panic and panic is contagious. There are numerous sounds, of which he is only vaguely aware because his mind is not processing them.

The two spotters have beat him to Ace, who is flat on his stomach. The two men are kneeling. Their faces tell him everything before he looks down.

He looks down anyway.

The red coat. The sawdust. The frayed section of net under him like something that was not expecting to be ripped apart. Again. A thin trickle of blood at the corner of Ace's mouth. His blue eyes open, fixed, already absent of the thing that made them Ace's eyes.

Theo digs his radio from his pocket. Brings it near his mouth. Presses the key that addresses every employee and performer who also carry the same radio.

“Code Blue. Ring one.”

He is back at the microphone within seconds.

“Ladies and gentlemen.” He has chosen, for now, to maintain the same warm, measured register he has used all season. Calm as a man discussing weather. “Please remain in your seats. Our medical team is on their way to Mr. Donahue right now. I ask for your patience and your cooperation while they assess the situation.”

The screaming has fractured into something more complicated—part horror, part confusion, part the sound of forty-five hundred people trying to decide what they’re supposed to feel. Some are standing. Some are frozen. Some are crying, including a small child who probably does not even know why, except that small children often sense the fear and anxiety of the adults around them.

The house lights come up.

In an instant the tent transforms—the theatrical darkness replaced by full illumination, every face suddenly visible, the magic of the circus collapsing into the ordinary reality of a large tent full of people blinking at the sudden brightness. Both big screens have been shut off.

Theo keeps his eyes on the audience.

Movement in his peripheral vision. Fast, low. Colorful. Coming from the direction of the performers’ entrance.

Dazzle, in full costume.

He steps away from the microphone and intercepts her cleanly, turning his body to block her line of sight to Ace… his hands finding her shoulders, steering her in a single practiced motion so she is facing away from ring one. She is making a sound he has never heard from her before—not words, not quite crying, something animal and desperate—and her hands are pushing against his chest but without real force, the pushing of someone who knows on some level that they are being protected rather than restrained.

"Hey." His voice is low and close. Not the microphone voice. Something quieter. "Hey. Look at me."

She doesn't look at him. Her eyes are trying to find Ace over his shoulder.

"Dazzle." Firmer now. "Look at me."

She looks at him. Her stage makeup is already smeared down her face.

"The medical team is with him. Let them work."

It is not a lie. The EMTs are coming through the performers' entrance at a jog, wheeling a gurney loaded with equipment. They will work. Protocol requires it.

Dazzle makes the sound again. Theo keeps his hands on her shoulders until he feels the pushing stop.

"Someone needs to be with her," he says quietly to Razzle, who has materialized at Dazzle's side. Razzle nods once and takes her gently by the arm.

Theo turns back to the microphone.

*

The EMTs are working on Ace. Theo watches them assess from the edge of the ring, his face arranged into something neutral and professional. He already knows what they are going to find. He watches them find it anyway.

They begin resuscitation efforts. Protocol.

Theo keys his radio again. "Danny—can you put on something quiet. Instrumental."

Soft music fills the tent. Not circus music. Something neutral. Something that gives the audience's nervous systems something to attach to while their minds catch up to what they've witnessed.

He returns to the microphone.

"Ladies and gentlemen, Mr. Donahue is being assessed by our medical team and will be transported to receive care momentarily. I want to thank each of you for your patience and your dignity tonight." A pause. "In a few moments our staff will begin guiding you toward the exits. Please take your time. There is no rush. And if I may ask—out of respect for Mr. Donahue and for everyone present tonight—please refrain from recording or sharing footage of this event. His family deserves privacy in this moment."

He knows the footage already exists. He knows it's already on dozens of phones and will be on the internet within the hour. He makes the request anyway. Because it is the right thing to do. Because the audience members who comply will feel that they have done something decent. Because the ones who don't will feel, however briefly, that they have been asked to be better than they were.

*

Theo steps back and watches the EMTs work with the practiced efficiency of people who do this for a living. They have Ace secured on the gurney and moving in under four minutes. They aim for the main exit, rolling through sawdust, and the audience parts around them in silence.

Theo watches them go.

His expression does not change.

He is already thinking about the next twelve hours.

*

"Thank you for your patience." Back at the microphone, his voice steady and warm. "Our staff will now guide you to the exits. Please move carefully and look after one another. Thank you for being here tonight. We are grateful for your support."

The audience begins to move.

*

The press are clustered near the stage-left bleachers where Theo had them seated. Two of his staff are already positioned with them—not blocking, not confiscating equipment, just present. Theo crosses to them directly.

"I'll have a statement within the hour," he says to the assembled journalists and photographers. His voice is matter-of-fact. "I ask that you remain on the lot until then. Anyone who leaves before the statement is released will not receive it directly."

A practical incentive rather than a restriction. Several of them nod.

One photographer raises a camera. Her tone is professional, but hopeful, when she asks Theo, "May I?"

Theo looks at her steadily. "Not tonight. Please."

The camera comes down.

*

Santa Fe PD arrives while the last of the audience is still filing out. Two officers first, then four more within minutes. Theo meets them at the entrance to ring one, his hand extended, his card already out.

"Theodore Crane, Operations Manager. I'm the senior staff member on site tonight."

He hands the card to the lead officer. Chief of Operations, it reads.

"I want to give you full cooperation," Theo says. "Whatever you need."

They cordon off ring one with tape. Theo watches them do it. The net. The wire. The platform. The sawdust where Ace fell. All of it has become evidence.

"We'll need to speak with you tonight," the lead officer says. "And we'll be back tomorrow for a more thorough investigation."

"Of course," Theo says. "I'll be here."

He is already thinking about the aerialists.

*

The audience is gone. The press have their holding statement—four sentences, reviewed and approved by legal counsel via phone, released at 11:40 PM. The lot is quieter now, the silence of a space that held forty-five hundred people an hour ago and now holds only the company and the police and the yellow tape around ring one.

Theo finds Marco at the edge of the performers' area.

"You okay?" he asks Marco quietly.

Marco's expression gives nothing, but he does manage a barely perceptible nod.

"Have the aerialists in the breakfast tent in one hour," Theo requests.

"One hour," he agrees, and turns on his heel.

*

The team leaders and senior performers gather in the breakfast tent at twelve-ten. Charlie. Brandon. The Tumbling Tropiques captain. The production heads. Marco, already seated when Theo arrives.

Theo stands at the head of the room. No microphone. No performance.

"Mr. Donahue was transported to Christus St. Vincent Regional Medical Center approximately one hour ago," he says. "I am awaiting word from the hospital. What I can tell you right now is this. We are staying in Santa Fe. For how long I will know more tomorrow. The police will be conducting a thorough investigation beginning in the morning. If anyone is contacted by investigators tonight or tomorrow, you are entitled to have legal representation present. I can arrange that for anyone who wants it. No one is obligated to speak to investigators without counsel."

He looks around the room.

“I know tonight has been….” He stops. Starts again. “I know what you witnessed tonight. I know what some of you are feeling right now. We will have time to process this together. Tomorrow. For now… get some rest if you can. I will contact each of you personally when I have more information.”

He pauses at the door on his way out.

“Thank you for how you handled tonight. All of you. Mr. Donahue would have—” Another stop. He does not finish the sentence.

He nods once. And leaves.

*

There is a chill in Theo’s trailer. He does not turn up the heat. Instead he changes into warmer, more comfortable clothing; it is going to be a long night.

He picks up his phone. Looks at it for a moment. Sets it down.

He picks it up again and dials Patty.

She answers on the second ring. Which means she was already awake. Which means she already knows.

“Patty.”

“I saw,” she says.

A pause.

“I need you here at six,” he says. “There’s a great deal to do.”

“I’ll be there at five,” she says.

He almost smiles.

“Thank you, Patty.”

He ends the call. Picks up a pen, opens his notebook. Writes down Roger’s name. Circles it. He’ll need to call Roger after the hospital calls him.

He stares at his phone's home screen for several long seconds, then dials Sophia.

She answers on the third ring. Her voice is alert; she was awake too.

"It's me," he says. "Something happened tonight… and I want you to hear it from me instead of the news."

"Oh," she says, half statement, half question. "Are you okay?"

"Yes. I'm okay. But Ace fell during his act. He's been taken to the hospital. But… it's bad."

"Oh." Softer. Acknowledging. "Are you… are you sure you're all right?"

"Yes."

Silence stretches for a few seconds before Sophia says, "It's… unfortunate. But I have to admit, I thought it was unwise to take up such a risky hobby at his age. Although… given his scotch and cigars habits, it's probably always been a matter of time."

"I suppose you're right. I keep telling… kept. I kept telling him. But he was an obstinate man."

"Do you know yet how—or if—the rest of the season is going to play out?"

"Things are a bit up in the air at the moment… oh. Sorry, no pun intended."

A laugh escapes his wife, and he smiles. The first time today.

"Is there anything I can do? I can't get away from work until next weekend, at the earliest."

"I can't think of anything at the moment. But I'll keep you posted."

Another lengthy silence. Then she asks, "Do you think you'll stay on with the company?"

"I'm planning to, yes. But… my role is going to change. And I want to tell you about it in person."

"Oh." This time there is surprise in her tone. "That sounds ominous."

"It's… it's some pretty big news. But I just want to tell you in person. It's not bad. If anything, I'll be able to spend more time at home."

"Ah. Well, in that case, I'll be patient."

"Thank you, babe."

"Love you."

"You too. Goodnight."

He ends the call. Sits for a moment in the cold trailer. Starts jotting down notes.

He's barely written two words when his phone buzzes on the desk. He looks at the screen.

Christus St. Vincent Regional Medical Center.

He answers on the first ring.

The call lasts less than two minutes. He says very little. *Yes. I understand. I will get word to his family. Thank you.*

He ends the call. Sets the phone down on the desk. Sits with it for a moment—the particular quality of a silence that is different from the silence before it, though nothing in the room has changed.

Then he picks up his notebook. Underlines Roger's name inside the circle. Picks up his phone. Dials.

*

The breakfast tent is quiet when Theo enters at one-fifteen.

They are all there. Marco at the far end, arms folded. Svetlana beside him, back straight, eyes on the door. Remy and Diego across from each other, neither one speaking. Jasmine at the end nearest the entrance, hands folded on the table in front of her. The others sit, carrying various attitudes of exhaustion and shock.

Theo pulls a chair from the nearest table and sits among them. Not at the head. Among them.

No one speaks.

"I owe you an explanation," Theo says. "And then I'm going to tell you what comes next."

He looks around the table. Takes his time.

"I asked you to switch the nets during the changeover after your final act tonight. Remove the new net. Put the old net in its place." He pauses. "I told you it was to teach Mr. Donahue a lesson. To make him see—at the halfway point, when he always looked down—the same net that was below Helena when she fell. I believed that seeing it would shake him. Frighten him. Force him to understand, in his body rather than his head, what his negligence had cost this company."

Another pause.

"I told you he would be wearing the harness. Because he always wears the harness." Theo's voice is steady. "Every performance. Without exception. You all know that."

Remy speaks without looking up. "He told me after he twisted his ankle in training. Said he wasn't stupid. Said he understood now what could happen up there." He pauses. "Said he would always wear the harness."

"Yes," Theo says simply. "We all heard him say it. We all had every reason to believe him." He looks around the table again. "I had every reason to believe him."

The room holds this.

"I did not know he was going to refuse to be clipped in tonight." He stops. "What I wanted was for him to look down at that net and understand—really understand—what he had done. He ignored my emails… my requests… the concerns I raised for two seasons. I wanted him to know what his decision had cost." His voice does not rise. It never rises. But it settles into something harder. “That was what I intended. Nothing more.”

Silence.

Then Svetlana.

Her voice is careful. Each word chosen.

“What if, Mr. Crane….” She holds his gaze across the table. “What if… you encouraged Mr. Donahue to refuse the safety harness tonight.” A beat of silence, then, “That would be convenient way to kill a monster.”

Her Ukrainian accent is thicker in the moment, Theo notes. And the weary managerial expression he has been wearing since he walked in shifts. Just slightly. Just enough. Something more precise surfaces underneath it.

“And yet, Svetlana,” he says quietly. “I never touched the net.”

There is a lengthy and heavy silence.

Then Marco. His voice has a finality to it when he says, “I’m okay with Ace Donahue being dead.”

Every head in the room turns toward him.

His expression is not angry. Not relieved. Not guilty. It is the expression of a man who made a decision a long time ago and has simply arrived at its conclusion.

Her name moves through the room without being spoken.

Helena.

The silence that follows is the most complete silence the breakfast tent has ever held.

Theo lets it sit.

Then he speaks.

“At some point on Sunday… later today… the investigators will want to talk to each of you. About the act. About the net.

About standard procedures for setup and changeover." He looks around the table. "You will tell them the truth. You switched the net at my request. I told you it was to frighten Mr. Donahue into confronting his negligence. I told you he would be wearing his harness, as he always does, as he promised Remy he always would after his fall in training. You believed me. You had every reason to believe me." He pauses. "That is the truth. Every word of it. I am asking you to tell it."

He turns to Jasmine.

She is watching him steadily. The newest member of this family. The one who came in through the door Helena left open.

"Jasmine." His voice is quieter now. "I gave you the opportunity to stay out of this. You chose not to take it." He holds her gaze. "I want you to know that I understand what that choice cost you. And I want you to know that the same truth protects you that protects everyone else in this room. You were told the same thing they were told. You believed the same thing they believed." A pause. "You are part of this company. And you know what happened to Helena, even though you came to us after her death. No investigator is going to see it any differently."

Jasmine nods once. Her eyes are bright but her jaw is steady.

Theo looks around the table one final time.

"I will arrange legal representation for anyone who wants it before speaking with investigators. That offer is open to every person in this room, tonight if necessary." He pauses. "Are there any questions?"

No one speaks.

Diego is looking at the table. Remy has his hands folded in front of him, his eyes somewhere in the middle distance. Marco has not moved. Svetlana is still watching Theo with the expression he cannot fully read and has not been able to fully read since this morning outside Ace's office.

Theo stands. Pushes his chair in.

At the door he pauses.

He turns back. Finds Svetlana's eyes one more time. His voice is quiet and certain when he says, "I never touched the net."

She holds his gaze. Her expression does not change.

He exhales slowly, then leaves the tent.

*

Theo's laptop has gone to screensaver mode and shows the time is 4:07 AM. The lot is eerily quiet. No generators running. No voices carrying across the dark. The Big Top stands against the star-filled night sky, its canvas sides moving slightly in the cold desert air.

He is sitting in his office. Other than the laptop, cell phone, and a small desk lamp, everything else is off.

The list he's working on has been reordered three times. It is currently twelve items long. He picks up his pen, circles items nine and seven, then draws an arrow showing he needs to swap those two tasks. Sets the pen down.

His eyes are doing that thing eyes do when it's been almost twenty-four hours with no sleep—a slight lag between looking and seeing, the words coming into focus a half second after he expects them. He reaches for the glass bottle of cold brew. Empty. He doesn't remember finishing it.

More caffeine, he tells himself.

He gets up and goes to his refrigerator. One bottle of La Colombe remaining. He takes it but stands there a moment, door still open, thinking.

There was something else; something he bought at a gas station a few weeks ago. Somewhere between Des Moines and Omaha. Grabbed it on impulse and then forgot about it entirely. He was almost certain he hadn't eaten them.

He closes the fridge, opens the cupboard above the coffee maker. A protein bar. Crackers. Paper cups. Advil.

Not in here.

He tries the next cupboard. Mismatched mugs. A box of tea he's never opened. A rubber band.

Nothing.

He crouches down and opens the cabinet beneath the sink, which makes no logical sense as a storage location but he is running on no sleep and at 4:00 AM logic sometimes reinvents itself. Cleaning supplies. A spare dish towel.

Nothing.

He straightens up. Stands in the middle of the small kitchen. Thinks.

Then he opens the cabinet above the refrigerator—the one he never uses, the one that requires him to stand on his toes—and there, behind a box of microwave popcorn he forgot he had, is a small bag, still sealed.

Chocolate-covered espresso beans.

Jackpot.

He takes the bag back to his desk, opens it, eats three. Then a fourth. Then decides the situation warrants a fifth.

He hits the space bar on his laptop. Enters his password.

All night he has been writing and reading emails. Making and receiving phone calls. Working on the list. Patty will be in her office in less than an hour and he needs to be ready for that conversation. The board has been notified. The lawyers have been notified. The former said they would contact his family, so… ostensibly the family has been notified.

But underneath all of it, running quiet but steady like a current beneath the surface of a river… Theo is thinking about Svetlana.

Her expression in the wings. The door to Ace's office open just a crack yesterday morning.

She definitely heard something, but what, and how much?

He may need a contingency plan. Just in case.

He opens Facebook. Types her name. Starts scrolling.

He was not expecting to find anything useful. But within a few minutes he sees something that could be…something.

Oh... what have we here, he thinks.

His fingertip moves toward the screen until it touches. He looks at it for a long moment. Taps the screen softly.

Then he picks up his pen and adds one line to the bottom of the list.

He caps the pen. Closes all the tabs on his laptop, except his email. Reaches for the cold brew. Remembers he hasn't opened it yet. Twists off the cap. Takes a long drink.

He sees a light come on in Patty's office, across the road and two trailers down from his.

Theo picks up his phone.

*

Patty has been in Theo's trailer since 5:30 AM and it is almost noon. She set up camp in his dining room and Theo has mostly been in his office. For the third time in the last hour she arrives in his doorway.

This time she is holding a legal pad and a pen, and the expression of a woman who has sixty-two things to tell him and is trying to decide which ones are most pressing.

He looks up from his notebook and is aware his eyes are stinging from too much screentime and not enough sleep.

"Patty." He sets his pen down.

Something in his voice makes her freeze in the doorway.

"Yes?"

"I need to say something to you."

She waits.

"I have not told you nearly enough—not once, actually, in almost two seasons—how much I appreciate what you do. What you've done. Not just today." He pauses. The caffeine is making him slightly more direct than he would normally allow himself to be and he decides this is acceptable. "You are extraordinary at what you do. And I should have said so long before today."

Patty is quiet for a moment. The legal pad lowers slightly.

"Well," she says finally. Her voice is not quite steady. "Thank you, Mr. Crane."

A beat.

Then, with the directness of a woman who has been in this operation long enough to know exactly what she knows, she asks Theo an important question. "When will you let the company know? About Ace's arrangements. That you're to succeed him."

Theo looks up at her from his ergonomic swivel chair.

"That will have to wait for the board and the lawyers to make it official. Could be a few days. Could be a week." He holds her gaze. "But until then… nothing changes operationally. I'm glad Ace told you, though. It's good that you know. Because I can't do any of this without you."

Patty nods once. The legal pad comes back up.

"The detectives called back," she says. "They'll want to get started at one this afternoon. In the Big Top."

"Good." He picks up his pen.

"You're first. Which probably is not a shocker."

"No, I already talked to Lieutenant Duran to get the scoop. I should be able to get some sleep after they interview me."

"That would be good."

"Yes. Much needed at this point." Even as he is saying the words he has to stifle a yawn. "So. What else you got on your list?"

She tells him. He writes it down.

*

He is dreaming when his phone pulls him out. Something about a mariachi band, he thinks.

He answers before he's fully conscious. His voice comes out even, which surprises him.

"Crane."

"Mr. Crane, this is Detective Zamora. Sorry to wake you."

He sits up. It's dark both inside and outside his trailer. He checks the time on his phone: 6:50 PM.

Four hours. It will have to be enough.

"Not at all," he says. "What do you need?"

"Just a quick clarification. When we spoke earlier you mentioned the safety harness was a gift. Something you had custom designed. We have it in evidence. I just need the name of the manufacturer. We may want to follow up with them directly."

Theo is already standing. Already moving toward his desk.

"Of course. That was commissioned through a company in Montreal." He finds his notebook. Flips three pages back. Reads off the name, the address, the contact he dealt with. "I can email you the original invoice if that would help."

"That would be great, yes. Thank you Mr. Crane. Sorry again for waking you."

"No need to apologize, Detective. You have a job to do."

He ends the call. Sets the phone on the desk.

Stands in the dark for a moment trying to orient himself. The only light in his trailer is from a splash of moonlight on his dining room table.

When he arrived for his interview he brought with him dozens of pages of documentation and a thumb drive of evidence. Camera footage. Emails. A file containing details about Helena's death, including the sparse police report and—notably—no mention of OSHA.

He did not think to include the Montreal invoice and is annoyed at himself for the omission.

He picks up a pen and adds it to his list. Crosses it out. A mistake noted and corrected simultaneously.

When he opens his refrigerator he is surprised to see four bottles of La Colombe on the top shelf. He smiles and thinks, *thank you, Patty.*

The microwave clock indicates it is 7:02 PM.

Even if Detective Zamora had not called, his alarm was already set for 9:00 PM. He needs to make another call then—what will be his third conversation with Roger since midnight. He takes a swig of the cold brew and reflects on his memories of the day which are, to Theo's mild surprise, relatively complete.

He addressed the full company at eight-fifteen that morning. All of them gathered in the breakfast tent—performers, crew, production staff, everyone. Someone had put away the tables and arranged the chairs into rows. He stood at the front of the room and told them what they already knew and what some of them didn't know and what all of them needed to hear from him directly.

That Ace did not survive the fall. That the company was staying in Santa Fe for the time being. That the detectives would need to speak with many of them, and that legal representation was available to anyone who wanted it before those conversations happened. That no one was obligated to remain on the lot as long as they did not have an interview scheduled. If anyone needed to get away for a day or two, that was completely understandable. He only asked that they keep their phones on and remain reachable.

He paused there. Looked around the room at the faces—exhausted, grief-stricken in varying degrees and for varying reasons. Some of them red-eyed, some of them carefully composed… and some wearing blank expressions that indicated they had not yet decided what they felt.

A choking sob reached his ears from somewhere in the back of the tent; Theo saw then that Shelby was hugging herself tightly, eyes squeezed tightly, her face red and crinkled. Katrina put her arm around her colleague and said, loud enough for everyone in the room to hear, "This was not your fault, sweetheart."

"I can't…" Shelby took in a gasp of air to continue. "I can't forgive myself."

Theo reassured her that she had done nothing wrong. "There was no way you could have forced him to use the safety cable, Shelby. You know how he was."

Sympathetic eyes shifted to the crying young woman who was alternating between nodding and shaking her head. Fighting a war inside herself.

"I want to let everyone know," he said, his tone calm, soothing even, "I understand this has been traumatizing. Not just Ace's death. But Helena's as well. I've arranged for a grief counselor to be available on site beginning tomorrow morning."

Most heads in the room swiveled to return their attention to him.

He continued.

"Her name is Dr. Sharma. She'll be available right here in this tent tomorrow, and through the end of the week, from noon to six o'clock. Talking with her will be completely confidential and completely voluntary. I would encourage anyone who wants to talk to someone… to take advantage of that."

Virginia started crying quietly in the third row. Brandon had his arm around Pip, who was watching Theo with great attention—present, serious, trying to understand something that the adults around her hadn't fully explained yet.

He was not able to look at her for very long.

He ended the meeting the way he ended everything: cleanly and without excess.

"Mr. Donahue built something worth preserving. I intend to preserve it. Keep an eye on your email for further announcements. A memorial service. Details about when we move on from Santa Fe. For now? Take care of yourselves, and each other. That's all."

They filed out quietly. A few of them stopped to shake his hand or say something brief. Charlie simply nodded at him from across the room on his way out. Theo thought about Charlie off and on the rest of the day. Quiet, dedicated, reliable. The only time Charlie ever surprised him was that morning in the breakfast tent when he made the dark joke about raw meat and the Ringmaster's coat and destiny. Every so often during the day the thought came to mind—even Charlie.

Theo arrived at the Big Top promptly at 1:30 PM, having eaten scrambled eggs and toast after Patty insisted he needed sustenance. His interview with Detective Zamora lasted ninety minutes. Straightforward. The detective was thorough and unhurried and asked good questions in a neutral tone that Theo respected. He answered everything directly and without elaboration, the way you answer questions when you have nothing to hide and everything to offer.

He left the interview feeling fairly calm, if not outright relieved.

Theo finishes off the bottle of La Colombe. Stands at the small kitchen window and looks out at the lot. Beyond the Big Top, the Sangre de Cristo Mountains are dark against the moonlit sky.

He thinks about Patty. He can see her office light is still on. Probably on the phone.

He thinks about Pip's face in the breakfast tent this morning. The way she was watching him. Trying to understand.

He doesn't let himself think about that for very long.

He picks up his phone. Checks the time. Forty minutes until Roger's call.

He returns to his office, wishing he had another bag of espresso beans. Opens his notebook. Finds the list.

Draws a line through items ten and eleven.

Circles number twelve.

*

Monday goes by in a blur, much like Sunday did. By ten-fifteen at night Theo sits at his desk with a cold brew, his notebook and a pen, and takes stock.

Spencer Donahue arrived that afternoon in a private jet. Ace's older son is CEO of one of Ace's other companies. Something entertainment-adjacent that Theo knows little about. The handoff was exactly what it was: a man picking up a box. No ceremony. No tears that Theo could see. They shook hands in the parking lot of the funeral home and Theo found himself looking at a younger Ace. The jawline. The larger-than-life presence. The way his eyes moved around a room, even when the room was a parking lot and there was nothing in it worth cataloging.

Theo offered to take him to dinner. Spencer politely declined. He climbed back into the limo in which he arrived, holding a box of his father's ashes, and was gone.

The last time Theo saw anything of Ace Donahue was walking away from him across a parking lot, carrying a box.

The press was manageable. Four statements released through the day, each one reviewed by legal counsel before going out. The narrative held: a beloved circus owner, a passion project turned into something remarkable, a tragic accident during a performance he loved. The word accident appearing in every statement. Consistent. Documented. Accurate.

He spoke briefly with Roger twice—the kind of conversation two people have when they are both aware of what cannot be said on a phone line. They agreed on the broad strokes. Roger would fly to Santa Fe on Thursday.

There are some things that can only be discussed in person.

He calls Sophia at ten-thirty. She answers on the second ring.

They talk for ten minutes about nothing consequential. Thanksgiving. Who will host this year. Whether her sister is coming.

She mentions that her executive assistant gave two weeks' notice today, so she will need to look for a replacement. She is not looking forward to that.

He mentions that some shameless opportunist snuck onto the lot in the pre-dawn hours… a photographer, looking for a shot of the tent or the net or whatever he thought he'd find in the dark. Someone called the police. The man ran off before authorities arrived. Sophia makes a sound that is equal parts sympathy and unsurprise. Some people, she says. He agrees and tells her he has hired security for the rest of the time they will be in Santa Fe.

Before they end the call, Sophia asks him what he wants to do for Christmas.

He tells her he wants to be home. Just home.

She is quiet for a moment. Then says that sounds perfect.

He ends the call. Opens his notebook. Finds the list.

Draws a line through items thirteen and fourteen.

Circles fifteen.

*

Tuesday. Theo sits at his desk just after 11:00 PM and thinks back on the day.

Patty left just after sunrise and said she would be back by eight. She went to visit her cousin and cousin-in-law in Taos, some ninety minutes away. Theo received at least three texts from her while she was gone, just checking in. She returned at 5:45 PM—earlier than expected—and Theo breathed an audible sigh of relief.

"Remind me to give you a raise," he told her.

He'd felt her absence keenly. He hadn't realized, until she was gone, how much of the operational noise she absorbs simply by being present.

Brandon took Pip to a hotel this morning. He mentioned it yesterday—a pool, room service, a couple of days away from the lot. Theo told him to take whatever time he needed. Brandon nodded but didn't quite meet his eyes when he took his daughter somewhere with a pool.

They crossed Theo's mind a few times during the day. Never for very long.

The eulogy gave him trouble in a way he didn't anticipate. Not because he didn't know what to say—he knew exactly what to say, he had been saying the right things about Ace Donahue for two seasons. But there was something about committing it to a page, in a form that would be read aloud at a service, that required a different kind of precision than he was used to. He wrote and deleted the opening paragraph four times.

He'll try again tonight.

Dazzle called at two. She's been in Albuquerque since Sunday—he knew this, he had been in contact with her. She sounded as though she'd been crying for three days and had decided to keep crying until further notice. He was patient and kind and told her the service would be an event worthy of Ace.

She said: *He was a difficult man... but he was my friend.*

Theo said, "I know." And meant it.

Two OSHA compliance officers arrived around three in the afternoon. The senior officer was a compact woman in her fifties named Lauren Ryser, who moved through the Big Top with the unhurried efficiency of someone who has seen every version of this before. Her partner was younger, quieter, taking notes while Ryser asked the questions.

Theo was first. His meeting with them lasted just under two hours.

He told them about Helena. All of it. The frayed net. The workaround the aerialists had developed. The five emails to Ace. The dates. The vendor he had on standby. He described the culture Ace had built—the climate of fear that made reasonable safety requests feel like personal insults, the reflexive dismissal of any concern that cost money, the firing of Dr. Block for asking reasonable questions about his own patients. He laid it out cleanly and without editorializing, the way a careful man presents a paper trail he has been maintaining for two seasons.

Ryser listened without interrupting. When he finished she was quiet for a moment, looking at the net still hanging in ring one behind the yellow tape.

"Mr. Crane," she said. "Your bigger concern—and I want to be transparent with you—is the Helena Danforth situation. An unreported workplace fatality is a serious matter."

"I understand," Theo said. "I want to be equally transparent with you. I reported the net condition to Mr. Donahue five times. I have the emails. I have his responses, or his non-responses. The decision not to replace the equipment was his, documented, and made over my explicit objection." He paused. "I did not have the authority to override him. I wish I had."

Ryser looked at him steadily. He held her gaze.

They were in the Big Top for another hour after that, walking the space, examining the rigging, photographing the net. Theo answered every question directly. When they were done with him he showed them to the small meeting room off the breakfast tent that Patty had set up for the remaining interviews. A folding table, four chairs, a window propped open to let in the afternoon air.

Marco was next. Theo returned to his trailer and did not allow himself to think about what was being said in the Big Top thirty yards away, because he already knew. He worked on the list. He waited.

When Marco's interview concluded, Ryser appeared at Theo's trailer door.

"We'd like to speak with the full aerial team tomorrow morning," she said. "Together, as a group. If their account is consistent with what you and Mr. Mura have told us today, we should be able to wrap this up and submit a final report within the next week or two."

"Of course," Theo said. "I'll make sure they're available."

Just as she started to turn around, he asked, "Oh, would it be possible for the office manager to attend? I would like her to take notes, if that would be acceptable to you."

"Yes," Ryser agreed. "That's fine."

*

The group interview was held at nine the following morning in the breakfast tent. Theo was not present for it. He did not ask to be. He stayed in his trailer and worked on the eulogy and did not look at the tent from his window more than twice.

Patty told him afterward how it went.

The aerialists had been consistent. The net, the requests, the workaround—everything aligned with what Theo and Marco had told Ryser yesterday. The culture of the operation under Ace came through clearly and without coaching, because it didn't need coaching. It was simply what had happened.

Svetlana had not spoken much. At one point she had stopped being able to speak at all. Marco had leaned forward and said quietly to Ryser, "Helena and Svetlana were best friends. They trained together for years. This season has been heartbreaking for all of us, but especially for her." Ryser had nodded and moved on.

Patty said Ryser had thanked the group at the end and told them they'd handled an impossible season with professionalism and integrity.

Theo set down his pen when Patty finished telling him this.

"Thank you, Patty," he said.

She nodded once and returned to her legal pad.

Before leaving the lot that afternoon, Ryser stopped by his trailer one final time.

"The Helena Danforth matter," she said. "The failure to report is serious. But the documentation you've provided, and what we heard this morning, paints a consistent picture. The negligent party is deceased. OSHA's interest is correction and prevention." She paused. "We won't be pursuing it further."

Theo thanked her. Meant it.

"As for Saturday—the old net was in place at the time of the fall. That's a violation. You'll receive a fine." She named the amount. It was significant but not ruinous. "Given the circumstances and the documentation, we're not recommending suspension of operations."

"The assessment," Theo said, "will be paid promptly."

She nodded. Paused at the door.

"Get your safety protocols documented before next season, Mr. Crane. Everything in writing. So there's never a question about who knew what and when."

"Already underway," he said.

He watched her cross the lot. Stood in the doorway until the rental car pulled out through the gate. Then he went inside, added two items to the list, and crossed one of them out.

That night, Svetlana came to his trailer at nine-fifteen. He heard the knock and knew before he opened the door.

She was crying. The kind that had been building up for days, but now the dam was burst. She stood in his doorway in a gray sweatshirt and darker gray leggings, and told him she was not coming back next season. Said she wanted to go be with her family.

He was compassionate. Patient. He had her come in. Offered her tea, which she declined. Then he asked her to wait—just a few more days, until Saturday's announcements—before making any final decisions.

He told her he was planning to end their season after the Albuquerque stand. Said he was still working on the details. Too soon to tell everyone. He asked if he could have one more conversation with her before she left for Pittsburgh. Told her she didn't need to perform in Albuquerque if she didn't feel up to it.

She cried harder. Said it wasn't just Ace. Said it was everything. The word hanging in the air between them in a way that could mean many things and almost certainly meant one specific thing.

He asked if there was anything he could do.

She shook her head.

He brought her a box of tissues, then called Marco. Asked him and Jasmine to walk her back to her RV. To stay with her for a couple of hours.

They came without questions—Marco in jeans and his Donahue's jacket, Jasmine in jeans and a turtleneck. They appeared at his door within four minutes, in much the way people appear when they have been waiting to be needed.

He watched the three of them move across the dark lot. Then closed his door.

Sat at his desk. Opened his notebook. Flipped back several pages until he found what he'd written at four in the morning on Sunday. The single line at the bottom of the list. The one he'd added after he tapped Svetlana's Facebook screen softly and looked at what he found for a long moment.

He copied his note forward to the current page and wrote underneath it:

Research AML, Mayo? Deep dive on Dmitri & Oksana Petrov.

Capped his pen.

Opened a new browser tab and watched the cursor blink. Decided the eulogy would have to wait another hour… and instead started googling.

He texts Sophia at eleven. She is in Dallas for a conference that runs through the rest of the week. She tells him Christmas is confirmed. New Year's is a possibility; she has friends in Charleston who've been asking for years.

He tells her he'll think about it.

She sends a smiley face emoji and: *You always say that.*

He types back: *I always mean it.*

*

By Thursday morning his list is down to seven active items: four circled, three flagged for follow-up.

Yesterday he worked on the ownership presentation off and on throughout the morning. He also made and received numerous phone calls.

One of those Wednesday morning calls was from Patty who wanted to coordinate the service details. She mentioned her niece's husband makes green chile stew and offered to bring two large pots for the reception. Theo said yes immediately. Patty also located, through means he didn't ask about, a photograph of Ace from the early Trentini years. Younger. Wearing the Ringmaster coat, grinning at something off-camera in a way that says he believes everything is about to go exactly the way he wants it to. She texted him the image and said she will have it enlarged and framed for the service.

The photo, Theo told her, is exactly right.

The eulogy found its shape last night around midnight. He was not entirely sure how. He was on his fourth draft and then suddenly it was simply there—the right opening, the right arc, the right ending. He read it back twice. Made two small changes. Called it done.

Detective Zamora called around two on Thursday. Interviews concluded. No concerns regarding foul play. The picture that emerged—consistently, across every interview, from every person who was present—was of a man who made an impulsive decision that cost him his life. Zamora used the phrase "open and shut" which Theo appreciated for its efficiency if not its poetry. He also expressed gratitude for Theo's cooperation and the thoroughness of the documentation he'd provided.

Theo thanked him and meant it.

Brandon sent a message at three-thirty. *We'll be back Friday morning. Pip wants you to know she's been practicing her bicycle bit in the hotel hallway.*

He read that twice.

Did not respond immediately.

Wrote the response carefully: *Tell her the hallway audience doesn't know what hit them. See you Friday.*

Then returned to the ownership presentation.

The board gave preliminary approval pending the formal legal process. Ace's lawyers confirmed the will and trust provisions. The announcement on Saturday was not premature—it was, as Theo preferred things to be, precisely timed.

Roger arrived at six-fifteen that evening. He parked his tan Chevy Malibu right next to the Tahoe, in front of Theo's trailer. They shook hands at the trailer door and Theo thought, not for the first time, that Roger Weber looked exactly like what he was: a careful man who'd spent over two decades making sure no one looked too closely.

Theo had half expected some residual wariness; the Chili's meeting had not been Roger's finest hour of discretion. But there was none. Roger had made his peace with Theo's role in all of this somewhere between Omaha and Santa Fe, and he'd arrived tonight ready to work.

Patty had been told no interruptions, from anyone. She enforced this well.

They ordered Thai delivery. Roger had a particular order… which did not surprise Theo. Pad Kee Mao, chicken, extra basil.

Theo had the same. Neither of them attempted the chopsticks. This went unacknowledged.

Their meeting lasted two hours and nineteen minutes.

Theo learned Roger and Ace went back a long way—further than Theo had fully understood from their Omaha meeting last year. Smaller structures over the years, Roger explained, eating his Pad Kee Mao with a fork.

He described how Ace had contacted him when he was working on acquiring the circus. Told him he had a specific vision for what he wanted to build financially and asked Roger to design it.

So Roger designed it.

What Roger built over seven years—using the circus as the vehicle Ace always intended it to be—was, in Theo's assessment, genuinely extraordinary. Cash heavy, jurisdictionally complicated, moving across state lines with the natural chaos of a traveling show providing cover for irregularities that would have attracted scrutiny in a fixed operation.

Roger told him the offshore accounts held just over twenty-eight million dollars.

Theo set his fork down. "The circus generates what—three, maybe four million in a good season. Where does twenty-eight million come from?"

Roger's expression settled into something between pride and satisfaction. He set his own fork down.

"The circus was never the primary vehicle," he said. "It was the cover." A pause. "Ace started two companies in his peak gameshow years. When his sons were done with their MBAs, Ace named Spencer CEO of the talent management company. Actors—some of 'em Academy Award winners. And Zane? *He's* running the luxury real estate business. Properties all over Hollywood and Beverly Hills."

Theo got a thoughtful expression. "Huh." A pause. "Very interesting." He looked at Roger steadily. "Do either of his sons... do they know what their father was..."

Roger picked up his fork. Speared a piece of chicken. Looked at Theo with the expression of a man who found the question genuinely delightful.

"Nope." He chewed. Set the fork down. Reached for his bourbon. "Not a clue."

Three revenue streams. Two unwitting sons. The circus as cover.

He thought about that December afternoon in Corpus Christi. Ace behind his desk, the color draining. Theo had said it with the calm of a man holding a complete hand—*I've talked with Roger a few times since you set up our meeting in September.* He'd been holding perhaps a third of one. Ace had assumed the rest existed and filled it in himself.

What he had just inherited was not a circus; it was an empire. Quietly built, carefully hidden, and now entirely his—along with every consequence that might come with it.

He did not let any of this show.

It was obvious Roger appreciated Theo's understanding of what he'd built. This man had spent over twenty years working for someone who never once understood what he'd built… but was now sitting across from someone who knew exactly how remarkable it was. Magnificent, even.

They discussed the transition. The shell companies. The offshore accounts. The one-day liquidity threshold—Roger explained he could make up to a million available to Theo within a single business day, the arrangement Ace had wanted. Theo said he would keep that threshold for now and revisit it in six months.

Roger nodded. Made a note.

Theo offered him a generous bonus. Roger accepted with the grace of a man who was genuinely pleased.

They finished eating. Roger declined a second drink. They shook hands at the door and Roger walked to the tan Malibu and drove into the night. Theo stood in his doorway for a moment looking at the lot.

Sophia calls him at midnight. They finalize Thanksgiving. Her sister is coming, which means her sister's husband is coming, which means Theo will spend four days being pleasant to a man he finds exhausting. He tells Sophia this. She laughs and says he's been pleasant to far more exhausting people than David.

He thinks about Ace and says, "Fair point."

She asks how he's doing. Really doing.

He is quiet for a moment. "I'm okay," he says. "I'll be better when Saturday is over."

"And after Saturday?"

"After Saturday," he says, "I think things will get quieter."

She says she hopes so.

He says goodnight. Opens his notebook. Finds the list.

Four items remain.

He draws a line through one of them. Circles the last three.

*****

A noise wakes Theo very early Friday morning. He sits up in bed. Tries to figure out whether it was something real, or something his brain manufactured in his sleep.

He remembers he was dreaming about two of the crew members (Derek and Ronny, he thinks) pounding an eighteen-inch stake into the ground to secure the Big Top. It's a sound that has woken him before, but they've been in Santa Fe for a week now. No one is driving steel spikes into the ground.

Must have been the dream, he concludes.

He stretches, then gets out of bed and heads to the kitchen to assess his caffeine situation.

Four bottles of La Colombe in the refrigerator. *No. Something hot*, he decides. Closes the fridge door.

There is Holler Mountain in the Mr. Coffee on the counter. *Also insufficient.*

He is dressed and in the Tahoe before the sun has fully cleared the Sangre de Cristos.

The lot is still, as if it is quietly telling Theo: *Something happened here and I'm not ready to be loud again.*

He doesn't look in the rearview mirror as he pulls out. He's been on this lot for a full week now. His decision to leave it—even briefly, even just to drive until he finds coffee—feels like the first fully voluntary thing he has done since that night. Since the last time Ace stepped onto the wire.

He makes his way through the streets of Santa Fe with no particular destination in mind. The dawn light is starting to creep over the Sangre de Cristos, low and unhurried. This leaves the mountains in silhouette, but allows the sunlight to bid good morning to the adobe walls and the yucca and the century plants.

He does not let himself think about Svetlana, though she is almost certainly the reason he's on the hunt for something stronger than the caffeine options in his trailer.

He finds the café almost by accident. It's a small place on a side street with a hand-painted sign and, improbably, a drive-through window barely wide enough for the Tahoe. A single car ahead of him. He waits.

When he reaches the window a young woman with electric blue fingernails takes his order without ceremony.

"Triple espresso. No milk. No sugar."

She nods. Then, almost as an afterthought, tilts her head toward the display case behind her. "We just pulled piñon coffee cake out of the oven. Goes fast."

He looks at her for a moment.

"I'll take a piece."

She smiles and disappears.

He sits with the engine idling and watches the street. A mutt trots from one sidewalk across to the other, as if it's learned cars can be dangerous. A man wearing an Army jacket walks past carrying a paper bag. The ordinary machinery of an ordinary morning, for most. He does not count himself in that group, because this evening he will perform Ace's eulogy.

The cup arrives first. Small. Paper. Unexpectedly heavy for its size. Then a square of coffee cake wrapped in wax paper, still warm, the smell of piñon and brown sugar reaching him before he even gets it into the Tahoe.

He takes the first sip of the espresso before he pulls away from the window.

The grimace is involuntary. The bitterness hits the back of his throat before anything else. Dense and immediate. Demanding. He holds it for a moment. Swallows. The warmth follows, moving through his chest with a directness the cold brew never quite achieves.

No one is behind him, so he sets the cup in the holder. Unwraps the coffee cake. Takes a bite.

He does not grimace at this.

The piñon is toasted and faintly sweet and the cake itself is dense without being heavy. There is something about eating it—warm, in the Tahoe, on a side street in Santa Fe at first light—that has nothing to do with sustenance and everything to do with wanting something simply because he wants it. He cannot remember the last time he said yes to something without thinking it through.

He finishes it before he pulls back onto the street.

By the time he is halfway back to the lot the caffeine is hitting his central nervous system. The sharpening has begun. The edges of things becoming more defined. Friday becoming navigable.

The sun is fully up now. He brings the empty paper cup into his trailer. Drops it in the trash can. The Sangre de Cristos catch the light the way they always catch it—indifferent, permanent, unchanged by anything that has happened in this city or on this lot or in this particular week of his life.

*

Svetlana Petrov arrives at his trailer at nine o'clock exactly.

Theo is already sitting at his desk when she knocks: two precise raps, nothing tentative about them. He has been in this office since seven-thirty. His notes for tomorrow morning's speech are in a neat stack to his left. The notebook is open to a page with one circled item.

"Come in, Svetlana."

She looks better than she did Tuesday night, Theo decides, *although better is a very relative term.*

Her swollen eyes have subsided but now have a haunted quality. She is wearing her dark hair pulled back and a forest-green jacket over a black shirt. She carries herself the way she always carries herself—spine straight, chin level—but there is something underneath the posture today that wasn't there before. She looks as though she has been holding herself upright through sheer will for days and is beginning to wonder how much longer she can manage it.

She sits in the chair across from his desk without being asked.

He looks at her for a moment. Then opens the bottom drawer and retrieves a contract. Sets it on the desk between them. Her contract. The one she signed in September, before any of this.

She looks at it. Looks at him.

He picks it up. Tears it in half. Puts the two ripped pieces together, then sets them on the corner of his desk.

The sound of it seems to surprise her more than the act itself.

"On Tuesday," Theo starts, "I told you that I wanted to have one more conversation before you made your final decision. I appreciate you being here."

She nods once. Says nothing.

"I understand you want to leave. I understand this season has been…." He pauses, choosing the word carefully. "Devastating. In ways that go beyond what anyone could have anticipated." He holds her gaze. "I'm not going to try to talk you out of your feelings."

Svetlana's jaw tightens slightly. She is waiting for the but.

"I would like to offer you something before you decide." He opens the desk drawer again and removes a single sheet of paper. Sets it in front of her. "A new contract. With different terms."

She doesn't look at it. She looks at him.

"Svetlana." His voice is quieter now. "I know about Irina."

Something moves across her face—not shock exactly, but the expression of someone who was bracing for impact and found it arriving from a completely unexpected direction.

"How." The word comes out flat. An accusation, not a question. "Why. How do you know about my sister?"

Her accent is thicker than he has ever heard it.

"Your Facebook page," he says. "You posted a photograph earlier this year. February twenty-sixth, to be exact. Your parents at her bedside. Irina." He pauses. "She was smiling."

Svetlana is very still. He can see her processing it. The page she never thought to make private, the photograph she posted without thinking twice, the window left open without knowing it. Her expression shifts from disorientation into something sharper. More wary.

"That is..." she begins. Stops. Starts again. "That is one photograph. From eight months ago." Her eyes are steady on his now. "She was so sick then." Her voice dropped to almost a whisper when she added, "She still is."

"I know," he says quietly. "And I think I can help her."

She looks at him. The confusion on her face is genuine—she has no framework for this sentence, no way to place it. Why would he know about Irina. Why would he want to help her.

"I wanted to understand your situation fully, before having this conversation," he continues. "I engaged someone to help me do that."

The wariness sharpens into something closer to alarm. "You had someone investigate my family."

Another accusation; not a question.

"I wanted to make sure that what I'm about to offer you is actually useful," he says. "Rather than too late."

A long silence. She is looking at him the way you look at something you are trying to decide whether to be afraid of.

"Irina is still in treatment," he continues. "The AML has not gone into full remission. Your father's insurance has covered some. But not enough. The gap grows every month." He pauses. "I know a transplant has been discussed. I know your parents are managing. I know it has been… a very difficult time for you and your family. And you've been here."

Something breaks slightly in her face at those last four words. *And you've been here*. A thousand miles away. Performing over a frayed net. Watching Helena die. Watching Ace ignore every safety concern that mattered. Sending money home when she could.

She pulls herself back together with visible effort.

"How." Her voice is careful now. Precise. "How can circus afford this? Mayo Clinic would cost over a million dollars. And that is not even including bone marrow transplant."

"The company can afford it."

She studies him. He lets her.

"If you stay," Theo says, "this company will pay for Irina's treatment at the Mayo Clinic. Every penny. For as long as she needs it." He pauses. "They have the best outcomes in the world for this type of cancer. Their clinical trials alone—"

"I know what Mayo Clinic is," she says quietly. Not rudely. Just—she knows. She has been researching. Of course she has.

"Your parents could come with her," he continues. "One, or both. Lodging. Travel. All of it covered." A pause. "The new contract also includes two weeks of personal leave for you next season. One week when Irina is discharged. Another week at your discretion, with reasonable advance notice."

Something flickers across her face. She had not expected that.

"You would need to stay through the Albuquerque stand. Honor the rest of this season. And sign on for next." He slides the contract toward her. "I'd encourage you to take it with you. Read it carefully. Have a lawyer review it if you'd like."

She looks at the contract.

He already knows she won't read it. Not today. Not in this room.

What moves across her face in this moment is not gratitude and not relief and not warmth. It is something more complicated than any of those things—the expression of a woman who is simultaneously horrified and hopeful and suspicious and grateful and furious, all at once, and cannot separate any of it from the rest of it. The expression of someone who has just understood the precise dimensions of a room she is standing in and found the walls closer than she expected.

She knows what this is.

She knows what she is being offered and what she is being asked to give in return and what it will mean for the rest of her time with this company. She knows he had someone investigate her family. She knows he found the February photograph and scrolled back through pages and pages of her life to find it. She knows the company can afford a million dollars in cancer treatment because she is not naive and she has been paying attention too, in her own way, for two seasons.

She knows all of it.

And Irina is barely sixteen in that photograph. Bald. Smiling weakly from a hospital bed in Pittsburgh while Svetlana was performing a thousand miles away.

She looks up at him. Her voice is quiet but steady.

"Why you are offering me this?"

Theo holds her gaze for a moment. "One of my goals going forward is to retain the best of this company. Especially those who have been here since the Trentini days. You'll learn more about that tomorrow." He pauses. "The Trentini legacy is going to be important to what we build next. I need people who remember what that looked like."

She studies him. He lets her.

She knows this is not the whole answer. He knows she knows. Neither of them says so.

Her words are quiet but demanding. "Give me pen."

He gets a pen from his desk. Uncaps it. Holds it out to her.

She takes it from his hand as if she cannot risk him withdrawing this offer. He won't, as long as she agrees to next season.

Svetlana Petrov signs the new contract without reading it. Her eyes are on his face while she does it—not blinking, not looking away—as if she needs to see him clearly while this is happening. A single tear slides down one cheek. She does not wipe it away.

She sets the pen on the desk.

Stands.

He stands.

"This offer," she says slowly, her words clear but quiet. "Is only good if I stay?"

"Yes."

She holds his gaze for one long moment.

Then she moves toward the door.

She stops.

Turns.

Looks at him with the expression of a woman who has nothing left to lose by saying the true thing.

"Ace was monster," she says. Her voice is steady. Certain. "You are worse monster."

She leaves.

The door closes behind her.

Theo stands behind his desk. Clears his throat and smooths down his tie.

He looks at the signed contract on the desk.

Picks it up.

Reviews it once.

Runs it through the scanner on his desk, then slips the page into a folder labeled Petrov, Svetlana. Puts the folder in his drawer, filing it between Pedersen, Trent—a crew hand; and Proudfoot, Eleanor—the veterinarian.

Before he continues working on the list, Theo walks into the kitchen and gets an orange from the refrigerator. Stands near the dining room window peeling it, casually glancing between the fruit and the view outdoors. He sets the orange on a plate and scoops up the peels. Discards them in the kitchen trash. Returns to the window and starts eating one segment at a time as he thinks through the rest of his morning.

When he sees the crow with the white scar on its beak, he stops chewing. It is perched atop another trailer across the road from his. He raps the window lightly, curious to see whether the bird will look toward him. It does not. He eats another segment without taking his eyes off the iridescent plumes.

Suddenly the crow lifts off. Theo tracks it, waiting for it to settle again. But today it only grows smaller and smaller in the distance. Until it is only a dot. And then it is gone.

*

The staff, performers, and crew arrive back on the lot throughout the day. By four o'clock most have returned and there is a comforting familiarity to their presence. Voices across the lot. The llamas humming. Bruno and Hazel stirring in their enclosure.

Theo stands at his office window for a moment and simply listens, then goes back to reviewing his notes for the eulogy.

Dazzle returns to the lot at four-thirty. He sees her from his office window. Still in black. Wearing sunglasses even though it is overcast. He raises a hand to offer a solitary wave. She raises one back.

*

The memorial service is held at six-thirty Friday evening, in the breakfast tent. Patty had transformed it—quietly, efficiently, without drawing attention to the transformation—into something that felt like Ace. String lights along the ceiling. The enlarged photograph of younger Ace in the red coat positioned at the front of the room where everyone can see it. A table of food along the back wall including two large pots of green chile stew courtesy of Patty's niece's husband, who drove down from Taos earlier this afternoon and stayed long enough to make sure the stew was properly heated before disappearing again.

There are flowers. Not tasteful restrained flowers, but large gaudy arrangements in red and gold that Patty ordered from a florist on Cerrillos Road and that were, Theo thought, exactly right.

The company fills the tent. Every performer. Every crew member. Production staff. The llama handlers, the riggers, the spotlight operators, Gloria from costuming, Danny from the sound booth. Razzle and Dazzle, the latter in black for the sixth consecutive day, seated in the front row with a handkerchief already in hand before anyone has said a word.

Charlie sits in the third row and later eats two bowls of green chile stew. From what Theo observed, the lion tamer did not say anything throughout the service.

Brandon has Pip on his knee. She is wearing her clown costume, which no one asked her to do and which is, Theo thinks, the most appropriate thing anyone in the tent is wearing.

Theo delivers the eulogy from the front of the room. No microphone. No performance. Just the words he wrote and deleted four times before they finally arrived somewhere around midnight on Tuesday.

He speaks about Ace's love of the circus. His genuine passion for performance and spectacle. The particular kind of courage it takes to stand in the center of a ring and demand that thousands of people look at you and mean it. He talks about the Trentini legacy and what it meant to Ace to be its steward—imperfectly, humanly, with all the flaws that attend any man who wants something badly enough to build his life around it.

He does not say what he was thinking at one point while writing the eulogy, which was, that even in his final moments Ace was performing. That he fell without making a sound, his Ringmaster coat billowing dramatically in his wake. That the last thing Ace Donahue ever did was give the audience exactly what they came for.

Instead Theo tells the company that Ace Donahue lived the way he wanted to live and died doing something he loved and that there were worse things to be said of a man at the end of his life.

He believes approximately half of that.

The room is quiet when he finishes. Then someone starts clapping—Virginia, he thinks, though he is not certain—and the applause spreads through the tent the way applause always spread through a tent… from one person to the next until it is everyone and then it is over, and people are getting up, moving toward the food, and talking quietly among themselves.

Dazzle finds him near the photograph. She looks at the younger Ace for a long moment—grinning at something off-camera, certain of everything—and then looks at Theo.

"He would have loved this," she says.

"Right?" Theo agrees. "That's why we did it this way."

She nods. Squeezes his hand once. Moves away and blows her nose into the handkerchief.

Theo stands alone in front of the photograph for a moment, taking in the details. Even in this image, his teeth are very white.

Then he heads to the food table. Gets a bowl of green chile stew and a warm flour tortilla. Both are very good.

*

He calls Sophia at ten. Tells her about the service. She listens without interrupting, which is one of the things he has always valued about her.

"It sounds like it was just right," she says when he is finished.

"It was."

A pause.

"Tomorrow is the big day?" she asks.

"Tomorrow is the big day."

"Call me after?"

"Yes," he says. "I'll call you after."

He ends the call. Opens his notebook.

The list has one item remaining.

He looks at it for a long moment.

Does not cross it out.

Does not circle it.

Just looks at it.

Then he closes the notebook and goes to bed.

Tomorrow is Saturday.

*****

The breakfast tent has been rearranged since last night. The string lights are still up but the flowers are gone. The photograph of Ace is gone. The tables have been pulled into a loose approximation of a U shape. There are some chairs along the sides for anyone who wants them. Perhaps forty people are standing. The rest—another thirty or so—have chosen to sit at the tables.

There are several quiet conversations overlapping, giving the space a somber feel. Some of that is residue from the memorial last night, but Theo is aware the people he is about to address are also uncertain about the company's future—or, more accurately, their own futures within the company.

At Theo's request, Danny has set up a laptop near the entrance, angled toward the front of the room. Two solid green dots indicate the board members in Texas are present and watching.

Brenda and Cassie are visible through the pass-through window, moving quietly, preparing what comes after.

Theo moves through the room briefly before taking his position. A handshake here, a kind word there. He sees Brandon near the side wall. Pip is at his side and already in her clown costume because of course she is.

As he approaches them, there is a brief moment in which he almost decides to pass by and speak to someone else. Instead, he reconsiders. Slows and stops in front of them. Crouches slightly.

Pip looks up at him with those greenish-gray eyes, the gold flecks not as visible when she is in here instead of outside.

"I heard the hotel hallway was very impressed," he says.

When Pip grins he notices she has lost another tooth. "I stuck every landing," she declares.

"I have no doubt." He flashes a quick smile. Straightens. Meets Brandon's eyes for a moment. Brandon gives him a small nod, which Theo interprets as the narrowest sliver of respect.

He makes his way to the front of the room. Steps up onto the low riser—eight inches, nothing theatrical, purely practical. The room settles without being asked.

He looks at them for a moment before he speaks.

"Good morning." A pause. "I need to share some important information, but I don't want to overload you. So, I am going to have a small booklet made and distributed to everyone in the next ten days or so. That booklet will go into detail about what is going to change and what will stay the same. Most importantly, I'm going to keep this meeting short… because Brenda and Cassie have a continental breakfast going up as soon as I'm done yakking. I will take questions at the end. And if you think of something later? Just email me, pull me aside, or find Patty. She's setting up some kind of suggestion box for anyone who prefers that."

A small ripple moves through the room. Recognition. He sounds like himself.

"Before I dig in, however, I want to take a moment to thank Patty. This company runs because she makes it run. I want to make sure that's said out loud, in front of everyone, at least once." He gestures toward Patty who is standing to Danny's right.

"Let's take a moment to let her know how much we all appreciate her."

He applauds warmly, aiming toward her, and the room follows. With this, the mood in the tent elevates a degree or two.

Patty turns crimson but accepts the gesture with grace. She smiles and bows her head in acknowledgment.

"So." The applause dies down and Theo puts his hands in his pockets. He is casual, deliberate. "I'm going to hit some of the highlights of what Donahue's Traveling Circus will be going forward. I've got some good news and some bad news." He looks around the room. "Which would you like to hear first?" He doesn't pause even a quarter of a second. "Oh good, I agree. Bad news first. Let's get that out of the way."

A few people smile. The mood lifts another degree.

"The bad news," he says, "is that you're stuck with me. Not just as Operations Manager. Not just as the person running things while the lawyers sort out the paperwork." He holds the room. "Mr. Donahue made provisions in his estate documents regarding the succession of this company. I was told he put careful thought into the future of all three of his companies, as well as his investments and the various properties he owned. And… he left almost everything to his two sons. But the provisions regarding this company… the circus. Those have been reviewed by the board and confirmed by his attorneys during this week. Effective within the next few days… I will be assuming full ownership of Donahue's Traveling Circus."

There are many shocked faces and murmurs at this news, almost certainly related to speculation of how this came to be. He watches the information move through the room, each person hearing and processing it differently. There is some level of surprise on almost every face. Mostly, though, he sees recalculation happening behind eyes that are suddenly doing math they weren't doing thirty seconds ago.

"I want to be clear about something," he continues. "I am not Ace."

From his left, someone immediately starts clapping. Loudly, and with admirable energy.

Theo sees it is Destiny, who is seated at one of the tables next to Charlie who is briefly startled by her enthusiasm.

She gets through five beats before she realizes she's the only one clapping and feels the awkward energy. Reins it in. Stops.

A blush creeps up Destiny's cheeks. She glances at Charlie sheepishly, then stares down at the table and sits on her hands.

Charlie does not acknowledge this just happened. Nor does anyone else.

Theo moves on.

"I will not try to be Ace," he continues, as if nothing occurred. "What I will try to be is the kind of owner this company deserves." He pauses. "What I want everyone to know… is that starting next season, I will not fill in for the role of Ringmaster."

More murmurs arise and several performers and staff glance around to see the other reactions. He only waits a moment before continuing.

"I won't pretend to be one-fourth as good as Ace was, at entertaining a crowd. So… that is a position I'll be looking to fill over the next few months, and I will keep you informed along the way."

He takes in a breath, then continues. "So now… for the rest of the bad news."

Theo walks them through the need for everyone to sign new contracts before the end of the season. Explains they will be digital, and that their reviews will still take place in person. He watches several faces tighten and acknowledges the learning curve. Mentions support will be available.

He walks them through his plan to shift to a bimonthly pay structure. Same annual income. But distributed across twelve months, instead of concentrated into the months of the active season. He explains the math carefully and watches people do it in their heads. He can tell some are fine with it, but others—in spite of the math—do not like this change. Theo understands some things feel like less, even when they aren't.

He walks them through the performance review structure. Annual. Documented. Based on audience response, technical proficiency, adaptability. A few of the older performers exchange a glance.

Then, "I am instituting a non-compete policy."

He explains it. Carefully and professionally. He uses the correct terminology.

Half the room nods with the vague understanding of people who have heard the words before. The other half wears the expression of people who have never encountered this particular combination of syllables in this particular order, and are not sure what has just been done to them, but suspect it is something.

From somewhere near the back: "Mr. Crane?"

It's one of the older clowns, Graham Jenkins, whose stage name is Patches.

"Yeah." Patches raises a hand halfway. "I do gigs between seasons. Birthday parties, office parties, that kind of thing. Does this mean I won't be able to do that anymore?"

"That's a good question," Theo says. "And I want to answer fully. But I would appreciate it if everyone would hold their questions until the end, at which point I will hold a Q&A session."

Even though Patches nods and sits back, Theo notes the damage is done. The people who understand what 'non-compete' means are now looking at Theo with a new quality of attention. Not hostile. Not yet. Just—watchful. The way you watch something you're not sure about.

He clears his throat. Moves on.

"And now for the good news," he says, and something in his delivery shifts. A degree warmer, a degree more direct. "Let's talk about the future of the company. Because I see great things on the horizon."

Some of his audience looks patient and interested. More of them look skeptical. Suspicious, even.

"This has been… a difficult season. We can all agree on that."

The majority of people in the room nod or otherwise murmur agreement.

"I will not ignore the fact that two very important people died under tragic circumstances this year. In fact, I am going to honor their contributions by creating two scholarships in their names. For Helena… who was so talented, and who represented four generations of aerialists. The Helena Danforth Scholarship will be awarded annually to a worthy student at the Circadium School of Contemporary Circus in Philadelphia."

This receives a smattering of applause. He continues.

"And the second scholarship, in Ace's memory. Some of you may be aware that the University of Southern California awarded Ace an honorary doctorate several years back. So, I have decided to create the Ace Donahue Scholarship. This will be awarded annually to a USC student in their entertainment management program."

Another small round of applause.

"I will be in talks with both of these institutions in the coming weeks, and these scholarships will go into effect for the next school year."

"Hear, hear," Bongo says, applauding loudly. Others join in.

Theo remembers seeing in Bongo's employment file that he graduated from the Celebration Barn Theater in Maine. Of course he understands the importance of scholarships.

The next major announcement he gives also results in wide applause: Theo says he is going to change the name of the company back to Trentini's Traveling Circus, effective on day one of next season. Not to erase the Donahue legacy, he says, but to honor the Trentini name which still has enormous brand recognition and belongs on the marquee.

He clears his throat and continues.

"Shortly after I came on board, Mr. Donahue decided to extend the season. I know that was a hardship for many of you to have such a short time to recover. Therefore, effective immediately, I am restoring the sixteen-week break between seasons."

A swell of murmuring erupts and travels through the room like a wave. Nearly four months, not two. The excitement has arrived, just as Theo knew it would.

He continues now that he has their rapt attention. Explains that they will end this season after their five shows in Albuquerque, pack up and head for Corpus Christi. This news, too, is well received.

Theo explains that starting next season, they will be offered comprehensive health insurance. Performers and crew. Virginia starts crying again. Happy crying this time, he is fairly certain.

"I have also decided to create a Human Resources department. This will go into effect next season… and will provide every single one of you—" he gestures broadly to the entire room "—the opportunity to be heard by someone whose entire job it is… to listen to *you*. This department will document problems, concerns, or grievances. And, they will make sure your concerns get addressed. No more hoping the information reaches the right person… no more hoping something gets done about your concern. This department creates the formal channel, and it *will* be used."

Light applause.

"And now, moving on to what I envision for the future of this company. I plan to expand and create at least two, or possibly three more regional touring companies. This will allow the brand to expand into other states. This means more audiences. More jobs."

He mentions he will make one of these a human performance circus—no animals, purely acrobatic and theatrical entertainment—and watches a flicker of something move through the room, but it's smaller than he expected. Charlie is giving him some side-eye, but he does not say anything. Not yet.

A hand shoots up. Gary Bartlett, one of the rugged crew hands. He does not wait to be called upon and instead blurts out his question. "The new regions… does that mean you'll be asking employees to switch to one of the other companies? I live in Laredo, and I don't want to move."

Theo adopts his most patient smile. "I mention the future growth because it is just that—something that will offer more opportunities. It is not a requirement to change to one of the newer companies, or to move."

Gary leans back, apparently satisfied.

"Please, hold onto your questions for just a few more minutes. I promise, I'm almost done. And this final topic is something I feel very strongly about, as I'm sure you do, too."

A restless quiet settles, and Theo can tell the smell of cinnamon rolls is eroding attention from his speech. He resolves to finish up quickly.

"Last but not least. Safety."

The room brightens noticeably. After everything this season. After Helena. After Ace. Safety feels like the right note.

"Under my ownership… safety is not a suggestion, and it is not negotiable. Every concern gets documented. Every request gets addressed. No one will ever be asked to perform on equipment that has been flagged." He pauses. "We will be implementing a comprehensive safety review across every aspect of this operation. Equipment. Animals. Audience interaction. All of it."

The room is nodding. This is good. This is what they needed to hear.

"As part of that review," he continues, "we will be making some adjustments to practices that present unnecessary liability exposure. For example… the pre-show photo opportunities with the llamas."

The nodding slows.

"Going forward, effective at the start of our next season, we will not be offering ticketholders the opportunity to interact directly with the llamas before the show. The liability is simply too significant."

The room is no longer nodding.

Pip's face has gone very still.

"I want to be clear… this is not a reflection on our handlers, who are exceptional. It is purely a matter of—"

"Mr. Crane?"

It's Charlie. Still seated, but now with his arms folded. His voice is just as quiet as always, which somehow makes it louder than anyone else in the room.

"Are Bruno and Hazel still going to be in the show? They're lions, after all. Not llamas."

The room goes very still.

Theo looks at Charlie. Charlie looks at Theo.

"That's not anything I'm considering now."

The word lands.

Now.

It takes approximately two seconds for it to detonate across the room.

Theo watches it happen in real time—the llama handlers exchanging a look, Katrina and Shelby going still, someone in the back whispering something to the person beside them, a rigger near the entrance shifting his weight.

Theo overhears someone grumble, "Ace was far from perfect, but he always said the animals are the best thing about the circus."

The room is slipping. Theo can feel it. The careful warmth he has been building all morning—the Trentini name, the sixteen weeks, the health insurance… frost is rapidly forming around the edges.

He needs to get it back.

He reaches, instinctively, for the tools that have always worked.

Structure. Precision. The language of boardrooms and business schools where things make sense and people speak the same dialect.

"What I want to do," he says, "is reframe this conversation around the larger paradigm shift we're undertaking as an organization. Because at the end of the day, what we're really talking about is a fundamental realignment of our operational priorities. And… I don't want anyone to feel like we're trying to boil the ocean here. The key takeaway is that we're not eliminating anything precipitously. We're being thoughtful and strategic about how we position our assets going forward—"

He stops.

Because the room has done something he did not predict.

Half of it has gone tight-jawed and flat-eyed, the expression of people who are genuinely angry and deciding whether to say so.

The other half is wearing a different expression entirely.

Virginia.

Virginia is in the second row and her face is doing something she is clearly trying very hard to prevent it from doing. The corners of her mouth. The slight trembling of her considerable shoulders. The pressing together of her lips with the desperate determination of a woman trying to hold back something that does not want to be held back.

Theo believes she is trying not to cry; he quickly learns it's the opposite.

She is trying not to laugh. And failing.

The last two words of Theo's sentence—*going forward*—die in the air between them as he registers this.

Theo Crane.

Standing on a riser in a breakfast tent in Santa Fe.

Having just said paradigm shift and boil the ocean to a room full of circus performers and riggers and crew hands.

It was all going so well, he thinks. *Why the hell did I have to mention liability.*

He does not say any of this out loud.

What he does in the three seconds that follow—in the silence of a room that is half angry and half trying not to laugh—is take a breath. Then pivot, hard.

Something in his delivery changes; he abandons the boardroom and arrives back in the breakfast tent.

"One more thing," he says. He believes he has smothered the trace of panic he is feeling.

"Before next season begins. Before any of what I've just told you takes effect…" He pauses. Longer than any pause he has taken all morning. "Trentini's is going to acquire two donkey foals."

The room changes.

Not gradually.

Immediately.

From somewhere in the middle of the room there is a small shriek. Involuntary. It is the sound of someone who has just been handed something she'd stopped letting herself hope for.

Pip.

She turns to her father and grabs onto his arm with both hands. Her eyes enormous.

"Daddy." Not quietly enough. "Did he say donkeys?"

Brandon looks down at her. Something moves across his face that he manages before it gets too far.

"He did, little Pip," he says. "He did."

The room is doing something Theo has not seen it do all week. It is moving toward something rather than away from it. Hope traveling from one person to the next—from Pip outward, touching the Tumbling Tropiques captain who almost smiles, touching Virginia who has abandoned all pretense and is now crying and laughing simultaneously, touching the llama handlers who exchange a different kind of look than before, touching Marco who looks at the ceiling, touching Svetlana who is still looking at the floor but whose jaw just visibly unclenched.

Theo watches it happen.

"You all know how I felt about Ace retiring Ravioli and Ziti. I felt it was premature. He disagreed."

Pip blurts out a word—tortellini—and Theo wonders if he misheard.

"What's that, Pip?" he asks.

"I've got the perfect names, Mr. Crane. For the donkey foals. Tortellini and Calzone."

Several people say *aww*.

Whether this is because they like the names, or because they are expressing their regrets over the donkeys who disappeared between this season and last, Theo is not sure. But he grabs onto the latter and leans into it.

"Tortellini," he says in a dramatic tone, "and Calzone. Those are the perfect names."

Another excited shriek erupts from Pip and she is practically floating from Theo's praise.

Theo and Brandon's gazes meet for a moment, but he looks away just as quickly because he does not like what he saw in Brandon's eyes. Or, for that matter, his facial expression or his posture. Pip is tugging at her father's sleeve and trying to get his attention.

"What do you say, everyone?" Theo asks, raising his arms in a gesture that suggests invitation. "Do we like the names Pip chose for the new donkeys?"

Nearly everyone in the room is nodding, while some are also clapping politely, and still others are cheering and clapping with abandon. Pip's hope is contagious and Theo smiles warmly at her. Applauds in her direction. This results in most of the company turning their attention to Pip, offering their appreciation.

Theo is still smiling at Pip. He sees Brandon rest his hands gently on her shoulders and give an affectionate squeeze. She is standing right in front of him at this point, her back facing him.

Her entire nine-year-old being is radiating happiness.

Somewhere between the paradigm shift disaster and Pip's shriek, he appears to have acquired two donkeys. He will have to put some serious thought into whether he meant it.

He decides he will deal with questions in the coming days and weeks.

This is the optimal moment to wrap up.

"That's all I've got," he says. "Questions, emails, Patty's suggestion box. Continental breakfast. Take care of each other. We've got one more show to do here tonight in Santa Fe, then the last stand for the season in Albuquerque."

There's a smattering of applause aimed at Theo then. He is not sure whether this is appreciation for his speech, or relief that he's done talking.

Regardless, Theo thanks everyone and aims his own applause at different sections of the room before stepping down from the riser.

Brenda and Cassie know this is their cue. They emerge through the kitchen door, one after the other, both women holding large trays.

The tent comes alive with voices and movement. A few people approach him and shake his hand.

Urns of coffee appear and several people head in that direction. Brenda and Cassie are setting out pastries and a variety of yogurt flavors, as well as two huge bowls of mixed fruit.

Theo navigates his way through the room, casually heading toward Brandon and Pip. Brandon's hands are still resting on Pip's shoulders, both of them eyeing the food on the other side of the room.

Pip is talking to her father again, and Theo guesses it is about donkeys because her expression is almost euphoric. The noise in the tent prevents him from hearing their exchange, so Theo casually moves in their direction. A handshake with Jasmine, a word with Danny, a nod to Dr. Ellie.

Relaxed chatter and the sounds of clinking silverware fill the breakfast tent.

Finally Theo arrives in a position where he can hear what Brandon and Pip are talking about. His back is to them when Danny approaches him again.

"You want me to save you a chocolate croissant?" Danny asks. "They're going fast."

"Very kind of you to ask," Theo replies, "But I'm good."

From behind him he hears Pip's voice.

"Daddy, do you really think we're getting donkey foals?" and, before Brandon has a chance to reply Pip adds, "Do you think I can help train them?"

Theo turns just enough to see the two of them in his peripheral vision. Pip is looking up at Brandon with adoration and the specific look of a child who has absolute faith in her father.

He squeezes her shoulders affectionately again, then leans down to wrap his arms around her. Kisses the top of her head. Straightens up again. Looks over at Theo, who is now directly facing the two of them.

The two men regard each other, and Pip is looking up expectantly at her father.

Brandon smiles at Theo. His expression is relaxed, as is his voice, when he finally says, "We'll see, little Pip."

THE END

ABOUT THE AUTHOR

M.K. Milligan has wanted to be a writer since she was eight years old. In the decades between that eight-year-old and this book, she was a legal secretary, earned a degree in hydrology, worked as an environmental engineer, became a medical transcriptionist, then a real estate agent, and raised three children. She currently is a full-time caregiver for her youngest child. Throughout the intervening fifty years, she was working up the courage to put her writing out in the world.

She has arrived. ***Come One, Come All*** is her debut novel.

She lives in Cedar Rapids, Iowa, with her middle child, who is in college and allegedly will move out someday; her youngest child, who has special needs; and seven cats who were not consulted about any of this, and judge her harshly, warranted or not.

WHAT'S NEXT FROM M.K. MILLIGAN

Crash Course ~ a family memoir spanning three generations, exploring how undiagnosed neurodivergence shattered her family for decades before it would illuminate her own journey as a mother.

Also in progress ~ ***Doors Unlocked***, a trilogy of science fiction short stories, as well as other genres currently under wraps.

www.ingramcontent.com/pod-product-compliance
Lightning Source LLC
LaVergne TN
LVHW100527110826
845146LV00002B/810